TOWER OF THE LORDS

THE RISE OF THE DRAGONS

RIGELS D. LAMCE

Copyright © 2015 by RIGELS LAMCE

TABLE OF CONTENTS

PROLOGUE 4
CHAPTER 1 8
CHAPTER 2 13
CHAPTER 3 21
CHAPTER 4 30
CHAPTER 5 39
CHAPTER 6 48
CHAPTER 7 57
CHAPTER 8 65
CHAPTER 9 74
CHAPTER 10 83
CHAPTER 11 92
CHAPTER 12 101
CHAPTER 13 108
CHAPTER 14 118
CHAPTER 15 127
CHAPTER 16 136
CHAPTER 17 145
CHAPTER 18 155
CHAPTER 19 164
CHAPTER 20 173
CHAPTER 21 182
CHAPTER 22 192
CHAPTER 23 200

CHAPTER 24 208
CHAPTER 25 217
CHAPTER 26 226
CHAPTER 27 236
CHAPTER 28 245
CHAPTER 29 255

PROLOGUE

The torch the old man held could barely cast its light on the winding stairs of the tower. The livery he wore was now too tight for him, although he had been wearing it throughout his life. He had yet to convince himself of what he intended to do. He clambered down the stairs with difficulty, making sure he didn't trip over anything and, when he reached the last level, headed towards the third cell. His boots grated on the rough stones and, although he heard drops of liquid splattered across the floor, he paid no heed. He leant the blaze towards the rails, and whistled through his teeth. "Young master…"

A skinny boy lay coiled up in the corner of the cell, dressed in rags, his black hair greasy and filthy. The servant took a bunch of keys out of his pocket and, picking one, opened the gate. "Young master," he repeated, this time in a somewhat louder voice. The boy opened his eyes and jumped up, clenching his fist, ready to attack…but he stopped as soon as he realised who stood before him.

"Velmar?"

The boy breathed with difficulty, as if he had just woken up from a nightmare, and now that he stood closer to the fire, he could make out the dried blood across his face, and his wounds that hadn't healed yet. "Quick, young master. Follow me. I'll help you escape."

"No. It's futile. I've tried it so many times before, and I've failed. Wherever I go, he's going to find me and drag me into one of these cells again."

His face was inscrutable, but pain and disillusion was painted across his eyes.

"It's different this time. Your father…"

"He's not my father, he is a demon!" His teeth gritted, and dark red rivulets of blood oozed from his lower lip.

"...Master Jenon isn't in the castle right now, and I don't know when he'll be back. Young master, you know that there is a place where not even your father will be able to track you down." The boy was hesitant for a while, until there were some heavy steps going down the stairs. Velmar grabbed him by the hand. "Hurry up! This is your only chance."

The old servant walked as fast as he could, he almost ran, while the boy was following him with ease. "We've got to get back," the boy suddenly said. "The stairs are on the other side. There's only a dead end ahead of us."

"There's a secret passage at the end of the corridor that only I know, young master. Trust me." When they came up against a wall, the servant brought the torch closer, and began to grope the bricks with the other hand, while the footsteps behind them grew louder by the second. All of a sudden, a dragging sound was heard, and under their feet appeared a new flight of stairs. "Hurry up, young master. We're almost there."

A strong, cold wind blew inside the passage, making the flame flicker and sway, while the boy shuddered with cold. Their feet waded through puddles of water, and Velmar was out of breath from running. At the end of the tunnel, far from the castle, a carriage with two impatient black horses awaited them. "We made it," the man wheezed. Thick droplets danced overhead, making the torch useless. He threw it to the ground, and took a change of clothes out of his black mantle. "Take these and go. Now! May the three ancient gods favour you."

The boy's face froze. "What do you mean?" he grumbled. "Aren't you coming? He won't forgive you if he learns you helped me. He'll punish you. Come with me."

"I can't do this. I have taken a sacred oath. No matter how harsh he is, I will serve Master Jenon for the rest of my life. Go now, before it's too late." The boy balked, but then obeyed.

The servant watched the carriage leave, and got back. When he reached the top of the tower, he was already out of breath, his back was killing him, and his knees cracked from ascending so many stairs. Another two towers loomed behind him, vying with each other in piercing through the clouds that engulfed them. Further below, wild waves, like frenzied monsters, were doing battle for supremacy.

"Master Jenon."

He saw him standing next to a thick wooden pole, from which hung heady chains, while his red coat was flapping in the wind, and his white, moist hair was stuck on his face. To that very pole, he used to tether the young master, leaving him with no food for weeks. This was just one of the multitude of tortures that poor boy was subjected to. "Is it done?" Jenon's voice sounded heavy and inhuman, like a hollow whisper.

"I helped the young master escape, as requested."

The man with the white hair turned towards Velmar. Despite his hair, his face looked young, as if he were only in his early thirties, while his right cheek was furrowed with three slashes that stood out as they were darker than his complexion. His red eyes that glistened like rubies turned black, as soon as he blinked. "Very well," he said. Just like his red eyes, his inhuman voice vanished. "From now on, his fate is in that person's hands—Zoloc."

"Master…I am aware that I am in no position to question your decisions, but still, I think it would be preferable for the young master to stay here, under your protection."

He gnashed his teeth. "We both know full well what happened last time I tried to protect someone."

"But that place, that horrible place…"

"I know." Jenon ran his fingers through his hair to pull some wisps away from his face, and then turned his head over in the other direction. "They want to kill him, Velmar, and I'm not going to allow this to happen. I have been planning this for the last sixteen years. Ironically, the safest place for him, right now, is the place that is known as the most dangerous. The Tower of the Lords."

CHAPTER 1

Small drops of rain were raging outside Nesto's window. It was a rainy day. He hated these days. His father had abandoned him and his elder brother on an overcast, dull day. It wasn't raining at the time, but every single time rain reminded him of his tears. Several years later, so did his brother. He hadn't cried on that occasion, but the sky did it for him. Ever since, he hated three things: his father, his brother and, most of all, the rain. In a way, he was relieved that his mother was already dead, otherwise she might have dumped him, too.

He lay in bed, groping the mark across the ribs with his fingers: three dark lines that looked like scratches. He was trying to remember when he got it, when a double knock on the door roused him. He put on his boots and hooded top, and went down the stairs. The house was empty and cold; two bodies weren't enough to warm it, let alone now that Garon, his uncle, was away, and Nesto was on his own.

His uncle was a hunter, the best ever, or at least that's what he was apt to say. He had been away for the last couple of days. Hunting lasted for at least three days, and there were times it went on for ten or more, but each time he came back with enough kill to feed the whole village. He gave it all to the local butcher in return for a basket of warm bread, cheese, meat and, sometimes, fruit on an everyday basis.

After another double knock, Nesto opened the door, only to see the butcher's daughter standing there, dripping wet, basket in hand. "You really needn't have brought it yourself, Lirelle," he said to her. "I would have come over to collect it." Just as he did every day.

"You were late, and I wanted to see you." Her hair was held back, revealing her pretty face. Blue eyes, red lips, and a curvy body. She was perfect, bar a small flaw—she was mad and desperate. There wasn't a single boy at Grakehall that hadn't received her flirting. Her obsession with marriage had led her to Nesto's door over the last couple of days. The other boys must have surely rejected her. Nesto had curly hair and brown eyes, while his medium height and thin hands didn't make him particularly popular with girls. *I guess she is that desperate.*

She gave him a slight push with her hand, and walked in. After placing the basket on the table by the wall, she let her hair down. "Garon must still be busy hunting," she said, having shot him a furtive glance. "Great. We are alone."

"I'm sure he's done with the hunting, and will be here any minute now," Nesto said. That was a lie. Most probably, the first he had ever told, and apparently not a very good one.

"He won't be back until tomorrow, I know that. I'm the butcher's daughter, silly boy." She flashed him a promising smile. "You'll soon turn sixteen, a grown man. I know that very well because, every time Garon visits my father, he mentions that we were born on the same day." Lirelle shortened the distance between them. She wore an olive green dress, which didn't manage to hide her cleavage, and Nesto's eyes always fell on it. She grabbed his hand and put it on her heart, while biting her lower lip. "Don't you think I'm beautiful, Nesto?" she asked, and she instantly received a nervous 'no' for an answer.

A second lie, and the fact that his hand still rested on her breast made it far less convincing.

As soon as he realised it, he pulled his hand away and took a few steps backwards, while Lirelle turned in the other direction, holding her body with her own hands. Her wet dress made her shiver with cold. Nesto offered to fetch her a blanket to keep her warm, but she paid no heed. "You like me," she stated after a while. "I've seen the way you look at me. Why don't you marry me, then?"

The third lie came more natural than ever. "I can't. I'm soon leaving Grakehall. I intend to challenge the Tower of the Lords," he responded, then he recalled his brother. Those were, more or less, his words when he abandoned Nesto. He wondered if his words had been just as phoney.

Maybe it was the memory of his brother and the rage that it incited, but Lirelle seemed to have believed him this time. She must have been truly desperate, for she left without saying a word, almost in tears.

His first lie came true as Garon returned from hunting that very evening. In contrast to Nesto, he was tall and stocky, with long black hair. He wore a dark green hooded coat, and strapped around his shoulder was his longbow. He carried no kill and, judging by the look on his face as he opened the door, he hadn't left it with the butcher. Nesto seldom saw that puzzled and sad expression; only on those rare occasions when hunting came to naught. He said nothing. He never did when his pride was wounded, and hunting was the only thing he was proud of.

While Garon was washing his hands, Nesto was preparing dinner. Even at the table, his uncle kept silent. "Lirelle's obsession with marriage has gotten even worse. This time, she's drawn a bead on me," said Nesto, in an attempt to make him speak, while avoiding any mention of the kill. Rubbing salt in the wound would do no good.

"It's not the girl's fault. I may exchange my kill with the butcher, but I don't like him at all; I never did. I'm sure the poor girl is suffering at his hands."

For an instant, he took pity on her, but what could he do? Marry her? *No way!* Ever since he was abandoned by his father and brother, he didn't want anyone by his side; he trusted no one, except Garon.

Silence reigned again, until Nesto blurted out: "Was hunting so bad?"

"I didn't go hunting."

"What? Why not?"

Garon huffed and pushed his plate aside. "I was hoping we could have one last peaceful dinner, but it seems that I can't prolong this anymore. I went to see an old acquaintance of mine to make some arrangements. First thing in the morning, you're leaving for the City of Kings, Nesto. You are entering the Tower of the Lords."

He let out a muffled laugh. Garon's completely stern face, though, showed that it was yet another lie of those Nesto told come true. When Almar, his brother, had decided, six years before, to leave for the "Tower," Garon had tried to talk him out of it. For a whole week, they had been arguing, until his uncle gave up. *He must think that I'm just like him.* "I'm not like my brother, I'm not going to abandon you. Only a fool would try to claim the title of a Lord."

"Shut up, you fool!" Garon shot to his feet. "Don't talk about your brother like that!" He walked into his room, by the stairs, and when he got back, he was holding a rag. Unfolding it, he revealed a small green weapon that looked like a knife, only a little longer. "Don't you remember a single thing of what he told you the day he left?" he asked, as he threw the weapon to him.

Nesto used both hands to catch it. Its handle was wooden, while its shining green blade was made of glass. It must have been really sharp as, at its very touch, his skin oozed blood. These red rivulets put him in mind of the rain he detested, and the memory he had been fighting back rushed through his mind. Tears. He didn't want to admit it, but he had cried once again. He had begged, chafed, bitten and, finally, got hold of the weapon his brother had always carried along, but still he didn't manage to convince him.

He looked at his hand. He cut himself in the very same spot, back then. He broke out in a cold sweat, when he recalled his brother squeezing and pressing his wound, hugging him, and whispering: "That mark of yours across the ribs, don't show it to anyone. They want you dead, Nesto. Trust no one!"

CHAPTER 2

The next morning came earlier than he had hoped for. He had been tossing and turning in bed all night, trying to put things into perspective. Who wanted him dead? And why? Garon had no explanation for either. The only thing he knew, the only thing Almar had told him during their altercation, was that Nesto had to enter the Tower of the Lords before he reached the age of sixteen. When he finally drifted off to sleep, he dreamt about his father. His face looked distorted; Nesto could only make out his green eyes and black thick hair. His purple mantle was flapping in the wind, while behind him flames had taken on the form of horrendous monsters. He could hear the wind hissing and whooshing, along with the song of the fire, but his father's words didn't reach him. He saw his lips move, then the rain set in…the tears.

Garon strode into the room just before sunrise. "Get ready," he said. "We're leaving." He didn't have to remind him where they were heading. The very thought was more than enough to have his stomach in knots. Their village storyteller had told them so much about the Lords, and so little about the Tower. All he knew was that it was a trial and, if you succeeded, you were given immense power and a status equal to that of a noble. But if you failed…you died. And almost everyone did fail.

His breakfast was the previous day's leftovers, then he got dressed to leave. They hurriedly walked through the village square. It was still very early and quiet, but soon the hammering sound coming from the forge would pervade the air, then he would hear the butcher's and all the other shops open up. He thought of asking his uncle to wait till all the square filled up with voices and laughter, so that he could bid farewell to the kind of life he had got used to, so far. But there was no one in the entire village he would really miss or say goodbye to. "Trust no one," his brother had told him, and it seems that he didn't, albeit unconsciously.

Garon's old acquaintance must have occupied a very important position as, a few miles away from the village, a black carriage awaited them—one of those used only by the noble and the rich. Nesto followed him inside. Only when the sound of the horses' hooves reached their ears, did Garon begin to narrate all that he knew. "Your father is a Lord," he said in a low voice, making sure no one else but Nesto could hear him.

This did not take him by surprise. It was something he had been suspecting since the day his brother decided to leave, but still, hearing it made the blood run faster through his veins. "He sent you to me with a letter, asking me to take care of you. As for the rest, I learnt it from your brother on the day of our argument. He knew who were the ones that wanted you dead, but he would not tell me. The only thing he did tell me was that, to be safe, you must enter the Tower of the Lords before you reach the age of sixteen."

"But I don't get it. Why did he decide to enter the Tower of the Lords? Did they want him dead, too?"

His uncle shook his head. "I doubt it. Almar is a brave kid. He probably saw it as his duty to protect you, to show you that becoming a Lord is not impossible. It seemed to me that he knew far more things than he confided to me, but I guess he must have thought it was imprudent for us to know. The last thing he told me before leaving was that he and your father were expecting you at the top of the Tower of the Lords."

Nesto lifted his shirt. "What about the…?"

Garon put his finger over his mouth, motioning for him to hush, and spoke more silently this time, almost whispering: "Be careful when mentioning the mark. You don't want anyone else to hear you. I don't know much about it, only that your father had a similar mark on his chest. But he got that the day he became a

Lord Candidate; he wasn't born with it, like you. His mark is referred to as the Mark of the ancient Gods, and it bestowed him with the fiery power of the Gods. I don't know who wants you dead, Nesto, but you'll be safe with the Order of the Lords." He didn't say so, but the words sneaked into Nesto's ears on their own. *If you survive the trial, that is.*

During their journey, Garon would recount stories of his father. How he always longed to become a Lord, one of those who protected the Kingdom from the monstrous tribes, one of those who had slain all the dragons. Those who had brought peace and prosperity to the human race. "Our parents, your grandparents," he said smilingly. "They were at the service of one of the noblemen and, because of one of your brother's dreams, they left his castle, settling down in Grakehall, where they became hunters. You see, the Lords were always at loggerheads with the noblemen, even with those at their service. And, if they didn't want to ruin your father's chances—no matter how slim— of earning the title, they had to rid themselves of the nobles."

Just before they reached the City of the Kings, his uncle took out of his pocket his brother's green knife. "I thought that maybe you'd like to keep it," he told him. What with all this, he had completely forgotten about the weapon. "It looks like a dagger, but it's definitely not a normal one." He wrapped it with a scrap of cloth. "Make sure no one sees it, or it may arouse suspicions."

They went through the silver grey gate of the city just as the sun went down, swapping places with the two moons across the vast sky. The city was surrounded by rocks, which made it impossible for the enemy troops to seize it. Not that it mattered. The Lords would easily fend off any threat. The first house that hove into sight through Nesto's window was of the same size as the one he lived in back in Grakehall, and was made of carved white stone. All the houses by the gate were small and short, and grew taller and bigger, as they walked on, until they came up against a snow-white, grandiose castle flanked by various towers, where the King and his noblemen resided.

Their carriage drew up in front of a black castle in the centre of the city, which looked like a shadow against the white backdrop. This was the sole exception, the only building that loomed just as tall and grandiose as that of the King and his noblemen. The Tower of the Lords. White and black. The former were entitled to power by birth, whereas the latter earned it by risking life and limb. Nesto recalled a story he had heard when he was younger from the storyteller of his village. There was a time when a thousand commoners tried, all together, to enter the Tower of the Lords, in order to gain the title…and every single one of them ended up dead. That was the harsh truth. If you were born a commoner, then you stayed a commoner. Those who asked for more only met death. The storyteller's words had scared him because, deep down, he knew they rang true. But now, he was here, in a last-ditch attempt to gain the title. Just like those commoners…

Just as Nesto was trying to get off the carriage, his uncle's hand stopped him. He had that worried and sad look again, and Nesto knew it was time to go their separate ways, bidding farewell, perhaps forever. He wouldn't cry; he had cried enough for his father and brother. *No more tears.*

"Nestal," his uncle finally said. "This is your father's name. You never asked." His tone blamed him for that.

Words came natural: "It's because I never wanted to know." No matter the reasons, it was his father that had abandoned him. "Farewell, uncle, and thank you for doing what my father neglected." That was harsh and, probably, not fair at all, but he could not keep in check all the hatred and rage bottled up inside all these years.

Garon stopped him again, this time after Nesto had got off the carriage. "What about Lirelle?" he asked. "Won't you send her your regards? I think you broke her heart, you know."

That made his face crack into a smile. He knew that this was his uncle's way to avoid parting, with only bitter words in mind. "Tell her I'm sorry. And that I lied to her. I actually do think that she is beautiful."

The man awaiting him at the gate was one of Garon's acquaintances, one of the Lords of the castle named Mendax. Short and plump, with a double chin and a grey wisp of hair, this Lord bore no resemblance to those he had heard of in stories. Those Lords could make your blood curdle with a single look. The only decent thing on him were his bright red clothes and his purple mantle that put Nesto in mind of his father's mantle—the one he had dreamt about.

He was trying to banish that memory, while Lord Mendax was leading him to the castle quarters, and explaining to him the ceremony that was to take place in a few hours, in order to endow the Candidates with the Mark of the ancient Gods. First, they would prepare his body, freezing it with cold water, and then he would receive the flame of the Gods. "The power of the ancient Gods can seize you, searing the life out of you if they do not deem you suitable to wield it. If they don't favour you," the Lord warned him. It was of rare occurrence to be favoured by the three ancient Gods together. Most of the Candidates were favoured by only two of the three, while there were also some unlucky ones, as Lord Mendax called them, favoured only by one.

What the Lord called the castle's quarters was a small, narrow room with a bed and a tiny table that, instead of a window, featured a small crevice. It looked more like a cell. "I know you must be scared, having heard all this about the Tower of the Lords," said the fat Lord, while he was about to close the iron door, "but I believe in you." He grimaced, probably trying to smile. "You have Garon's blood running through your veins. There is nothing you can't achieve."

"These words meant nothing to Nesto. They must have been the same words he had told all those vying to gain the title of the Lord. After all, he wasn't scared. *If that floppy man made it, then how hard could it be?*

But, as he closed the iron door behind him, Nesto felt the shadow of fear inside of him, its hands gripping his lungs tightly, and he started to choke. He was on his own now, together with his thoughts, and whatever he had learnt over the previous two days had just sunk in. His father was a Lord, his brother became one or, at least, tried to, in order to protect him. There were people out there who, due to a mark across his ribs, wanted him dead, and Nesto would soon go through the most lethal trial. All of a sudden, marrying Lirelle didn't seem such a bad idea, whatsoever.

He sat on the bed and, instantly, something jabbed his belly. He had hidden his brother's dagger there, inside his trousers. The green colour of the sharp glass turned orange and red in the light of the oil lamp. As he gazed at his dark reflection in the glass, he felt a pang of remorse for all those times he thought his brother had abandoned him, for all the rancour he had felt against him. *I'm going to survive and meet at the top of the Tower, no matter what,* he thought, as he hid the dagger under the mattress. As Garon had said, if someone found it, it would arouse suspicions.

The shadow of fear was still lurking inside Nesto's body, when Lord Mendax came to lead him to the baths hall, where the ceremony would be held. Nesto would have to doff his clothes for the ceremony, and the very thought that the mark across his ribs would be there for everyone to see terrified him. The Lord must have read the disquietude across his face when he opened the door, as he said, to soothe him: "Most of the Candidates lose their lives before entering the Tower, but almost none have died during the ritual."

If that was supposed to calm him down, then it didn't work.

The hall was one level below ground and, as soon as he set his foot there, Nesto felt a cold aura engulf his body. Big chunks of ice jutted out of the surrounding walls, which gave off a faint white and blue light. "They are called crystals," Lord Mendax explained. Except for a piece in the middle of the hall that looked like a corridor, the rest of the surface was gone, and in its place he could only see water. *Frozen,* Nesto supposed, seeing the other Candidates shaking while scrambling out of the water onto the corridor. At least, he wasn't the only one to take part in the ritual.

He carefully took off his clothes—his top was the last one he doffed—, while trying to hide the mark with his right arm. He dipped in, feeling his muscles contract and his heart throb frenziedly, as the water pierced through him like countless frozen arrows, preparing his body to accept the Mark of the ancient Gods. He recalled the thousand commoners who had lost their lives, and wondered how many of them perished during the ritual. *Almost none,* Lord Mendax had said. *All of them,* he heard the storyteller whisper in his ears.

When he finally got out, his breaths were short and fast, while his limbs were numb. Fear oozed away and the cold settled in its place. A second Lord was already in the hall, holding two small crystals. A white and a black one. He wore the same apparel as Lord Mendax, only he was two heads taller, with a square face and a slash across his chin.

The first step, preparation, was over, and the second, and last, step was about to begin. All the Candidates, more than twenty persons, had formed a line, with Nesto bringing up the rear. Lord Mendax took the white crystal from Lord Cornius, as he called him, and placed it on the first Candidate's chest. The Lord's face smiled when the crystal turned dark blue, and said: "Two of the three ancient Gods favour you." Then, he immediately touched the black crystal at the same spot. Sparks flew out of it, and the candidate slightly flinched backwards. Then, the mark appeared.

The other Lord was jotting down the names and the number of the ancient Gods who favoured them, while Lord Mendax was endowing them with their fiery power. *Surely, they want to keep track of how many of us will survive.* Every time the crystal turned blue, Lord Mendax smiled, while these couple of times it turned red, his face cracked into a sad grimace. "Only one of the three ancient Gods favours you," he said, and everyone roughly knew what this meant. He wouldn't be alive for much longer.

Frozen drops trickled down Nesto's hair, while his body shook like a leaf, when his turn came. He stood naked, with his arms stuck to his ribs, trying to hide the mark as well as he could. Lord Mendax placed the white crystal on his chest, and Nesto wished its white colour would turn blue…but it didn't. It didn't even turn red. It remained white, and both Lords exchanged surprised looks.

Then, Lord Cornius turned his gaze upon Nesto, and said in his heavy voice: "I'm sorry, child. No God favours you."

CHAPTER 3

"We cannot endow you with the Mark of the ancient Gods. Their power will burn you," Lord Cornius explained to him. "I'm sorry, child, but you won't be able to enter the Tower of the Lords."

Two days ago, if someone had told him that he wouldn't be able to claim the title of the Lord, he wouldn't have cared. He might even be happy about it. But, now, things were different. 'They' wanted him dead, his only salvation was the Tower of the Lords, and his brother was waiting for him at its top. "No, you don't understand. I must go, I must enter." He raised his hands, in an attempt to plead with them, but he stopped as he remembered that the mark could be revealed.

"No, it is you that don't understand. If we endow you with the Mark of the ancient Gods, you will die, and you are not allowed to enter the Tower without it."

He felt his only hope ooze away from his grip. The emotions slashed him like a knife. Was it fear? Frustration? Anger? Probably all of that together as his throat closed up, and the only thing he could do was simply hold back his tears.

"So what?" said Lord Mendax. "Most of them will die before they even enter the Tower. If the boy wants to take the risk, I say we let him." The shorter Lord turned towards Nesto: "You want to, don't you?"

Nesto gritted his teeth and gulped with difficulty, trying to clear his throat. "I do," he said. "Yes, I want to take the risk."

"As Lords, we have no right to turn him down." He took the black crystal, ignoring Lord Cornius' advice, and slightly placed its edge on Nesto's chest. "Prepare yourself, this might hurt…a lot."

But it didn't hurt, it burnt. It was as if he had inhaled fire. His lungs were engulfed by flames as the Mark was formed across his chest. Then, the burning sensation crept downwards, in his entrails first, and then pierced through his bones. He knelt down when the burning reached his limbs. He wanted to scream for help, but it felt like fire was going to spit out of his mouth. *This is it. I'm dying.*

The others were, surely, watching him die. Watching the power of the Gods burning his life. The first candidate that failed. *That's me*. He felt a leg kick him; he barely managed to raise his eyes and see Lord Mendax. He was smiling. He revelled in it. He was probably trying to dispose of Nesto's body, so that the other Candidates wouldn't see where they would end up. But he was enjoying it. And he was supposed to be a friend of Garon's. One last kick threw him into the water, and he was sure he was going to die, for instantly relief overtook his body. A cooling sensation. Everything stopped burning, and the pain faded away. His ears were ringing, and his vision went blurry. His heartbeats reverberated throughout his body. That's what made him realise he was still alive. This along with the hand that grabbed and dragged him out. He could tell that someone was half carrying, half walking him. He used all the energy he had left to coil his hand around the mark across his ribs, and then everything went black.

He had that dream again: His father's purple mantle flapping in the hissing wind. Only the flames were different; they didn't have the forms of monsters, but had engulfed the house, burning it down. His father's hand didn't let him see the spectacle. His lips began to move, but his voice didn't reach Nesto and…the tears started again.

When he woke up, he found himself lying in his bed, naked. In his damp bed. He wasn't sure if it was sweat or just water. It took him a moment to realise what had happened. He had managed to survive, at least the ritual. The Mark that had appeared on his chest resembled that across his ribs. They had the same black colour, only the Mark of the ancient Gods was bigger, and the three lines ended in an apex.

Yet another mark on his body. Hopefully, this, he wouldn't have to hide.

He got out of bed and put on the white clothes someone, a maid maybe, had folded up and left on the small table. He surmised that all the Candidates wore the same clothes. He felt his body lighter, thinner. This was, most probably, due to the fact that he hadn't had anything to eat since the previous morning, but, strangely enough, he wasn't hungry. Lord Mendax knocked on the door the moment Nesto was lifting the mattress to check if the dagger was still in its place.

"Oh, you are still alive?" said the Lord, almost surprised, when he opened the door. It was probably a good-natured joke, but it wasn't that funny. *Not when my life is on the line.* "I thought that you might have turned to ashes while you were sleeping."

He faked a smile "No, not yet, at least."

"I'm glad you are so optimistic. Now that you and the rest are officially Lord Candidates, you will have the privilege of being taught by Lord Cornius all the things that you must know about the boring story of the Order of the Lords. Since, unlike the others, this is officially your first day in the castle, I am going to show you around before I hand you over to him."

"What about the Tower? When are you going to allow us to enter it?"

"Hold your horses. You still don't know what exactly the Tower is, and where it is situated. If we sent you there in your present condition, you would surely lose your lives within less than a single day."

He followed Lord Mendax across the paved corridor, illumined by torches. The sun must have gone up, but its light couldn't reach them down there. There was no window in that part of the castle where the quarters were, except for some small slots in each room. "In case you've forgotten about it, right underneath is the baths hall," said the Lord, while calmly pacing.

How can I forget? Actually, he had been so nervous the previous night, he couldn't remember the castle's interior. All he could recall was a purple mantle that he kept following, and the baths, of course. The burning sensation that he felt during the ritual, and the fact that the baths were the only ones that could control the fiery power of the ancient Gods had seared the location of the hall into Nesto's memory.

Right before them turned up the reception hall. The sun rays beamed down at the big colourful windows, casting various shadows on the marble floor. They were small pieces of a uniform portrait: a dragon with sharp jaws that received the spear of a Lord.

Lord Mendax noticed Nesto's fixed stare, but he did not remark on it; he actually said: "Towards the left of the staircase is the kitchen. Of course, one of the maids is ordered to bring you food in your rooms, but no one can forbid you to raid the kitchen as often as you like. You won't be feeling hungry for the rest of the day, I can vouch for that, but tomorrow, you will be starving."

"Why not?"

"Because of that Mark of yours."

He instantly felt his stomach in knots. *The mark!* Had he seen it? There was no doubt, Lord Mendax was the one that carried him to his room. He could have seen it. His thoughts were interrupted when Lord said, "When they receive the Mark, all Candidates do not feel hungry or thirsty the following day. Maybe because their body has not got used to the power of the Gods, I am not sure."

Nesto did not speak; he only wondered for a second what Lord Mendax's reaction would have been if he had really seen the mark Nesto was born with. Would Garon's friend try to kill him? He wasn't a friend, he remembered. He was just an old acquaintance. *Of course he would…*

He went on to say that, next to the kitchen, there was an armoury. A place he had to remember as he would often use it. They went up to the first floor, and he hastened to point out that the second floor was out of limits for the Lord Candidates. There was something in his voice telling him that there was no leeway for questions. On the first floor, there were the Lords' rooms, and the library, where Lord Cornius would teach them about the dull history of the Order of the Lords. Practically speaking, the only halls he really needed to remember were those of the baths, the kitchen, the library, and the armoury, where history and weapon practice were taught.

The corridor leading to the library was lined with paintings that portrayed all the Lord Commanders that had passed through the Order of the Lords. Nesto observed that their apparel and the sword they wielded were the same on all occasions, only their faces were different.

One of the other Lord Candidates, of the very few that was around Nesto's age, stood at the end of the corridor, looking intensely, almost spitefully, at one of the paintings. He looked taller than Nesto, with short black hair, which jarred with his pale complexion. He tried to recall his name, but to no avail. He hadn't retained any names during the ritual.

"Lord Candidate Daemon, it's a pleasure seeing you again. It's truly an honour having a nobility amongst the Lord Candidates." Lord Mendax's voice sounded too thin. He was clearly pretending.

Lord Candidate Daemon must have realised it, as well, for he gave him an indifferent look, and went away. "Despicable nobles. They have realised that their authority is limited, and now they seek to claim the title of a Lord. He won't admit that he is a noble, but his clothes and conduct, when he set foot in here, gave him away. The only redeeming feature is that only one of the three ancient Gods favour him. His body will most probably turn to ashes before he even enters the Tower." It took him a moment to understand what he had just said, and then turned to Nesto. "Oops," he said apologetically.

If he thought that Daemon wouldn't even manage to enter the Tower, then what was he supposed to say about Nesto? No God favoured him! *Yes, exactly. Oops.* He wanted to bear him a grudge, but he couldn't. Lord Mendax had saved his life during the ritual, dragging him to his room. "Thank you," Nesto told him after the Lord had shown him to the library, "for throwing me into the water."

"I had no other option. If you had died on the very first day you stepped into the castle, I wouldn't have been able to face Garon again." A little voice told him that, if he died on the second day, then Lord Mendax would have no problem to face Garon, but this was merely his instinct warning him not to trust anyone. "However, you should bear in mind that, now that you are officially a Lord Candidate, you can't receive or give help. Even if one of the others lose control of the ancient Gods' power in front of you, and goes up in flames, don't you even think of helping them. It will cost you your life. There are eyes all around watching every single move you make."

He was tempted to ask him how and why, but the Lord left hurriedly. The library was a spacious room lined with shelves full of thick, leather-bound books, parchments, various maps, and age-old artefacts in glass displays. Lord Cornius gathered them around an old garment placed above a lighted fireplace. The fire was so big that Nesto felt his whole body flare up.

The Lord's eyes were burning with fire as he narrated the story of the garment. It belonged to the first Lord. The first one Gods had chosen. A commoner, not a noble, as he stressed, looking at Daemon. The noble Candidate was sitting alone by the window, and didn't seem to be affected by the Lord's words. "He united all the separate human races into one, and created the kingdom of men," he added. When he was done with the first Lord's achievements and began to tell them about the dragons, Nesto had already broken out in a cold sweat, and could barely keep himself from opening a window.

The other Lord Candidates were listening attentively, as if it were the first time they had ever listened to these words. All the storytellers used to tell the same stories in all towns and villages, at least his own. He was only nine years old when he first heard them, before his brother left for the Tower of the Lords. Dragons were monstrous beings that reigned over the skies, the lands, even the seas. Human beings looked like flies before them. Whenever they pleased, they would fly down from the skies and burn down villages and towns. They devoured everyone in their wake. Nobody dared oppose them. Not even the strange northerners with their superhuman power, or the allomorphs and the giants. The storyteller always finished, saying: "Of all creatures, only the elves with their magic could threaten them, but they chose to become their loyal servants." Lord Cornius, however, finished by saying that the Lords, thanks to the Mark of the ancient Gods, slew the dragons and elves, and freed all creatures from their tyranny.

The Lord and the rest of the Lord Candidates walked on to see some more exhibits and learn more stories, but Nesto stayed behind. It was so hot in the hall that his chest frantically went up and down. He had seen that Daemon was no longer at the window, and almost ran to open it and stick his head out to draw in some fresh, cool air. The window opened up with a slight creaking sound, but the cool air never entered his nostrils and lungs. When he put his hand on his chest, he realised why.

The Mark of the ancient Gods was burning his body.

He turned over to go away and run towards the Baths, but his legs failed him, and he plumped to the ground. He was about to call out for help, but he remembered that no one would do that. He gritted his teeth and tried with all his might to stand up on his feet. He pushed the wooden door with his body, and it opened wide. The fiery force of the Gods was searing his throat now, and he knew which parts of his body would follow. He only hoped to make it before his knees failed him, as well.

He couldn't hear his steps as he ran across the marble corridor. The only sound that reached his ears was that of his heartbeats. *Ba-dum, ba-dum, ba-dum.* His vision got bleary, and not even for a second did he think of going down the stairs. He jumped right downstairs. It must have been more than seven metres high, yet he felt no pain. A bone must have surely been fractured, but the searing sensation had reached his entrails, and he wouldn't dare stop running. *Ba-dum, ba-dum, ba-dum.*

His mouth seemed to be blowing fire when he reached the Baths hall. He dipped into the frozen waters with his clothes on, feeling their cold embrace smothering the flame that longed to reduce his body to ashes. He was slowly sinking towards the bottom, where there were crystals all around giving off a blue glow that made them look like the stars turning up over Grakehall every night. Small bubbles came out of his body, and in one of them he thought he saw his brother's face. Where was he? he wondered. Had he gone through the same torture? Had he acquired the title of the Lord? *And if he had, why didn't he come to see me? Why did he say he would wait for me at the top of the Tower?* So many questions left unanswered. He only hoped to live up to his brother's expectations as going up to the top of the Tower now seemed an impossible feat to him.

His heartbeats subsided when danger was gone, and his body began to surface on its own. Although the water was frozen, he preferred to stay in a little longer to make sure that the power of the Gods was under control.

A plash made him realise that he wasn't alone in the baths. He saw Daemon clamber up to the corridor, on the other side. His body must also have been engulfed by the power of the Gods at the same time as Nesto's. Yet, he had had time to take off his clothes. He leant on one knee for a second, taking a breath, and then stood up. Nesto noticed that his body was full of scars. A huge slash tore his chest in two, while another one sprawled across his heart. He wondered why the body of a noble was so worn down.

As Daemon turned around to leave, Nesto saw another scar. This was across his ribs: three dark lines that looked like scratches. *Just like mine…*

CHAPTER 4

His body froze. The water was frozen, but that was not to blame. Nesto froze in fear. It was almost funny how fear could, one moment, look like fire raging through his body, and the next, take the form of frozen hands tightening their grip on his heart. A part of him wanted to climb up to the corridor, to run and make it to Daemon, asking him about the mark. Another part of him, though, was afraid of the answer he might get. His brother knew what that mark meant, and had decided that Nesto shouldn't know, at least not yet. This knowledge was so dangerous, it had kept their father away from them, forcing Almar to put his life in danger.

He tried to convince himself that it wasn't the same mark, that he just thought it was but was wrong. In vain, though. "You may not have inherited the big hands and the tall body of our family, but you surely have a hunter's sight," his uncle once told him. He would have been able to make it out, even from fifty metres away.

Later at night, he tossed and turned in his bed, unable to get a wink of sleep, trying to decide whether he should ask Daemon about the mark, thus risking revealing what his brother insisted that he keep a secret. It would be, without a doubt, foolish to take that risk. Daemon would have answers to many of Nesto's questions, though. What did the mark mean? Who wanted him dead? Was someone waiting for Daemon at the top of the Tower, too?

Maybe, he could learn without revealing anything, by lying to him. But he soon realised that this wasn't a very good idea. Daemon wouldn't trust him. *And let's face it, I'm not the most convincing liar.*

When morning came and the first sunlight pierced through the crack, he decided that he couldn't stand not knowing any longer, although his instinct bade him not do it. After all, most probably, one of these days, he would turn to a handful of ashes.

Just like Lord Mendax had said, as soon as he made his first move to get out of bed, Nesto felt hungry like the wolf that sees his prey after many lean days. On the table, the servant had left a jug of water and a platter of sausages, fried eggs, and freshly-baked bread but, before he tasted it, Nesto knew that this food wasn't enough to satisfy his hunger. He had another half-eaten sausage in his hand when he made it for the kitchen. He gulped it down in one go. After all, he wasn't the only one to raid the kitchen. More than half of the Lord Candidates had thought the same.

Fortunately, the cooks had made provisions for that as in the middle of the kitchen there was a counter full of fried meat from chicken, deer, wild boar, lamb, even horse, which Nesto had never tried before. At the other end of the table, they had put a variety of pies and pastries, and around them were several baskets full of fruit. All the Candidates had gathered in front of the counter, frantically biting at whatever they could lay their hands on, while talking to one another. They looked like a pack of wolves that had just finished their hunt and were now enjoying their kill. Nesto made a dash for the deer. "The best meat a hunter can ever catch," Garon used to say.

When deer's meat was over, he proceeded to the wild boar, while at times he stuck his fingers into various pies. His belly was swollen, and his hunger quite sated, when he saw Daemon walk into the kitchen. He was carrying his own platter. He put some pieces of horse meat, cut a piece of apple pie and, after stuffing his platter with fruit, he sat alone at a table in the corner. None of the Candidates took any notice of him; they chose to ignore him, except for two brunettes who were stealing glances at him and, all of a sudden, polished their table manners.

Even in the library, he had chosen to sit on his own, away from the other Candidates, Nesto recalled. Maybe he didn't want to consort with commoners, or maybe the other candidates didn't want to be close to a nobleman so much loathed by the Lords. It didn't matter which of the two was true. What counted was that he could approach him more easily, without having to think of a way to isolate the rest of them.

His hunger was almost assuaged, yet he grabbed a big horse thigh, and headed towards Daemon's table. He introduced himself and sat down.

"I know who you are," Daemon told him curtly. "The other Candidates have placed a bet how many days you are going to hold out until the Gods' fire burns you. What do you want?"

That took him by storm. Nesto himself was just as curt with almost everyone in Grakehall, but this behaviour was due to Almar's flight and his last words, which had been seared into his subconscious, not to trust anyone. Probably, before that, he must have been normal. What excuse did Daemon have? "How many of them have lost so far?" He wasn't particularly good at conversations, but something inside was telling him that it wouldn't be an exceptionally good idea to ask him directly about the mark.

"At least half of them. They betted you wouldn't hold out for more than a day."

"That long?" That made the noble chuckle. "Were I in their shoes, I'd bet I wouldn't live through the night. No God favours me, remember?" He was an awful liar, of that, he was sure, but it seemed he wasn't that bad at conversations, after all. He took a bite of the horse thigh, but he found it too hard for his liking. "What about you? How many days d' you think I will hold out?" he asked.

"Probably a day less than me. Only one God favours me, remember?" That made both of them smile.

For as long as they engaged in conversation, the two girls were flashing Daemon glances all the time. It wasn't hard to see the reason why. Apart from his haughty style, Daemon had high cheekbones, captivating dark eyes, and a charming smile. Everything that Nesto lacked, in a few words. At least, there was a girl who wished to marry him, although his looks didn't exactly attract others' attention, and she was much better-looking than both of them.

"That Lord Mendax," the noble finally said, after biting and chewing an apple. "If I were you, I'd keep him at arm's length. He's weird. I've been in this castle for ten days now, and I've only seen him three times, while the other two, I get to see them almost every day."

"So what? He may have been away on a mission or something."

"That's the thing. The Lords of the Castle cannot leave their posts. It's forbidden. And it's not only this. When in front of the other Lords, he tries to act as normal as possible, but when he's alone, his character changes completely. He tends to talk to himself, and he smiles like a fool." The noble made a grimace. "Besides, I don't like his smell."

"I'll keep that in mind." Nesto did not mention that the short Lord was an old acquaintance of his uncle. He had built some kind of intimacy with Daemon, and he feared that this knowledge would bring them back to square one. "Did he tell you the second level is out of bounds?"

Daemon snorted. "His exact words were that he would kill me if I didn't obey that order, although I am a noble…especially *because* I am a noble."

"So, not even you know what lies up there?"

"I'm sure that the Lords are full of secrets, which they wouldn't reveal even to the King himself, let alone me!"

Nesto tried to direct the conversation towards the mark, mentioning the incident at the library, which made him run in the direction of the baths. That made Daemon confide to him an unexpected piece of information that could keep him alive until he could enter the Tower of the Lords. "Don't use the baths only when you feel the Mark of the ancient Gods sear your skin," he told him. "The more often you use them, the fewer the chances of the Gods' fiery force getting out of hand." Something that the Lords had failed to mention.

He was so happy, he had almost forgotten that his goal was to learn as much as possible about the mark across his ribs—not so much about the one on his chest. When it finally dawned on him, all the Lord Candidates were walking out of the kitchen, leaving behind bones and an empty counter. So did Daemon. "Come on," he told him, "we don't want to be late for our first lesson at the armoury. They loathe me quite enough already; we don't have to make the situation any worse." Nesto followed him.

The walls of the corridor that led to the armoury were adorned with various words that seemed to be in the ancient language spoken by people before the First Lord united them. Try as he might, Nesto wasn't able to make head or tail of them. It didn't strike him as odd that, when he stepped into the armoury, he saw a huge place. All the halls—the baths, the library, even the kitchen—were spacious. He was pretty sure that even the Lords' rooms were equally big. *Only ours look like cells.* That was probably due to the fact that the castle had been built with the aim of housing hundreds, maybe thousands, of candidates, who obviously ignored the peril the Mark of the ancient Gods entailed. With so many deaths in the history of its Lords, it was really strange that he wasn't the only Lord Candidate.

The place smelled of metal and rust. There were various weapons hanging from the grey walls, and there were even more of them piled in a corner. Anything ranging from duty swords to sharp spears, big bows and heavy bats that hadn't been properly preserved. Further afield were three steps that split the armoury into two zones: the place where all the weapons were stashed, and the training area.

Out of the three Lords, this one—the one in charge of their training in guns—was his least favourite, Nesto concluded. She was a stocky woman with relatively short hair and shoulders broader than those of Lord Cornius that called herself Lord Ereina. She had a stern, scary face that made her look like a wild beast. But this wasn't the reason why Nesto liked her the least of the other two. It was what she did. She locked the iron door of the hall! She locked it, dooming with this act all those candidates that would be unlucky enough to lose control of Gods' fiery power.

If I judge by yesterday, I'll probably be the first one...

Right after that unexpected surprise, the Lord bade them hold a sword.

Nesto hesitated for a while; long enough for Daemon to ask him what was going on. "I don't know how to wield a sword," he admitted. He was good at the bow and knife, but Garon had never shown him the sword.

"Of course you don't; you're a commoner," said Daemon in a haughty style befitting a noble. Suddenly, it was pretty clear to Nesto why everybody loathed Daemon. The noble took two swords, gave one to Nesto, and they both headed towards the training area, where the paved floor was full of nooks and hollows that must have been formed by various fights.

Their first lesson had to do with the Mark and all the gifts it bestowed. In theory, their body was stronger and faster than that of an ordinary human, while their skin was as hard as iron. Impenetrable, as the Lord pointed out. And she didn't stick with theory alone; she even showed it in practice. She took a sword and, after lining them all, she tried to stab them without hesitation.

Thankfully, her words came true as no candidate bled. The only thing left behind was a small rash and pain. Unbearable pain! "Iron swords won't be able to kill you anymore," said Lord Ereina. "Only the flame simmering inside of you. Even this, you will be able to tame, at least some of you. You will learn how to erase the Mark at will, and the danger of going up in flames will cease."

Afterwards, the Lord showed them only two simple moves, how to attack and how to block, and had them practise all day long. The clangour of steel striking steel reverberated on the walls. The force hidden behind every single strike made it sound like thunderclaps. *It feels weird,* Nesto thought, as he held onto the sword with both hands, and charged at Daemon with all his might. His body was unexpectedly light, and shortened their distance in the blink of an eye. The sword felt extremely light, too, despite its size. Daemon's blade was shaken by Nesto's attack, but his hands remained steady.

Nesto got back in position and prepared for the block. He lifted his sword horizontally overhead, as Lord Ereina had shown them, but Daemon's attack came from below. A powerful thrust with the point of the sword aiming at his heart. The blow hurtled him onto the hard ground, and the pain was acute. The blade didn't pierce through his flesh, but Nesto was sure a bruise would appear at the spot the following day.

"You know that I'm still a beginner, right?" he grumbled after standing on his feet. "Can't you hold back a bit?"

Daemon's arrogant smile turned up across his face. "I'm sorry, that was actually me trying to hold back," he said.

"Well, you weren't trying enough." Nesto kept down the urge to punch him.

"Don't blame me. It's not my fault that I was never taught how to hold back."

Clearly, he wasn't lying as, every time it was his turn to attack, Daemon struck with incredible force, aiming at spots that, but for the ancient Gods' power, would have cost Nesto his life.

By the end of the day, all the Lord Candidates were drenched in sweat, their bodies breaking out in a rash at the spots the tip of the sword had missed. Some of them were throwing up their breakfast, while others looked at the door patiently, their hands stroking the Mark on their chest. When, finally, the Lord unlocked it, all of them stormed outside, pushing and jostling their way towards the frozen baths. Strangely enough, Nesto didn't feel his body hot, nor there was any sign that would have him believe the ancient Gods' power was going to engulf him in flames. Still, he preferred to follow the other candidates to the baths, along with Daemon.

Nesto and the noble came last, while the rest had already taken a dive. Their bodies stayed afloat, tinged with a blue hue, thanks to the glow of the crystals. That was the first time, after the day of the ritual, that all the Lord Candidates had gathered all together in the Baths Hall. "All but one," Daemon noted. "I'm the only candidate that is favoured by only one God. They found the other guy's ashes on his bed this morning."

Nesto could easily have been in his place. But such thoughts were absolutely meaningless, that's why he tried to ignore them, dipping into the water. His body relaxed, and he felt fatigue ooze away. Bubbles came out of all the bodies, and there were so many of them that they sounded like music to his ears. A smile formed across his lips, while he was musing over that morning's incidents. The food in the kitchen, the conversation with the noble, the practice with him, his company. He was surely arrogant, and the haughty tone of his voice was so irritating, but it wasn't unbearable. It was nice having someone to talk to. Someone to help him, someone that he could trust…a friend.

All the doubts that had wedged themselves in his mind since that morning were now gone. He was bent on revealing Daemon's mark. He waited till all Candidates went away, and then, when they were on their way to their rooms, Nesto went up to him. "Daemon, wait," he said. "There is something I want to tell you."

His wan face shone in the torchlight when he turned in Nesto's direction. "If it's to do with today's practice, then I'm sorry. I will try to hold back some more," he told him in his haughty tone of voice.

"No, it's not that." Of course, he wouldn't mind if he really tried a bit harder. His stomach was in knots, and he was almost shaking. He didn't know how to initiate the discussion, and decided to cut to the chase. "I've got the same mark as you," he confided, anxious to see his reaction.

"I know," said Daemon. "All candidates have the same mark."

"I'm not talking about the one that appears on all Candidates' chests…I have a second mark across the ribs."

The noble's face turned even paler, as if there were no blood in his head. He hurriedly looked behind him, then his black eyes were menacingly glued to Nesto's. He didn't even have time to see Daemon's hand tighten its grip on his throat, pulling and locking him against the wall. His pressure was so immense, he could barely breathe, while he felt his vision go blurry. "I knew it was you from the start." Daemon's frozen breath made him shiver. "Die," he said.

I guess I should have listened to my brother. I should have trusted no one.

CHAPTER 5

He didn't have time to think why Daemon did such a thing. He desperately tried to extricate himself from his clamp-like grip, but to no avail. He stuck his nails into the noble's hand, and tried to push him back, but he felt drained out. His vision was black when Daemon suddenly turned his head away and released him.

He could hear his steps fade away, as Nesto was gasping for air. He didn't know who, but someone had turned up, and their presence must have prevented the noble from chocking him to death. "There are eyes that watch every single move you make," he recalled Lord Mendax's words, and suddenly he felt grateful for those eyes. He staggered to his room, coughing, and tried to take a deep, unimpeded breath. His body was in a state of shock, so was his mind. *We have the same mark. Why is it, then, that he tried to kill me?* He racked his brains, but he couldn't make sense. His thoughts were garbled, and always ended in the same phrase, "They want you dead, Nesto." He started shaking at the very thought. He listened to his uncle and followed Almar's steps, for some people wanted him dead. But it looked so unreal. Just like a dream, just like a scary dream…but now it had become reality.

The maid had left his dinner on the table: fish cooked with onions, and two pears beside the plate. He made an effort to gulp down two morsels of food, but it was difficult to swallow. He only drank a few drops of water with difficulty. He decided he had to sleep to put his thoughts in order, but sleep didn't come, despite his exhaustion. For two nights in a row, he stayed wide awake and, when the following morning came, his eyes were puffy and red; he could barely keep them open.

When the maid came, carrying a tray full of figs, warm bread, and honey, he devoured them in no time. He ate the figs first, then he spread the honey on the soft bread, and finally licked his fingers. Lack of sleep wouldn't help him in Lord Cornius' lesson, and lack of food would make him feel even worse. *He'll be there, as well. I must have enough energy to face him.*

He didn't know what would happen if they were left alone again. Would he try to kill him at the first opportunity? That's why Nesto waited until he heard footsteps along the corridor, then he mingled with the rest of the candidates, where he would be safe. In the library, he found Lord Cornius indifferently leafing through an old book. For an instant, he thought of telling him that…that what? That the noble wanted him dead due to a mark he wasn't supposed to reveal to anyone? Would he make the same mistake, trusting someone, while his brother had clearly told him to trust no one?

Daemon was nowhere to be found, which was a relief. Nesto wished Daemon had lost the power of the ancient Gods while he was sleeping, and his body had turned to ashes, just like the other Lord Candidate, who was favoured by only one God. But his wish wasn't granted as he saw the noble walk into the hall and head towards the window, shooting him a fixed stare. He knew what those dark eyes were telling him. *Die!*

The Lord began to read some heroic deeds of the Lords from the book, but Nesto couldn't absorb a single word. He recalled Daemon saying, "I knew it from the start," and he started to bite his nails in anguish. He had surely seen the mark on the day of the ritual, when he almost went up in flames. He wondered how many others had seen it. Perhaps someone of the two Lords always present?

He reproached himself for being so open with Daemon. He should have seen through him. At first, he had looked brusque, but soon he became overly friendly, and confided to him the secret, so that he would survive until they entered the Tower of the Lords, thus gaining Nesto's trust. In fact, the only thing he wanted was to find the right opportunity to kill him. He remembered the way he had been charging at him with the sword in the practice area. Every time the tip of the blade aimed at Nesto's heart, throat, and chest. Maybe he hoped that, if he exerted enough force, the blade would manage to pierce through his skin, although the Mark protected him. *And no one would ever blame him for such an…accident.*

The question was, why did he want him dead, since they had the same mark? But it didn't really matter now, did it? Only one thing counted, and that was to survive. And he wouldn't let anyone steal life way from him. Not even the Mark of the ancient Gods, or Daemon. He looked at him, wondering why he feared him so much. He was simply good at the sword, nothing else. Just a spoilt noble.

And then it hit him. The one who tried to kill him was a noble. What if "They," meaning the ones who wanted him dead, were the nobles? It made perfect sense. It explained why his brother insisted that Nesto enter the Tower. The nobles and the Lords were at loggerheads and, if someone could protect him from the former, then that was the Order of the Lords. And there was a Lord among them that had saved Nesto's life. Someone that could help him.

Lord Mendax.

When the history lesson was over, Nesto watched Daemon walk out of the hall. Then, he went up to Lord Cornius and asked him about Lord Mendax's whereabouts. Nesto hadn't seen him for the past couple of days. "I guess he is in the kitchen," the Lord told him, somewhat annoyed by the question. "We used to hang out together a while ago, but now he prefers avoiding me."

"What if he isn't in the kitchen?" Nesto asked.

"Then, he's surely in his room. He's usually cooped up in there for hours on end, and he doesn't want to be disturbed." He gave Nesto a cold look. "I doubt it whether he would like to be disturbed by one of the Lord Candidates," he told him.

At the third door after the library hall, he found Lord Mendax's room. On the wooden door was carved the Mark of the ancient Gods, and right beneath it was his initial letter, "M." Despite Lord Cornius' advice, Nesto knocked on the door. He knocked for a second time, but he didn't get a reply. He looked for him in the kitchen and, when he drew a blank, he went to the armoury. He looked in almost every nook and cranny of the castle, until he thought that probably he was on the second floor. Eventually, he decided to make a beeline for the baths hall, just in case.

With his body frozen and his mind mulling over the mark and the nobles, Nesto found himself standing at Lord Mendax's door again. After a few strong knocks, he heard the Lord's voice. "Haven't I told you not to disturb me when I am in my room?" he said, his tone of voice betraying his irritation.

"I am sorry to disturb you, Lord Mendax. It's me, Nesto. I would like to talk to you about…"

"Oh, it's you, Nesto. Please come in." He did. The window was closed, and the only light that crept in came from the lighted fireplace. Two paintings of the plump Lord adorned the walls, and it was apparent from their quality that they had been made by the same person. In the middle of the room stood a table and two chairs, the one slanted at an angle. The room looked untidy, while there were muddy footsteps across the red carpet. "I thought it was one of the other Lords again. They tend to become really annoying," said the Lord. Nesto noticed that he wore the same garment even when he was in his own room, and his shoes were full of mud. None of the three Lords was allowed to leave the castle, so how had he soiled them? He wondered if Daemon was right, until he remembered that it was Daemon who wanted him dead.

"I'm glad that you have survived so far. Of course, I always believed you would, but it's good witnessing it with my own eyes. Do you want something to drink? Wait here for a moment." The Lord went into the other room and, when he came back, he was holding a decanter full of red wine, and two glasses. "This wine is of excellent quality. Only the King and His few select nobles, apart from us, have the opportunity to taste it," he said as he filled the glasses. He gave one to Nesto, and he began to drink out of his own.

That was the first time he had ever tried wine, and its taste was particularly sharp and rich. The Lord lifted the chair that had fallen over, and had Nesto sit. "How do you like its taste?" he asked.

Nesto took some time to speak. "Strong," he finally said.

"Good, but don't drink too much. I have heard that wine is not particularly helpful in keeping Gods' power under control."

The sip he took instantly spurted out of his nose. "You could have told me that before you offered me some," Nesto complained.

"It's alright. This small quantity is not enough to do you any harm, trust me," Lord Mendax said, and offered him a handkerchief. Trusting someone was the most difficult thing for Nesto right now. Wiping himself with the handkerchief, he put the glass on the table, and decided that he would be better off, from now on, without a drink.

"So, tell me, Nesto. Is Lord Cornius' history lesson still as boring as it always was?"

He couldn't tell if it was really boring or not. Both times he had attended, he was busy. On the first occasion, the fire of the Gods nearly burnt him alive, and on the second, he was preoccupied with the thought that Daemon and the others wanted him dead. The lesson was far from boring, on that score. "No, it was quite interesting," he was forced to say.

"Really? I guess his lies have become more interesting."

"What do you mean?"

Lord Mendax hesitated. It was obvious. That was something he wasn't supposed to mention. "Oops," he finally said. "Sometimes, I tend to speak without thinking first." He gazed at his empty glass. "Even more often when I drink. I guess it won't do you any harm if I tell you about it." He re-filled his glass with wine. "All the new candidates, just like most of the Lords, are taught that they are powerful enough to kill a dragon. That's a lie. Only a special few of them can actually harm one." The Lord looked at Nesto, and smiled. "Do you know what that means?"

"What?"

"It means that the Lords weren't the ones that killed the dragons and ended their dominance. It was the elves."

"But I thought that the elves were loyal to the dragons."

"They were, at first, but in the end they saw their mistake, and the loyal servants betrayed their masters. Do you want to know how they managed to kill them?" Of course he did. Nesto nodded.

There was a spark in the Lords' eyes, and it didn't come from the reddish light of the fireplace. "If you look carefully at the paintings in the corridor, you will see that all the Lord Commanders wield the same sword. The Dragonslayer. A sword made solely for slaying dragons. It is said that its handle is made from the bones of the First of the elves, and it contains his enormous magical power. It was crafted by the elves themselves, and the legends have it that they had so much confidence in their craft that they used it directly on one of the dragons. Just one slash was enough to penetrate his scale and steal his life."

"So, they used the sword to slay all the dragons?"

"No, only one dragon was slain by the Dragonslayer. One sword wouldn't be effective against hundreds of dragons now, would it? In terms of force, the dragons would lose to no one, so they changed their tactic. Instead of a weapon, they crafted a gift. A tower whiter than snow and brighter than the sun. The magnificent White Tower, as it was called. Thanks to the magic of the elves, it hovered over the Mountain of the Dragons, and it became their second home…and also their doom.

"Magic has so many ways to harm you. But the best way is to make you harm yourself. The constant effect of magic blindfolded them, and those they used to see as friends became their foes. After a bloody battle, the White Tower was blown to smithereens, and their kind went extinct by their own hand, or I should better say their own claw." The Lord laughed, as if he were the one to have devised that devious scheme. "That's how the era of the dragons ended, and the era of the Lords started. There is a legend, though—actually, it's more of a tale that some storytellers narrate to become more dramatic—, that one of the dragons survived. It took a human form and still wanders our world, waiting for the right moment to reclaim the skies. But that's just silly."

"But, if it was the elves that wiped out the dragons, why does everybody believe that they were slain by the Lords?"

"Well, if you keep repeating a lie, eventually it will become the truth. Besides, you have witnessed what the Mark of the Gods is capable of. It wouldn't really seem impossible to slay a dragon with that kind of power. Now, if…"

A heavy knock on the door interrupted him. "How many times have I told you not to disturb me when I'm in my room?" he said at the top of his voice.

"Lord Mendax, Lord Commander Legris just arrived and requested your presence on the second level," a female voice said, probably a maid.

"Lord Commander Legris is here, at the castle? Oh, well, that's a first. My apologies, Nesto, but him, unfortunately, I cannot ignore."

The Lord escorted him to the stairs, and then went on the second floor, out of bounds for the Lord Candidates, while Nesto descended them, heading towards the baths. The Lord's words about the wine had affected him a lot, if not frightened him. The sun had set and all the corridors were illuminated by torches. He hadn't found the opportunity to talk to Lord Mendax about Daemon, but he certainly would the next day. The more he delayed, the greater the danger. He surely couldn't trust the Lord completely, but he was an old acquaintance of his uncle, and had already saved him once. That was worth something, wasn't it? Besides, what other option did he have?

He wasn't alone in the baths, and he was grateful for that. Daemon might be lurking somewhere, biding his time, waiting for the right time to kill him, but Nesto had no intention of making it easier for him by isolating himself.

Drowsiness spread all over his body like a wave, and the frozen water couldn't keep him awake. He hurriedly went back to his room, and lay in bed, without even glancing at the tray with his dinner. His eyelids closed, and he felt his body hover in midair and float in water.

His sleep brought back the same dream. He stood on a small hill teeming with pine trees, while in front of him his father's purple mantle flapped in the wind. The wind had picked up, and there was another sound that resembled a baby's cry. A house was engulfed in flames further afield, and Nesto felt his chest hurt. There was something in the house, something he would miss, something that caused him the pain in the chest. A hand forced him to turn around his head and fix his stare into his father's green eyes.

"Look at me and listen carefully." This time, his father's words reached him. "I need you to be brave, alright? Listen, they want him dead…" Tears trickled down his cheeks. "No, don't cry. You are not a child anymore, you have to be brave now." His father wiped off Nesto's tears with his thumbs. "I want you to make sure that he will enter the Tower of the Lords. Do you understand?" Nesto nodded. "Good boy. Remember, he has to enter the Tower before he reaches the age of sixteen. Because of the mark, they will hunt him down. The Lords will want him dead, Almar."

CHAPTER 6

Dawn found him seated on the floor, with his back against the wall. The intoxicating slumber that had visited him the previous night gave him only one nightmare, and then disappeared, leaving him breathless, his body drenched in sweat. His face must have become bony from lack of sleep over the last days and the meagre portions of food he had, while there were black circles under his eyes from the very first day. All through the night, every time he shut his eyes, they stung, and his eyelashes grew heavy. But they would open up instantly when he pictured a pair of green eyes close in on him from behind and slash his throat. He couldn't bring himself to sleep; sleep might mean death.

What he had seen can't have been just a dream. He knew it, he felt it. The pain he had felt was much too real. And his father's hand on his face…was a memory, a weird memory, well hidden in his mind that showed him who his real enemy was. *The Lords.*

When the maid came carrying his breakfast, Nesto caught himself nervously tapping his fingers on the floor. He tightened his jaws and clenched his fist. Everybody looked like enemies, people who wanted him dead; even the maid, who would just bring him food. As she left one tray and took the other, she looked at Nesto. She saw the awful state he was in, but she was courteous enough not to speak—or she may have been too indifferent. He made an effort to have a few spoonfuls of the mushroom soup, but in vain. His stomach was in knots, and he was off his food.

He went out in the corridor, heading for the armoury. The torches were aglow, yet the corridor looked strangely dark. His gaze focused more on the dark places. Perhaps, it was because he was hungry, but his senses were heightened now, and that almost drove him mad. At every step he took, he could hear his boot grate on the floor, and see the shadows scurrying along the walls to kill him. He would turn his head around every so often to defend himself, to react, but the shadows were his own, not of any Lord with green eyes. *Calm down. You need to calm down, Nesto.* His heart hadn't ceased to beat fast, ever since he woke up, and now it was driving him up the wall.

A hand that touched his shoulder from behind made him jump, and instantly blood rushed through his head. That was definitely not his shadow. Instinctively, his own hand moved with a jerk, and his elbow hit the shadow's face. The thrust was so strong, he pushed the shadow over onto the ground.

"I guess I deserved that," said the shadow, and the tone of voice made him breathe more heavily. "Since I tried to kill you." Daemon stood up and rubbed his jaw with his hand, the flame of the torch nearby reflected in his dark eyes. "I came to apologise, but it seems that I don't have to, anymore. Now, we are even."

That was a lie. Another deceit of his. "Your tricks won't work on me again."

"What tricks? It wasn't a trick. I'm telling you we're even. Don't expect me to apologise now."

He wouldn't fall for that, he wasn't that foolish anymore. "Don't come closer again. Next time, I won't hesitate to kill you," Nesto warned him, and hurriedly walked away, covering himself.

He got to the armoury, looking behind rather than in front of him. The Lord Candidates had gathered outside the door, waiting patiently. Nesto joined them, until a maid appeared, who informed them that the three Lords were on the second floor, conferring with the Lord Commander. *Great!* thought Nesto. He couldn't stand being locked up all day in a hall full of people who wanted him dead. Now, they were only candidates, but soon some of them, if not all, would gain the title of the Lord, and they would surely want him dead.

This thought made him flush, and he felt even worse when he tried to think what kind of mystery was behind that mark he had across the ribs. He had a headache, and felt his body sweat profusely. This time, he knew what exactly this meant. The Gods' fire was trying to sear the life out of him.

He took a few deep breaths, and took to his heels. Things were getting worse and worse. Daemon wanted him dead, the Lords wanted him dead, even the ancient Gods wanted him dead. Well, at least the Gods, he had a way to stop them. He got to the baths hall, huffing and puffing. He took off his clothes and dipped with no hesitation. Instantly, a wave of freshness and relaxation gripped him. As soon as he shut his eyes, he felt them bleed from within. He hadn't slept a wink for three days now, and his body and mind were suffering. Only water could offer him that serenity. And security. He felt more secure here. Everyone and everything wanted to kill him, while these baths were the only thing that tried to keep him alive.

He didn't realise how and when, but he dozed off, and woke up restful, his body floating on the water surface. The burden he had felt on his chest all these days that crushed his bones was gone. What threatened his life wasn't yet gone, but the solution was there, plain to see, all along. He snorted when that thought sprang to mind. He wouldn't have to trust Daemon, Lord Mendax, or the Order of the Lords. The only one he had to trust was his brother. He surely had a plan according to which Nesto had to be under the same roof with those who wanted him dead. And maybe, Daemon wasn't one of his enemies, after all. They had the same mark. The Lords might want him dead, as well. *He even came to apologise to me.*

He couldn't be sure of Daemon, but there was only one solution, and that was confronting him. His stomach began growling. First of all, though, he had to make a dash for the kitchen. He was starving.

The sun was about to set, as he noticed on his way to the kitchen. He had been sleeping for the best part of the day. After eating a whole hot loaf of bread and two big deer thighs, he headed towards the corridor with the paintings. Daemon couldn't be in the library or the armoury, and he certainly wasn't in the baths or the kitchen. Nesto hoped to find him shooting black looks at some of the paintings, just like the first time. At any rate, the fact that he took a dim view of the Lords' paintings was a good sign. He gave Nesto yet another motive for approaching him again.

He didn't find Daemon there but, when he turned to go, he met Lord Mendax. The meeting with the Lord Commander was obviously over. "Oh, Nesto," he said. "I was looking for you. We left our discussion incomplete, and I have the impression that there was something you wanted to tell me." Nesto stared at him, his receding hairline, green eyes, weird smile, and purple mantle touching the marble floor, and instinctively took a step backwards. He was a Lord, one of those who wanted him dead. He looked weak, but the Mark of the Gods was surely etched in his chest—and there was nothing weak about the divine flame running through him. He felt his neck tighten, but he loosened it up again. Lord Mendax wouldn't kill him. Not as long as he didn't know about the mark.

He tried to come up with a plausible lie, but in vain. "No, it wasn't something special. Has the meeting with the Lord Commander come to an end?" he asked, trying to steer the discussion away from himself.

"Yes, our beloved Lord Commander was trying to convince us that the castle doesn't need all three Lords to prepare the Lord Candidates and, when he saw he couldn't, he forced Lord Ereina to follow him. She needed her for a personal mission. Then, they left." He heaved a sigh. "Yes, Lord Commander Legris really counts on our opinions," he said jeeringly.

"What did he need Lord Ereina for?" Not that he really cared; on the contrary, it gladdened him. Nesto would have one less Lord to fear. And that was probably the most frightening one.

The Lord took some time to think. "Has Lord Cornius ever mentioned the story of the White Lords?"

Nesto had no such recollection. "No, he hasn't," he finally replied.

"Yes, I wouldn't expect him to do so. The very memory would wound his pride as a Lord. The White Lords—there were ten of them—were the elite of the Lords. Handpicked by the previous Lord Commander himself. Among them were Lords strong enough to wound a dragon. They were the ones favoured by all three of the ancient Gods. Yet, despite their strength, almost all of them were cut down by a single person."

"Only one?" Nesto found it hard to believe. "Is that even possible?"

"Still, it is. Because that person hid a demon inside his body. Normally, demons cannot enter our own world because of the barrier between the two worlds erected by the ancient Gods, but in some way that demon managed to pierce through this. He single-handedly slaughtered all the Lords that dared attack him, and then vanished without a trace. Of course, the Lords kept their humiliation well hidden."

"What does Lord Ereina have to do with the story of the White Lords?"

The Lord smiled, and his voice sounded different when he said: "Because the demon is back." He coughed and his voice got back to normal. "He got out of his hiding place, and he left traces, so that they might find him, and another bloody fight takes place, similar to that sixteen years ago. Lord Commander Legris is trying to gather the strongest Lords to face him, and Lord Ereina is a Lord favoured by all three of the ancient Gods."

Good, let them kill each other. So much the better for me. "If Lord Ereina is gone, then who's going to be in charge of lessons in the armoury?"

The Lord proudly crossed his arms above his chest. "You needn't worry about that," he said. "Lord Cornius and I have taken care of that. Tomorrow, you are practising the sword, as usual, or whatever you're practising. If I were you, I'd me more concerned about other more urgent issues. For example, the flame of the ancient Gods that is burning inside your body."

"What do you mean?" There was something in the Lord's voice that made Nesto swallow with difficulty.

"Oh, nothing special. It's just that, were I you, I'd make sure I controlled the flame, for shortly you will be in for a little surprise, and then the Portal to the Tower of the Lords will open up."

Nesto headed towards the Lord Candidates' rooms, still remembering Lord Mendax's last words. Soon enough, he would be one step closer to his brother…and his father. He didn't yet know what he felt for his Lord father, but he had no intention of forgiving him so easily. At the same time, he was preoccupied with the surprise Lord Mendax had mentioned. It must surely be an awful surprise if he mentioned it.

He was thinking that it was already too late to meet Daemon, when he saw him leaning against the wall, next to his room door, arms crossed. "My apologies," said Daemon when he saw Nesto. "Are you satisfied now? This is a lot more than being even. My jaw still hurts."

Nesto was on the defensive. "How did you know which one was my room?"

Daemon gave him a look that said: typical commoners. "Your name initial is carved here, right? You see it?" he said, after pointing at a spot on the iron door.

"Why did you try to kill me?"

Daemon's smile was gone. "When you mentioned the mark across the ribs, my mind went cloudy," he said, trying to justify himself. "I thought my father had sent you to kill me or, worse, to take me back to his castle."

"It couldn't possibly be that bad living in a castle," Nesto said, before he recalled the slashes he had seen in Daemon's body.

"Oh, you don't know my father. You don't know what it is like living with him. Whoever was in my position would rather enter the Tower of the Lords than live in my father's castle."

He felt sorry for him for an instant, until he realised that this could be yet another lie. He mustn't make the mistake of trusting him so easily. "What makes you think that your father didn't actually send me to take you back?" he asked in a serious tone.

Daemon's haughty look came back across his face. "That's easy," he replied. "I should have realised from the start, but my judgement was clouded. My father would never send someone like you. I mean, you can't even hold a sword properly, let alone use it. This may come as a shock to you, but you are really, really weak, Nesto."

That extra 'really' hurt him a little bit. "If I was that weak, then your jaw wouldn't still hurt."

"It doesn't. I just said it to make you forgive me more easily." Daemon paused for a while. "We're still friends, right?" he finally asked.

Nesto nearly snorted at the sound of that word. "Yes, we're still friends." *Until he betrays you again,* a voice whispered.

He walked into his room with yet another predicament. He wasn't sure if Daemon's words were real, but at least now he wouldn't be completely unsuspicious. He would pretend to be his friend, and this way he would watch his every move. If Daemon did want to kill him, he would discover that Nesto wasn't so weak as Daemon would like to believe.

His dinner included fried hare, sausages, apples, and pears. Only a few hours had passed since his previous meal, but his stomach kept asking for food to make up for the ones he had skipped. When he was done, his stomach asked for more, but he thought it would be better not to overdo it. He lay down, with Lord Mendax's words at the back of his head. Whatever that surprise was, it couldn't be something good. What he mentioned about the fire of the ancient Gods worried him. *Could that be connected somehow with tomorrow's lesson in the armoury?* It wouldn't strike him as odd if the new Lord in charge of the lesson forced them to stay in the hall, until one of the Lord Candidates lost control of the power of the ancient Gods and went up in flames.

And that Lord would probably be me or Daemon...and somehow I doubt it would be Daemon.

That made him get out of bed. He had spent the best part of the day in the baths; that was certainly enough to keep him from turning to ashes during the night. Still, he would feel more secure if he dipped his body into the frozen water one more time. It limited the Gods' fire. The following day would probably prove the worst.

He went out and, as he tried to walk as silently as he could, he heard some alarming voices coming from below, from the baths hall. He wasn't the only one headed there. Other Candidates had got out of their rooms, while some of them were running, as if their Mark were searing their innards. Nesto found them all gathered outside the iron gate leading to the baths. They were all agitated, while two of them bent over a third one, wrapping a piece of cloth around his belly. After a while, he noticed the blood over their hands and the garment. It took him a second to realise that, normally, no blade could pierce through the flesh of a Lord Candidate as he was protected by the Mark.

He turned around to figure out who could be responsible for that, and then he saw them. Two shadows standing in front of the door seemed to be hovering in midair, but Nesto finally made out their black feet treading on solid ground. They were dressed in black, and looked like scarecrows. But for the white masks covering their faces, he wouldn't have been able to discern them in the torch light. Overhead, carved in the heavy door, shining like green flames, were several words that formed a clear message:

NO CANDIDATE MAY ENTER THE BATHS HALL

That did really, really surprise him. For all he knew, Daemon could still want him dead. The Lords surely wanted him dead. It seemed, though, that the ancient Gods were the ones that were actually going to kill him. Or, more precisely, their fiery power.

CHAPTER 7

Nesto moved aside, as the two Candidates went past him, transferring the wounded man possibly to a room of a Lord to treat his wound. He wondered if, in that case, the Lords were allowed to help or not. If he had to guess, then probably not. There was no doubt that one of the two masked men was responsible for that wound. The Candidate, in an act of despair, must have tried to force himself into the baths hall, and one of them must have used something sharp to pierce through his skin. Enter the hall and you die, don't enter the hall, and you die again. Not much of a choice there.

He looked all around, and saw angry, scared, and desperate faces. They didn't look like wolves now, as they had seemed to him the morning of the third day, when he went to the kitchen. Then, they were drooling, and charging at their prey without hesitation. Now, they were the prey, shaking before Death's jaws. They looked like a herd of deer that had been cornered. Deer would use their horns in a desperate attempt to escape, but these Candidates wouldn't dare. Not yet, not as long as the ancient Gods' flame was not threatening their lives.

Under normal circumstances, that would have been his own reaction, but for some reason he was weirdly calm. *Now, all of you will experience the ordeal I have been through so far, when they told me that no God favoured me.* All these who were favoured by two of the three Gods would now feel the terror Nesto felt every time he lay in bed and shut his eyes, without knowing if he would be lucky enough to open them again the following morning.

He was being mean, but so what? They were all enemies. Someday, they too would want him dead.

"That's not really good news, especially for us." Daemon went closer to him from behind. He must have turned up that very moment; Nesto hadn't seen him earlier. He looked quite calm. Maybe, death would be preferable to going back to his father's castle.

"Why do you think they are doing this?"

"Doing what?"

"I mean, trying to kill us." Nesto's mind scurried to the mark both of them hid across their ribs. "Especially us," he said in a lower voice as he turned to look him in the eye.

Daemon showed no signs of comprehension; he might have pretended not to understand. "This way, they're preparing us to survive in the Tower of the Lords, where there will be no baths hall. Or they may simply be perverted. There are so many people like that. The more power they've got, the worse they become." He was certainly hinting at his father.

He was in for another surprise in the armoury the following day. Lord Mendax was their new weaponry instructor. Compared to Lord Ereina, he wasn't that strict. Actually, he was extremely lenient. They found him sitting on a chair in the corner, with his legs splayed out on the table, and his hands behind his head. When, after some time, he decided to occupy himself with their practice, he stood up and carefully picked the sword he would use.

His ability regarding the sword was astounding, but not in a positive sense. In an attempt to show them how to attack from below, the Lord's sword slipped through his hands and landed on the opposite wall. "It seems I am a bit rusty," he justified himself with a chuckle. "It's been a long long time since I last had to use a sword."

"He's even worse than you, Nesto," Daemon noted. "Aren't all the Lords supposed to be fierce warriors with excellent swordsmanship? I told you he's weird."

Lord Mendax didn't bother to wield the sword again. He simply told them to practise what Lord Ereina had shown them, and then he left them alone in the armoury.

The unbridled clangour pervaded the room again, with the swords clashing so fiercely, Nesto wondered what kept them from smashing into pieces. Daemon's attacks were exactly the same. They were all meant to kill. Even the look in his eyes resembled sharp blades, and these managed to pierce through him. Whenever Nesto complained about it, he would reply in the same haughty tone, and many a time he would compare Nesto's abilities to those of Lord Mendax.

Half way through the day, the Lord turned up again. At every single move he made, he left muddy steps behind. When he ensconced himself on his chair, one of the Candidates asked him what had become of the wounded Lord Candidate. "Dead," the Lord replied. "Just like any one of you who will try to enter the Baths Hall. Those treacherous things have orders to kill whoever goes too close to the door."

Their image flashed through Nesto's mind. A dark aura engulfed them, and their snow-white mask, which did not give away any characteristic, made them look fierce. "What are they, and how did they manage to wound a Lord Candidate?" he wanted to know. "Even a sword can't penetrate our skin."

All the Candidates had stopped practising, and gathered around the Lord, curious to know more about the masked men. "With the appropriate weapon, even maids can kill you," explained the Lord. "As for them, they're damned creatures. We call them the Cursed Ones. They watch your every move, and hear all your conversations. There are more than one in this castle. But they move like shadows, and the uninitiated cannot perceive them. Their existence is known only to the Lords, and are only accountable to the Lord Commander. Their strength does not compare to that of the Lords, but a Lord Candidate doesn't stand a chance against them, so do not make the mistake of messing with them."

Daemon snorted. "If I ever have to choose to oppose the power of the ancient Gods, or that of the *Cursed Ones*, then I will take my chances with the masked men."

"Then, you will die," the Lord said with a smile.

"Maybe, maybe not," Daemon stated, shrugging his shoulders.

"Definitely, I will make sure of it. Rules are to be adhered to by everyone, even by the nobles. After all, there is a way to control the fire of the Gods, until your bodies manage to tame it." He paused, and it seemed to Nesto that he did it on purpose, as if he really enjoyed seeing them all anguished. "Take deep breaths, and simply try to relax. The more you panic, the faster the fire will spread over your body. That's it. So simple." Nesto hated him for these words. Something so simple, they could have mentioned it on the day of the ritual, but no Lord had even bothered.

The first day passed without any Candidate turning to ashes, although, on certain occasions, Nesto wished Daemon went up in flames. It wasn't his poignant remarks or his dexterity in the sword that had irritated Nesto. He wasn't sure, but it was something deeper than that. He realised it when he lay down in bed and thought one more time of his brother and father. His own father had abandoned him, while Daemon's, no matter how mean, had found the time to teach him. He had no other recollection of his father, except the one he constantly saw in his dream. Still, it seemed that there were some parts missing from that memory. *He didn't even bother to pay me a single visit.*

On the second day, during Lord Cornius' lesson, he noticed that there were fewer Candidates attending. At least five of them must have lost their lives while sleeping. That relieved him, making him feel more secure. His enemies were dwindling in number. Although he didn't want to admit it, he was glad to see that Daemon had made it through the first day.

His joy was short-lived, though. He had spent a whole day in the Baths hall, that's why he had managed to keep the fire of the ancient Gods in check for almost two days, but at the end of the second day the first signs appeared. The flush in his chest forced him out of bed. The burning sensation in his throat got him out of the room, while his stomach, which was on fire, dragged him to the baths. When he realised what he had done, he stopped and went down on his knees. He had nowhere to go. The Cursed Ones were going to kill him before the frozen water of the baths managed to tame the Gods' fire. Was death the only choice? If so, then he would prefer to die fighting the masked men, just like Daemon had said.

He tried to stand up, but his legs wouldn't obey, so he began to shuffle. *I don't want to die here.* He stuck his nails into the cracks along the paved floor, and dragged his body. If his nails were to open up under the pressure, there would certainly be no blood, only flames. *Not this way.* He gritted his teeth with all his might, and kept shuffling. His eyes stung and, all of a sudden, there were more torches along the corridor than he had seen in the entire castle. For an instant, he thought it had gone up in flames, but it was only his eyes that were burning.

He was almost blind when a hand grabbed him by the shoulder. He figured out he had reached the heavy gate. Now, all he had to do was overcome the obstacle of the Cursed Ones. They didn't try to kill them on the spot. He heard the door open, and they dragged him in. "Drink this," one of the two men told him, taking him by storm. His hand touched a cold jug of water. Why weren't they killing him? Had they decided to spare him his life, or did they simply want to torture him?

Amid his delirium, Nesto knew that plain water wouldn't do him any good. "No, I have to dip in the baths," he said, and felt his throat melt.

One of the masked men snorted. "Commoners," he said, his tone of voice sounding much too familiar. "Why do I even bother?" He felt a hand forcefully open his mouth, and some cool water refresh his whole body. The fire inside of him began to die down, and his vision got back to normal. He expected to see a white mask right before him, but what he saw was Daemon's arrogant face.

"You…" He coughed. His head was reeling, and he found it hard to collect his thoughts. "You are one of the Cursed Ones?"

Daemon's eyes flew open. "Don't be ridiculous. I'm a noble," he said. "And the one that saved your life. Don't compare me to such…stuff!"

Nesto leant on to his elbows. He wasn't in the Baths hall, like he thought, but in a small room similar to his own. "You shouldn't have done that." He was grateful for his help. And this, he didn't really like. "Lord Mendax expressly said that whoever helped a fellow candidate would die." And he didn't want Daemon to die. He didn't like that, either. Gradually, he trusted him again, and each time he trusted someone, it didn't turn out well.

"Can you tell me how exactly I helped you? The baths hall is being guarded, and the only way you can save yourself is dipping into its waters."

"I keep asking myself the same thing. Water alone cannot have such an effect. If it could, every Lord Candidate wouldn't be threatened by the fiery power of the ancient Gods."

"It doesn't have the same effect," Daemon admitted, and brought him another jug of water. Nesto gulped it down greedily, and felt even better. "But, if you mix water with pieces of the crystals you find in the baths, then it does."

He shot to his feet. He had regained all his strength. "How did you come by these crystals?" he wanted to know. "Did you somehow manage to sneak inside the baths hall?"

"Of course not! I'd taken them before entrance was prohibited. That fool, Lord Mendax, helped me realise that such a thing was possible. Not that he wanted me to. His goal was to scare me. Like a stocky Lord could ever do such a thing. He cannot even wield a sword. I used my last crystal on you, by the way. You are welcome."

"I guess now we are even," said Nesto, and what he feared had come true. Daemon had saved his life, risking his own, and had used his last crystal on him. How could he possibly not trust him now?

Daemon looked furious. "NOW, we are even? We were even the moment you hit me with your elbow. Now, you owe me, A LOT! You ungrateful commoner."

To appease him, Nesto had to reveal to him the information he had obtained from the stocky Lord that the portal to the Tower of the Lords would soon open up. But, obviously, that wasn't enough as, even when Nesto was going to his room, he heard Daemon shout they weren't even.

On the third day, there were only twelve Lord Candidates. More than half had lost their lives. Only two of those who died had followed Daemon's advice to attack the masked men, as Lord Mendax told them. *There would have been three if it hadn't been for Daemon.*

Towards the end of the day, there were eleven Candidates as Nesto, with his own eyes, saw one of them lose his life. Just like Nesto, he had been trying to drag himself towards the baths hall as his knees had failed him. Up until then, he had never seen a Candidate go up in flames and, when he did, he wished he'd never see it again. Blue flames flared up in his eyes, and then seared his skin. What was left were ashes, as all the Lords claimed, and his hair-raising howl still echoed in Nesto's ears.

He believed that such a thing wouldn't affect him, but he was wrong. It was a totally different thing seeing the agony and fear in their eyes than seeing the horror painted across the Candidate's face, while the power of the Gods was robbing him of his life. He had to remind himself for several times that they were all enemies, in order to swallow his food and stay there. The worst thing was, it would soon be his turn. His body had already begun to sweat, and this time Daemon wouldn't be able to help him.

Calm down, calm down. He recalled what Lord Mendax had told them, as he went up and down in his small room. If the Lord's words were real, then the only one way he would survive was to stay calm. But how could he remain calm when the flame was burning his insides? He started taking some deep breaths but, every time he felt calm, the Candidate's picture going up in flames and his screams came rushing through Nesto's mind, and his chest was burning again. He needed something that could help him focus on his goal, to remind him his brother, to remind him that he had to reach the top of the tower.

The dagger! That was it. That would calm him down.

He bent over the sides of his bed, and stuck his hand under the mattress. He didn't find the dagger at his first attempt, and that made him panic. *Calm down.* He searched more carefully, ran his hand from corner to corner, but the dagger was nowhere to be found. Then, he decided to remove the mattress altogether. A thick drop of sweat trickled down his forehead, and he gulped. The dagger was gone…

Alright, now you can panic!

CHAPTER 8

A kick sent the bed flying towards the roof, while more images of the bloodcurdling spectacle came out of his unconscious, but this time it wasn't the candidate burning that he saw—it was himself. He didn't stop there. Now, it was the turn of the small table. He kicked it and, when he saw it hadn't broken, he went closer and hit it with his feet, until it smashed into pieces. When there was nothing else for him to kick, he began to punch the wall. All the tension, the rage, and the indignation he had felt all these days he was in the castle, he gave free rein to now, and whatever he saw fell prey to his outburst.

There were already some cracks across the wall when he suddenly felt his stomach turn. His dinner—fried eggs with sausages and chilly peppers—came out of his mouth and nose. Surprisingly, that helped. He calmed down, and the burning sensation in his chest ceased. Something told him that it wasn't calmness that had helped him, but rage.

Someone had stolen his dagger, and a new burden weighed heavily on Nesto's chest. It wouldn't come in handy as a weapon—actually, its sharp blade wouldn't be able to pierce through his flesh, let alone that of a Lord if Nesto's secret were to be revealed, and he had to kill—, but it was the precious reminder his brother had left behind, and he didn't want to part with it. Most probably, the maid had taken it; she was the one to come and go, fetching him food. However, it would be useless to her. It looked valuable, but she would never be able to sell it. A common maid would never account for being in possession of such a weapon, and no one would buy it.

For a moment, he thought of reporting it to Lord Mendax, but that might trigger undesirable questions. Questions that he wouldn't be able to answer without resorting to lies. And lies were not his forte. He had resolved to confront the maid, when he recalled the image of furious Daemon shouting they weren't even. The dagger would only be useful to him, he thought. And that, only so that they would be even. It had to be him…He hoped it was him.

All the rooms were the same, so it took him some time to find the door with the letter "D" carved on it. He knocked on the door and, when that opened, he was ready to shout at Daemon and grab him by the neck, just like he had done to him, but his hand stopped in midair, while his mouth opened only to let out an incomprehensible mumble that sounded like choking. Instead of Daemon, at the door turned up a girl with long black hair, honey-yellow eyes, and fleshy lips. She gave him a puzzled look for a while, and then raised one eyebrow. "Yes?" she said.

"I'm sorry. I thought this was Daemon's room," Nesto replied when he finally found his voice.

"You thought right," said the girl and made space, showing with her glance a point where the bed could only stand.

There, he saw Daemon in another girl's embrace. She was flushed, her brown hair tousled, and her hands reluctantly trying to push Daemon's hands away from the buttons of her blouse. Nesto coughed, and Daemon turned his head in surprise. "I remember telling you to get rid of whoever it was, not inviting him inside," he complained to the standing girl.

"He is kind of cute. I say we let him join us."

That was the first time a girl had found him "kind of" cute, and he almost instantly blushed. The thought of the dagger, though, brought his cheeks back to normal. "NO" both of them said, after exchanging looks.

"Daemon, I need to talk to you."

"Does it have to be right now?"

"Yes!"

"Are you sure it can't wait for a while? I promise it won't take too long."

"Yes, I'm sure. It's really important."

Daemon looked at the two girls, then at Nesto. "Commoner, I…"

"It's alright, you two lovebirds can have your private time, we are leaving," the girl in Daemon's bed said, obviously disappointed, and left, along with her friend, after doing up her blouse and straightening her hair.

Daemon looked at him with the same murderous eyes with which he always did during the sword practice. "You know, I spent two of my crystals on them both. You could have waited for a while, until they paid me back."

Suddenly, a fire appeared in Nesto's chest, only it had nothing to do with the power of the ancient Gods. It was a fire seething with rage. Rage because, a few moments before, he had nearly died, while Daemon had spent his crystals to save two persons bent on gaining the title of Lord. "Why did you use two of your crystals on them?" he wanted to know. *Doesn't he know that the Lords want us dead?*

"I couldn't just stand there and watch two beautiful girls get burnt to death. I guess you would, but you are a commoner. I wouldn't expect anything more from you. Besides, I have already managed to tame the fire of the Gods. I can erase the Mark whenever I like."

That was good. It was reasonable that his own body would do the same shortly. But he couldn't be absolutely sure of that as none of the Gods favoured him. "Daemon, do you know the secret behind the mark across our ribs?" He had decided not to ask him until they managed to enter the Tower of the Lords as he didn't trust him, but now things were different. And, honestly, he couldn't understand Daemon's behaviour. If he were in his position, Nesto would never help anyone what would want him dead in the future.

Daemon's face went completely pale, as if blood had oozed away from his head. "It's just a scar that my beloved father gave me," he said in a bilious voice. "One of the many. There is no secret behind it." Obviously, he didn't know about the mark or the Lords.

"Make sure you never show that mark to anyone. Especially the Lords, or one of the Lord Candidates," Nesto told him. He didn't bother to explain why. Not that he himself knew anything but the result.

"Was this the important thing you wanted to tell me about?" Daemon asked.

"No, not that. I came to get back the dagger you stole from my room."

"Are you calling me a thief?"

"Yes. Can I have my dagger back now?"

"Why would I even bother stealing a stupid dagger from you?"

To get even he intended to say, but it was clear from Daemon's reaction that it wasn't he who had stolen the dagger. The expression on his face told him he was a noble and, apparently, stealing was something that only commoners would do. "It's not a stupid dagger, alright? It's got a green shine, it's made out of glass, and it's really precious to me," he said, and slammed the door behind him.

Since it wasn't Daemon who had stolen it, chances of retrieving it were slim. Come to think of it now, it was highly unlikely—and insane—that the maid could have been the culprit. Why would she even bother to search his room?

He returned to his room, and wondered if the maid would complain about the mess the following morning. He only made his bed, so as to be able to sleep, and lay down, hoping that no dream would visit him during the night, unlike the previous days.

But it wasn't some kind of dream that came while he was sleeping, although that's what he took it for at first, but a Cursed One. Shivers went up and down his spine and, when he opened his eyes, he saw the expressionless mask lurking above his head. His gloved hand grabbed Nesto by the arm, and led him out of the room, without saying a single word. If he wanted to kill him, he would already have done so, while still in his room. He must have been carrying out the Lords' orders.

It couldn't be about the dagger, right? There was no chance the dagger would betray his mark, even if a Lord had taken it. His heartbeats got back to normal when he saw other Candidates accompanied by masked men. Just like Nesto, they seemed oblivious to what was going on. Their steps echoed in the dark and the dead of silence. They went up the stairs on the first level, and then the second one, the forbidden. Then, it dawned on him.

It was time to enter the Tower of the Lords.

The stairs led in front of a huge copper wide-open door to welcome the Lord Candidates. A black carpet showed them to a pedestal where the Lords were seated, and there was an empty chair between them, probably intended for Lord Ereina. Behind the Lords was a grandiose fireplace, while its flames looked like a huge burning dragon that hulked overhead. The Cursed Ones took their seats; half of them on the side of the pedestal, and the other half on the other side, after arraying the seven Candidates in line before the Lords.

"Some of you, I never expected to make it so far," said Lord Cornius, as he stood up from his chair. It wasn't necessary to come and stand before Nesto for him to figure out he was referring to him, but he did. "While others"—the Lord walked and stood before Daemon, two seats away, giving him a grim look—, "I hoped they wouldn't. But that's not of any importance right now." He walked between two persons, and then strode towards the door, which made the Candidates turn in his direction. Nesto gave Lord Mendax a furtive glance before he joined them. The Lord yawned and placed his hand over his mouth. He looked sleepy. That could be it, or he was preparing for yet another dull story of Lord Cornius, as he himself would say.

"The time has come for you to follow in the footsteps of the most heroic Lords," stated Lord Cornius, and looked above the door. It was the boring story, after all. Several designs and drawings adorned the walls and the roof, and the Lord had fixed his stare on a specific painting, which depicted a white tower surrounded by some dragons and Lords locked in battle. He began to narrate the final countdown between the cruel dragons and the courageous Lords, and Nesto knew that it was a story riddled with lies. It wasn't the Lords who had defeated the dragons, but the magic of the elves. It wasn't the Lords who had destroyed the White Tower, thus marking a new era, but the dragons themselves, who had been mesmerised by the magic of the Tower.

When he mentioned the Tower of the Lords, Nesto figured out that most of his words were real as he didn't hear even a single thing that praised the Lords; besides, his story was much too short. After all, Lord Mendax's yawn was suddenly stifled. It was quite clear what he was implying.

The Tower of the Lords was, in fact, four islands formed by the pieces of the White Tower, and connected with one another through magic portals. Thanks to the magic of those pieces, all the islands, except the first one, hovered in midair, one on top of the other, forming a mental tower. They were all inhabited by most dangerous creatures that needed the presence of a Lord, so that they wouldn't kill one another, the Lord said to them very briefly. *I guess that was a side effect of the magic used to turn the dragons against their own kind.* "Don't be killed by the monsters. Pass the trials of the Lords that rule each island, and reach the last portal. That's all you need to do to obtain the title of the Lord," he concluded. Quite simple. And, of course, deadly.

Some cooks walked in, carrying platters of the last supper for the Lord Candidates, while a maid bringing up the rear fetched some new clothes to replace the old, tattered ones. They were of a dark red colour, like blood. They got undressed in front of everyone else, just like Nesto, albeit more carefully, lest his mark be revealed. He hoped Daemon would be just as careful. One of the two girls and one more Candidate had managed, just like Daemon, to erase the Mark of the ancient Gods at will, as Nesto noticed. The girl caught him staring at her, and winked at him, thus making Nesto's face turn red as her blouse. He was appeased by the fact that there were others whose bodies hadn't yet managed to tame that flame.

Lord Mendax went up to him, while Nesto was tasting the chicken and the sweet pastries. "I told you you needn't worry, didn't I?" he said, while his hair-raising smile flashed across his face. That smile jarred with his wide mouth and puffy cheeks. "I didn't have the slightest doubt that you'd get that far. Garon would be proud of you, just like I am." *Yes, but Garon wouldn't want me dead, just like you would, if you knew about the mark.*

The Lord came even closer and stuck his fingers into the pastries. "The first part is over," he said in a low voice, almost muffling his words with the licking of his fingers. "Now is the hard part, but rest assured: in this part, you will be able to get assistance openly."

Does he know that I received help from Daemon? If he weren't an acquaintance of his uncle, or if he was another Lord, then both of them would be dead by now. For that, he was grateful. He must surely have noticed, during the lessons in the armoury, that they were intimate with Daemon, and he must have surmised that they were helping each other to the bitter end. Of course, Daemon and Nesto hadn't come to such an agreement. However, since he saved his life, such a thing would be expected. Especially if you add in the fact that they both carried the same mark. "There won't be any rules that will keep us from helping each other?"

"Oh, there won't be any rules at all. Just survival."

Survival? "I have been trying to survive from the moment I set foot in this castle."

"Yes, but soon after you enter the Tower of the Lords, it will begin for real."

He wouldn't even dare think what he had to go through to reach the top. Perhaps, it was Lord Mendax's fault, or he might still be angry at him for calling him a thief, but Daemon didn't speak to him at all during lunch. He only flashed him a look, when Lord Cornius had them gather in front of the engraved wooden door by the fireplace. "It's the Portal that leads to the first islands," the Lord explained to them, and that led him to the narration of another story. No wonder why Lord Mendax would rather keep him at bay. His stories were enough to kill a dragon. They were that boring! It had nothing to do with the way his village storyteller used to narrate the stories of the Lords. You could listen to him for hours on end, but you couldn't hear Lord Cornius even for a second.

After finishing his story, Lord Cornius ordered two of the Cursed Ones to open the wooden door. They moved silently like cats, black cats, to be more precise. The door split in two, as the masked men dragged its two parts, and a wall with circular lines appeared. It turned into a black sea when the Lord took a small crystal out of his pocket, got hold of its two ends, and turned it upside down.

One by one, the Lord Candidates nervously began to walk through the Portal. Only Daemon and Nesto were left behind, when something on the masked man standing on the right side of the Portal caught Daemon's eye. The noble turned and signalled to him, and Nesto figured out what he asked him for. His eyes sized up the Cursed One, until a small green shine grabbed his attention. It was a small blade strapped around his waist that sheened. The difference was that this blade was glassy, and its handle was wooden.

My brother's dagger!

His white mask was expressionless, but Nesto could almost see the faint smile hidden behind it. The hair around the neck stood on end, and a shiver went up and down his body. He felt the dark eyes of the Cursed One pierce through his mask, and jab him in the ribs. The masked man didn't speak, yet Nesto heard his voice, as the darkness of the Portal engulfed him.

It was heard like the hiss of the wind. *"I know,"* it said to him. *"I know about the mark..."*

CHAPTER 9

Everything was dark around him, as if the black sea had swallowed him. At first, he felt like he was walking in a vacuum, then the earth was gone under his feet, and he began to fall, which made his stomach jump to head, until he fainted.

When he came round, he was dizzy, while his body was sore. He tried to open his eyes, but his eyelids were too heavy, and the only thing he managed to see before they closed again was a faint light in the dark, and several thin shadows that looked like bars. His numb hands stood over his head, in their own right, and something kept his legs from moving. It didn't take him long to realise the situation he was in. Hands and legs immobilised, darkness, and bars. He was no longer in the Tower of the Lords, but in their castle, inside a cell.

There was no mistake about it: the faint smile of the Cursed One, his gaze, and his words wasn't just a fantasy Nesto's mind had created out of fear. They were real. It wasn't the maid or Daemon who had taken the dagger, but one of the masked men. Most probably, they had orders to search in all the rooms, for as long as the Candidates were busy listening to stories, practising, and trying not to turn to ashes. It should have been easy for them. They moved like shadows.

Then, they must have informed one of the Lords, or even the Lord Commander. Maybe the Lord Commander's visit had to do with this. This showed how important, or rather how dangerous, the mark was for the Lords. He still didn't know how he ended up bound hand and foot without realising it, since he was sure he had followed the rest of the Candidates through the Gate. But that didn't really matter now, did it?

He felt his consciousness slipping away. When he woke up again, he couldn't tell if several hours or days had passed. Hours, he guessed, as he still felt weak. Although he could open his eyes, the only thing he saw was a blur. Screams came from all around, and they were so loud, for an instant he thought they came from beside him. There must have been a special torture chamber in the castle, which Nesto hadn't been to before. Up to now, of course. He wondered what kind of torture was in store for him. He had heard his uncle say that in the city of the Kings stealing was punished with cutting both hands and, if you made the mistake of robbing some eminent noble, punishment was death.

If that was true about stealing, what kind of torture was he worthy of for carrying the mark?

The door creaked, and a figure approached him. He couldn't make out who it was. One of the Lords, he supposed. He stood in front of Nesto for a moment, like he was examining it with his eyes, and then took a few more steps beside him. "Just two so far," he mentioned, his voice too thin to belong to Lord Mendax or Lord Cornius.

Just two so far? Was there another one chained in the cell? Of course there was.

Daemon!

He shared the same secret with Nesto. But what gave him away? *Was this my fault for getting too close to him? That's just great. If, by any chance, we manage to get out of this alive, I will owe him for life. He is never going to forget this.*

He lost consciousness again, but not before he heard some of the figure's words, as it walked away. "Tomorrow…dead."

The cries still echoed in his ears when he woke up. Dizziness and pain had ceased, while his vision was back to normal. He tried to free himself, but to no avail; the chains were so tight. He was in a dark cell, just like he had imagined. It was damper and bigger than he expected and, while he smelled something burning, there was no fireplace or fire anywhere.

Maybe, the smell was coming from the torches hanging on the walls.

"Daemon…" He turned to look at him, but there was no one beside him. All he saw were some empty chains, gathering dust, like they hadn't been used for a long time. Countless thoughts reeled in his mind, and they were all trying to hold on to something to reach the conclusion that Daemon was still alive. One of these thoughts told him that the noble had managed somehow to escape, while another one said that they hadn't caught him yet, it was just a dream, and the dust over the chains fuelled this thought even more. He knew it, though, that he was just fooling himself. He had heard the words uttered by the figure: "Tomorrow…dead." And tomorrow might have already gone.

He heard footsteps close in, and instantly his father and brother crossed his mind. Whatever their plan was, it was in vain. Nesto never made it to the Tower of the Lords. He expected to see Lord Mendax or Cornius or even Lord Ereina, but another female Lord turned up instead. A red mantle was tied on her shoulders, while the scant remains of Lords' apparel was of a gold colour, especially revealing. She opened the gate and walked in. She strode towards Nesto, holding his brother's green dagger, and stopped only when she got so close that, despite the dim light, Nesto could make out her grey eyes and her thin red lips.

"You have survived so far," stated the Lord, while pointing the dagger to his throat. Nesto intended to survive even longer. He had already devised a plan. As soon as the Lord set him free, he would somehow distract her and then run as fast as he could to escape. With the ancient Gods' fire inside of him, they would find it hard to kill him, he remembered before he recalled Lord Mendax's words: "With the right weapon, even a maid can kill you."

The Lord abruptly lowered the dagger, and cut Nesto's shirt down to his chest. "Your body managed to tame their fire," she said, after checking his chest. Her breath was hot, stroking his neck. "Unlike the rest, who turned to ashes."

The rest? Were there more people with the same mark, apart from Daemon?

"What are you going to do now? Kill me or lead me where the other Lords are?"

She looked at him in surprise. "I have no reason to kill you. And it would be hard, even impossible, for me to lead you to the other Lords. All I can do is open the Portal to the second island if you successfully pass your test."

Nesto wasn't sure he really understood what was going on. "What about my mark?" he asked.

"It's erased. Now, you can show it or erase it at will," she replied to him.

But that wasn't the mark he was asking about. Was she not aware of the mark across his ribs? He asked one more question to make sure. "The dagger that you are holding, where did you get it?"

The Lord brought it to the same height as her face. "What was it that caught your eye? Was it the green glow? Some of us Lords have several of them in our possession. They have magic inside, although it's useless to us as we don't know how to use it. As you are going to find out soon, they are very sharp, even for our own skin."

Great! he thought. His secret was still safe. The Cursed One that had robbed him of the dagger hadn't informed the Lords. Anyway, even if he had, there was no clue that would lead them to the mark. Maybe, this way, they would discover that his father was one of the Lords, but that would certainly not be enough. *But then...* "Why am I chained?"

"When you went through the Portal to enter the Tower of the Lords, only the bodies of three Lord Candidates had managed to tame the Gods' fire, so the Portal didn't affect them. But that was not true for the rest of you. No one without the Mark of the ancient Gods can go through the Portal without losing their lives, and it is just as dangerous for those who have not been able to tame it. Their fire would have burnt you alive. For as long as you were in the castle, you used the baths halls to keep the fiery power of the Gods in check, but there are no such luxuries on my island. The only thing I could do to help you was immobilise you."

"And how did that help?"

"Well, you are alive, aren't you?"

"And what about the others who hadn't tamed the power of the Gods? Where are they?"

"I confined you all to the same room. Where do you think they are?" Nesto looked at the chains again that were full of dust. Only it wasn't dust; it was ash. He recalled the screams he had heard and the burning smell. Of the four men, he was the only one to survive.

The Lord released him, and Nesto plumped to the ground. His feet were stiff, while his hands were in a worse state. They were more than just numb; he felt like these limbs belonged to someone else. He must have been chained for several days. Blood began to run through the veins of his hands, and that was such a pleasant sensation.

"Rest for now, bur prepare for tomorrow as your test begins," she said to him, as Nesto stood on his feet. "Only when you gain the title of the Lord, will you be taught how to materialize weapons by using the ancient Gods' power. That's why in your trial, you will have to use such daggers." The Lord threw the dagger to him, and then turned around to leave. Under normal circumstances, he would have caught it with ease, but his hands were still numb, so the dagger stuck to the hard floor.

His hands were back to normal when one of the Lord's henchmen walked into the cell, bringing some food, enough to sate another three men—the ones that hadn't survived. When Nesto asked him if he too carried the ancient Gods' Mark, he nodded in the affirmative. He hadn't gained the title of the Lord, he explained to him, but he wasn't a Lord Candidate, either. He and another one had the duty to serve and satisfy every need of Lord Asaer. Apparently, the Lords of the islands were top of the Lord hierarchy, and on the islands their authority went even beyond that of the Lord Commander, that's why they could have as many servants carrying the Mark as they wanted.

He drooled over the roasted meat and the sweet grapes and, when he tasted them, they were as delicious as he had hoped for. The meat tasted like horse, only it was somewhat more tender. He ate it all, and wished there were more for him. Dinner on the second floor of the castle seemed to have taken place the previous night, yet his stomach made him wonder if more time had passed. "How many days was I unconscious?" he asked the man, swallowing his last mouthful.

"Almost two days. Usually, all the Lord Candidates go up in flames or manage to tame the ancient Gods' fire, by the end of the first day. However, for some reason, you took longer than that."

It wouldn't have taken me that long if I, at least, had had one God that favoured me. "And the other Candidates, have they already passed the test?"

"No. The Lord postponed the trial for tomorrow, and that holds for everyone. Actually, this made one of the other three Lord Candidates complain," the man mentioned.

It wasn't difficult for Nesto to guess who that was. It was Daemon, for sure. At least, he was alive. "Are we allowed to know what our trial will be?"

"Four persons survived after the Gate, but only half of you will proceed to the next level of the Tower of the Lords." He looked at the dagger stuck to the ground, and then back at Nesto. "You will fight with each other to death."

This cruelty was to be expected. They didn't mind shutting the baths hall and letting the Candidates burn to death. This was just one of the many reasons that prevented any sane man dare challenge the Tower of the Lords. But still, hearing that almost made him throw up what he had eaten. He could think of an excuse for whatever the Lords did in the castle. It wasn't a very good one, but preventing the Candidates from entering the baths hall, so that their bodies would tame the power of the ancient Gods, was somewhat acceptable. But this, the sole purpose of this trial was to reduce the numbers of the Lord Candidates to half…"

Which, actually, wasn't such a bad thing. It just meant that the numbers of his enemies would be reduced. He should be more grateful for that. When the man left and Nesto was alone, together with his own shadow, he took the dagger, and started swinging it around to get used to its weight. He would find it hard to use some other sword, but with a knife he wasn't inferior to anyone. After practising with the dagger, he lay on the floor to take a breather. He thought which of the candidates had survived, in order to predict his possible opponent the next day. One of them was Daemon, the other two… and then he realized it. One of them was Daemon!

Killing one or all of the Lord Candidates, he wouldn't mind, but Daemon wasn't just a Lord Candidate. He had the same mark, the same secret, and he had saved him from burning to death. The idea had wedged itself in his mind that they would help each other survive, not the other way round. What would he do if he were forced to fight with Daemon to the bitter end? *Would I try to kill him? Would he try to kill me? Somehow, I don't think that he will have any problem with that.* He could imagine him saying in his arrogant tone: "I'm sorry, commoner, but you didn't really expect me, a noble, to give my life for you, did you? I mean, you don't even know how to wield a sword. You should be the one to die." And that would sound perfectly reasonable to him.

He couldn't go to sleep, his body was already well-rested, while his mind too preoccupied to drift off. The following day was already there, and he hadn't yet managed to convince himself. What counted more than anything else was his own survival, he knew that, but his remorse and doubts weighed heavily on the hand that wielded the dagger.

The same servant with the Mark that had brought him food led him to the arena through a tunnel lit by torches and some strange crystals that gave off a green, almost yellow, glow. They resembled the ones underground, in the ruins of the White Tower. Lord Asaer was obsessed with magic, and everything to do with the elves.

The arena was a bit bigger than his room cell, as he noticed when he walked in, and the wired iron door slammed shut behind him. The place was damp, and it stank, but at least it was bright. Yet, on reflection, it would be preferable to fight in the dark, without having to see his opponent.

But he saw him stand in the middle of the arena with his dagger in hand, and he knew that only one of them would walk out alive.

The good thing was that he wouldn't have to fight the noble. The bad thing was that he would have to fight with the girl that had found him "somewhat" cute.

She had been smiling last time he saw her, and she had actually winked at him, but now her smile was wiped off her face, and her eyes looked focused and wild. She had already prepared herself. Her red clothes gave the impression that she was covered in dark blood, and Nesto couldn't help imagining his dagger piercing through her flesh, and blood gushing out in rivulets, covering her whole body. For some stupid reason, her face was replaced with Lirelle's innocent and desperate one. If only he hadn't talked to her and she hadn't smiled at him, it would have been so much easier to kill her.

Oh, well, at least it wasn't Daemon.

CHAPTER 10

"No hard feelings," she said, her fingers clenched around the dagger handle.

"Not at all." He couldn't afford to show any weakness. His opponent might take advantage of that. He felt the power of the ancient Gods running through his veins, making him stronger, faster, and somewhat fearless, as the Mark began to scorch him across his chest. He could hear his opponent's short and heavy breathing, and her heartbeats. It could be his own heartbeat. He couldn't be sure in that confined space.

She started circling around him slowly but steadily, biding her time until she attacked, her eyes always locked with his. After each of them coming full circle, Nesto heard the sound of the skin shuffling on the rock, and then he saw her charge at him. Her movement was so abrupt and quick, Nesto could barely move to fend off the deadly blow right in his heart. He stepped aside and her dagger stuck into his arm, cutting him deep.

The pain was sharp, and it felt so weird. An iron sword couldn't even scratch him, and that had given him a false sense of security against sharp objects, but this dagger could so easily steal his life. He ignored the pain, as he saw his opponent charge again. Her movements were fast, but so were his. He pushed her blow back, then hit back, making her dagger slip her fingers and hurtle away from her. He tried to deal a final blow, but a kick threw him on the wall, leaving him almost breathless. When he raised his eyes, he saw her run towards the dagger. He stood up and ran after her, while she had already grabbed the dagger.

Nesto's dagger was only a breath away from her throat, when it happened. His feet slipped along the damp stone, and both of them plumped to the ground. Blood trickled under his eye, at the spot where he had been cut, while they were falling, and his own weapon had stuck into her chest. Her face was over his, and he could watch her breathe her last. "No hard feelings," she whispered, frittering away what was left of her life. Her lips were red, covered in blood as they were, while her eyes gradually changed colour, turning from honey-yellow to green, then a bright blue, covering all the white. They looked like crystals.

Not at all…

He stood still there, only looking at her eyes' blue glow, captivated by their beauty, and the horror hidden in there. He didn't know how long he had been standing there in this state, when one of the Lord's henchmen came to drag him out of the arena. The next thing he could remember was that man treating his wounds. That cut under his eye only took a good rinsing with plain water, but the one in his arm was more serious. After rinsing it with water, the servant had to anoint it with some kind of herb, then dress it to staunch the flow of blood.

He tried to ask about Daemon, but he felt so weak, so exhausted, that he couldn't speak. Had he won too or had his eyes turned into blue crystals? It was Daemon, he probably shouldn't be worried about him. Nesto knew how remarkably good he was with the sword. He had proved it on so many occasions during their practice, although in this trial they had to use daggers, not swords. But still, how bad could he be? He felt his strength ooze away, as the Mark of the ancient Gods faded away from his chest, and his eyes grew too heavy to keep open.

A slight sound woke him up that was repeated every so often. He leant on his elbow, and saw someone in the cell throwing small stones at the iron bars. He stopped when he saw him waking up. "I didn't expect you to survive the battle, commoner. I mean, I know how bad you are with a weapon." He felt glad to hear his voice…and also irritated, but a slight feeling of irritation was always expected, when Daemon opened his mouth to speak. His worries weren't for nothing as he found him rather worn out after his own battle. A thin gash ran across his face, while his left hand and thigh were dressed in bandage.

"Well, I'm not as bad as you, judging by your cuts. What's your excuse? Are you really that bad with the dagger?"

"Don't be stupid," said the noble. "I'm really good with all the weapons, and I'm even better when I'm not using any. It's just that my opponent happened to be almost as good as I am. If you had been in my position, you'd be dead now."

Strangely enough, he felt the need to defend, not himself, but the girl Candidate he had just killed. "I'm sure my own opponent was just as good as yours, perhaps even better. It was one of the girls I had seen in your room, you know."

He must have sensed some sort of guilt in Nesto's words because he immediately said: "I would have killed her, too." And there was no arrogance or bragging in his voice. "And I would also have killed you, without a second thought." But now there was.

"Me, too. Without even a hint of hesitation." In his thought, it had seemed so difficult to kill Daemon, but now, words came out almost like reflexes.

"Really? After all the things I have done for you! You are really ungrateful and cruel, commoner."

"One's own survival always comes first."

"I will remember that, next time you need my help."

When he made an effort to stand up, he leant on his injured hand, and the wound opened. So, when food came, Nesto had to patiently wait until they anointed it with that herb, and covered it in bandage, before he could fill his mouth with grapes, hard liver, pieces of heart, and offal. When he asked when they would be allowed to leave for the second island, the servant told him that, shortly enough, Lord Asaer herself would open the Portal.

The servants with the Mark of the ancient Gods had said 'shortly enough', but more than an hour had passed, and the Lord wouldn't turn up. The wait and the boredom made him tighten and loosen his arm to see if the wound would open up again, while Daemon began to remove all bandage. "I'm not much of a healer, but I'm pretty sure that your wounds haven't healed, yet," said Nesto, looking at him.

"These," said Daemon, showing him his wounds, after removing the bandage, "are just minor scratches. I have had a lot worse than that." He thought of competing with Daemon over who had sustained the most serious wounds during their short lives, but that thought was gone as quickly as it appeared. The truth was, Nesto had sustained quite a lot of injuries on those few occasions he had gone hunting with his uncle: wolf bites in the legs, a rib broken by a deer's horn, and a bear's scratches across his shoulder, just before Garon stuck an arrow in the back of its head. But all this, no matter how spectacular at first, was minor scratches compared to the inhuman wounds that dotted the noble's body.

The Lord took some time to appear, but that wasn't the worst part. When she finally turned up, she refused to open the Portal, claiming that they had to be properly trained before she let them pass on to the second level. Apparently, the training they had back in the castle was inadequate, and Nesto couldn't argue down that statement. They only had one day of proper training with Lord Ereina, the days they spent training under Lord Mendax didn't really count. And, according to the Lord, any kind of exercise that lasted less than two months would be insufficient.

They were given one more day of rest, and the next morning one of the Lord's henchmen would lead them beyond the tunnels, at the surface, where their training would be held.

Before she left, the Lord took two daggers out of her waist case. "These are the weapons with which you killed the other

Lord Candidates. You can keep them as mementos. I have enough," she told them, and threw the one to Daemon and the other to Nesto. Nesto used his right, uninjured hand to catch it but, for some unexplained reason, when he got hold of it, his palm was cut, just like the first time Garon had thrown him Almar's dagger. And what happened next was even more weird.

Dark clouds surrounded him, and he felt like he was in one of his dreams. Maybe he was, after all, as he didn't see Daemon or the Lord anywhere, when the clouds cleared up; only two flames were flickering next to the iron throne, where a man was seated, wearing a black mantle that covered all his body—in fact, he was lying down, using his hands as a pillow.

"No one sits on my throne, Zoloc!" That female voice, which belonged to Lord Asaer, made the man turn his eyes in her direction. The woman's eyes had become two slits that looked at him angrily, while her sharp boots grated on the marble floor, as she walked towards him. Behind her, the fiery red mantle she wore flapped, just like the two flames next to the throne. Neither of them looked at Nesto. It was as if he didn't exist.

"Not even me, my love, your soon-to-be-husband?" he said, after standing up. He straightened up his crumpled clothes, and then strode towards her, while she stopped short, and kept giving him the same angry look.

"Stop playing games with me. I'm not here to ease your boredom. You are one of the Lords of the islands. You know what happens when a Lord leaves his island."

The man walked around her, touched her blond hair, and his fingers stopped at her pretty face, as he stood in front of her. "The monsters lose the small sense of logic they barely possess, and start killing one another…and, of course, they won't stop until every monster is dead, including themselves. The magic of the elves is really terrifying, don't you think? Last time I left the island, I found more than a hundred bodies, including those of the Lord Candidates."

"Yet, you left the island again"

"It's not my fault" said the man, and walked around her again. "Your beauty is majestic," he then whispered in her ear.

"If you don't tell me right now what you really want, I'm going to kill you and ask for the Order of the Lord to elect a new Lord of the island," said the Lord, whose patience seemed to be wearing thin.

"Oh, I see…it's that time of the moon, again. But, you know, I don't care about the blood." He brought his lips closer to hers. Her grey eyes were glued to his, while her hand touched his chest, and started to go up, slowly but steadily, scratching him with her nails, until she grabbed him by the neck and began to strangle him—with all her might, Nesto figured out as he noticed that the man could barely breathe. The Lord bit his lower lip, then took a dagger out of her waist case, and brought its tip over the man's heart.

The man dressed in the black mantle looked at the weapon she held, and raised his eyes to look at her, smilingly. The Lord must have surely tried to jab him with the dagger, but the man, miraculously, vanished and, in the blink of an eye, appeared on the iron throne, leaving her choke the air. "One of these days, I'm going to find a way to catch you. And then, I will kill you slowly and painfully." From her lips oozed some drops of blood, which was his own, not hers.

"You hanker after the impossible, my love. I cannot be caught or killed…but I will stop bothering you if you do me a small favour," he said, and then wiped the blood off his lips.

"Why couldn't you say that from the beginning?"

"I wanted you to appreciate what I'm offering…"

"What do you want?" she asked curtly, almost angrily. "I have already changed my trial, so that only half of the Lord

Candidates survive each time, just like you asked me to, last time. What is it that you ask for now?"

The man twined his fingers, and crossed his legs. It was clear from his smile that he enjoyed playing with her, torturing her, and seeing her eyes and body sizzle at his touch. "How many of the Lord Candidates survived this time?"

"Just two."

"And they're both still small boys. They have yet to become men, I presume."

"Yes. How did you know that?"

"It doesn't matter. I want you to lead them to the only Lord, apart from you, who lives on this island, and make sure they stay there to train under him for at least two months."

"You mean Lord Raizel, the only one of the White Lords that is still alive? He won't accept any disciple after the incident with the demon, which resulted in wiping out almost all of the White Lords. You should know that."

"He will if you are the one to ask him. He owes you one as you allow him to reside on your island."

"Maybe he will, but I won't do it," she took delight in replying.

"What? Why?" Her reply seemed to surprise him.

"Because now I know what you want, and I'm going to make you suffer by not giving it to you."

The man smiled and scratched his lower lip with his teeth, at the spot where the Lord had bitten him. "Fine. I will make another offer, an offer that you can't decline," he said, and stood up from the throne with a jerk. The flames dancing beside him flared up and engulfed him.

"If you are offering me your body, then I'm not interested, unless it has stopped breathing," she told him, looking at him with murderous eyes.

The mysterious man walked towards her, while the flames followed him, scorching the marble floor. He bent forward and whispered in her ear.

"And how would I know that you are not lying to me?" she asked, squeezing his throat again. Her eyes had no sign of trust.

"You already know the answer to that, my love. Those who can use the words of magic…can never tell a word of lie."

The Lord let go of his throat, and ran her hand through his dark hair, lifting it up to reveal his green eyes. "Are these two Lord Candidates so special that you would disclose your secrets for their sake?"

"Well, let's just say they have piqued my interest."

Nesto suddenly woke up, panting. He held on to the dagger tight and, when he looked around, he didn't see Lord Asaer or that mysterious man, or even the iron throne with the two fires next to it. He only saw Daemon eye him with a look that implied, "Finally, you have woken up." "Did you have a good sleep?" the noble asked him. "You collapsed out of nowhere. Your body must have been exhausted."

But Nesto didn't respond. His collapse couldn't have been related to exhaustion. That dream gave him the same feeling as the one he had seen while still in the castle, the dream where his father was telling him that it was the Lords who wanted him dead. He remembered the Lord telling him that the daggers hid magic. The daggers must have been related somehow. He couldn't find any other explanation. It was as if there were memories hidden deep inside of them.

His breathing was still heavy, and his heart was pounding. There was something else, as well, apart from the daggers, that united these dreams or memories. He began to sweat, and his hand wouldn't stop trembling as he reflected on it. His dark hair, his green eyes, his look…that mysterious man in his last dream looked exactly like Nestal, his father.

CHAPTER 11

Could it really be him? *I mean, I never imagined him being like that.* The picture he had of his father had nothing to do with what he had seen. What kind of father would have been so easy-going, flirting, and playing games, while his son risked losing his life? That made Nesto hate him even more. But, on the other hand, this could just be an act. He hadn't revealed anything to Lord Asaer about Nesto being his son, so that meant he didn't trust her. And he had kept track of him, and Daemon, too. This shouldn't come as a surprise. It was the mark. Somehow, everything revolved around the mark across their ribs.

But then again, he could be wrong. Just because that man looked like Nestal didn't mean it was his father. In the end, he barely remembered his face.

The Lord must have wanted to make sure that White Lord Raizel would accept them as his disciples, as she led them to her quarters to wash away all that dirt. In contrast to the arena and the rooms where the Lord Candidates were held, the Lord's quarters was mainly snow-white, and the walls gave off a white-gold glow. Walking past the hall with the iron throne that Nesto had seen in his dream, they entered another bigger hall with dark walls, lit only by the white glow coming out of a statue of a dragon, over ten metres tall. It wasn't only light that came out of it; cold, crystal-clear water oozed out of its wide open mouth, forming baths that resembled those in the Black Castle of the Lords.

They took off their clothes, and dipped into the cool water. Scrubbing hard but carefully, so that their wounds wouldn't open up again, their black, dirty bodies shone like the dragon's statue, when they stepped out. The Lord had replaced their tattered garments with clean clothes that weren't so worn out—they must have belonged to her two servants. When

Daemon covered his scars with his sweater, Nesto noticed that the scratch across his face was gone. "How long has it been since I passed out?" he asked him. Such a wound couldn't have healed in a few hours.

"A little longer than half a day," the noble replied, rubbing his hair dry. "The Lord was worried about you. For a moment, she thought you were a goner, until she heard you snoring."

"That's a lie. I don't snore. And I must have been sleeping for more than half a day. The scratch on your face has already healed."

Daemon seemed to have been taken by storm, and was on the defensive. It gave a strange sensation like he was hiding something. "Trust me I know what I heard, commoner" he said. "And that scratch on my face was a tiny one. Half a day was more than enough for it to disappear."

"Alright, I will admit that I might snore" said Nesto. The phrase 'trust me' still bothered him so much. It felt like a stab. "But let me see your hand." He grabbed Daemon's hand, and saw that, while the wound hadn't yet healed completely, it looked as if it had been quite some time since he sustained it. There was only a long, thin scratch along his palm. There was nothing serious that called for special care. "You're lying" he accused him. "I must have been unconscious for days! What are you and the Lord hiding from me?"

Daemon pulled back his hand, and he looked irritated. "I already told you, didn't I? These were just minor scratches and, besides, the herb they anointed them with must have done a really good job. What's wrong with you, commoner?"

The noble's angry look made Nesto realise how paranoid he must have sounded. "I'm sorry, you're right," he admitted. "I just had a strange dream." Daemon had no reason to lie to him. It can't have been more than a day. It was just his instinct that bade him not trust anyone, especially the noble, who was too close to him now.

The Lord prepared a kind of dinner that looked like soup, and tasted even worse, and then later she had one of her men lead them beyond the tunnels, outside the ruins of the White Tower, where the White Lord was supposed to be. Under normal circumstances, Nesto's priority would have been to reach the top of the Tower of the Lords to meet his brother, but now he had no other option but to stay on the first island as his father or, at least, the man who looked like his father, wanted Nesto to train under Lord Raizel for two months, making him stronger.

Strong enough to deal with a Lord? I don't know. What he knew was that, completely by chance, Nesto would turn sixteen in exactly two months' time. And his brother and father desperately wanted him to enter the Tower before he came of age. This was just as mysterious as the mark across his ribs.

After some miles and a while later, they reached the cave where the Lord dwelled. Almost two weeks had passed since the last time he felt the sun burning…no, not burning. That's what the flame of the ancient Gods did. The sun was warming him, giving him hope, not despair and sleepless nights. Next to the entrance, between the huge rocks, flowed a stream that ended in the verdant forest behind them, while along the stream were ten vertical burning sticks. The island, especially the forest, was full of bizarre monsters, but not even one dared approach the cave where the Lord lived.

They learnt why the monsters didn't get close, when the servant left them standing there, telling them that they would be better off staying outside, rather than entering the cave, as Lord Raizel was ruthless and a half-lunatic. Such an intrusion would even cost them their lives. Both of them decided to follow the servant's advice.

"How come you have the same weapon as a Lord?" Daemon asked him, while waiting outside the cave. His question gladdened him as he wasn't sure if the noble was still angry at him. For as long as they were in the Black Castle, he had blamed him for stealing his dagger and telling him lies, and that he and the Lord were hiding something from Nesto. Daemon, probably like most nobles, seemed to be oversensitive to such insults. "That's what the dagger stolen from you looks like, right?" he said, while holding the dagger.

"I think it belonged to my father. He was a Lord," he replied. Nesto took his own dagger out of its case. Carrying it around was a bit tiring. He didn't like that dagger; he preferred his brother's. He felt it heavier and, although it looked sparkling clean, he could still see on it the blood of the Lord Candidate that had been his opponent. Yet, he couldn't throw it away. It was the only weapon that could pierce through the skin of a Lord. *And you never know when it may come of use.* Especially if his enemy was ruthless and a half-lunatic.

He gave in to the temptation of sharing with the noble the reason why he had entered the Tower of the Lords and the few things he knew about the mark, but it was so difficult for him to trust someone that, at the very thought, he felt two frozen hands gripping his throat. Maybe Daemon had a share in that.

Anyway, he had managed to enter the Tower, and the noble had already proved he was trustworthy. So, no matter how hard it was, he decided to ignore the voice that kept whispering to him not to trust anyone, and confided everything to Daemon.

The threat that the mark imposed on them, Nesto had already revealed to Daemon, when they were in the castle, so that part wasn't too hard to believe. Convincing him, though, of the dreams-memories he had had, and that training with Lord Raizel must probably have been his father's idea, was a little bit harder. *And by little, I mean A LOT harder.* He was laughing and saying that the flame of the ancient Gods had inflicted permanent damage on Nesto's head. Until he heard that Nestal had not only kept track of Nesto, but him as well. That silenced him up for some reason. The last part, he couldn't be entirely sure of, but it was quite satisfying seeing him flinch, almost terrified.

"So, what happens when you reach the age of sixteen?" Daemon finally asked.

"I don't know. In my village, I get the right to marry the woman I want, and raise my own family."

"That's it, then, commoner. The Order of the Lords is aware that you don't know how to treat a lady, and they want to kill you before you get the chance to marry one."

"Very funny. Do I need to remind you that they want to kill you too?"

"I'm a noble. Do I need to remind you that they wanted to kill me from the day I was born, just like every other noble? Now, they just have another reason to want me dead."

"Are you sure you don't know anything about the mark? Isn't there anything your father might have mentioned to you?" Nesto asked. It was almost scary the way his blood kept disappearing from his face whenever his father was mentioned.

"No, we barely even talked." His voice had become solemn and strict. It was as if there were a wall between them. "And the few words we exchanged had nothing to do with the mark or the conversations a father can have with his son. Unless you discussed with your father how badly you wanted to kill him, and the way in which you would go about it. Oh, wait. Your father abandoned you," he said with a grin. "We're not all as lucky as you are!"

Any more questions about the castle where Daemon lived, or about his father only managed to turn his answers into virulent remarks and jokes, that's why Nesto finally stopped insisting.

They waited for long, but only the countless stars turned up in the sky as it got dark, not the Lord.

When he opened his eyes the following day, he saw two big fangs drooling blood over his head, greeting him good morning. He got startled and tapped his feet on the ground, dragging himself backwards, until his back landed on a tree trunk nearby. "You can count yourself dead," the old man told him. On one shoulder, he was carrying the carcass of a four-legged monster, a little bigger than a wolf, while one of his legs pressed on Daemon's throat, who lay still on the ground, struggling to let go. "While you," he said to the noble, "you have, at least, good instincts. You might have survived, if your opponent had been a wild beast."

"Are you White Lord Raizel?" Nesto asked him, propping up his neck. He thrust the dust off his clothes, and tried to remove the blood stains, but to no avail. The man did not respond, but it was definitely him. He could figure it out from the look he gave him. It was as if he had heard something that annoyed him, a name maybe that he hadn't heard for years. Besides, how many people, apart from Lord Raizel, could be residing on the surface of the island? Probably none.

"You two must be the Lord Candidates that Lord Asaer told me about." After carefully looking at them, the Lord told them—it actually sounded more like an order—to take off their shoes and hop into the stream, with no further explanations, then he went back into the cave.

Judging by the Lord's tone and the way he had woken them up, their decision to take up the servant's advice not to intrude on his privacy was certainly the right one. Both of them did what Raizel told them, and stood barefoot in the cold water, ankle-high. Daemon's face had lost its arrogant look and, for some reason, he seemed to be shocked. "Normally, no one can catch me unawares," the noble explained to Nesto. "Even while sleeping, I can hear the slightest sound, I can feel any presence…but this time it was too late, and his foot was already on my throat."

Just then, the White Lord came out of the cave. He wasn't carrying the wild beast on his shoulder, and Nesto was now much calmer to examine his characteristics. His grey beard was almost as long as his long thick hair, while there was a big scar in his throat. Under the rags he wore, his broad shoulders and wide chest were easily visible. His gait was scary, and made you swallow with difficulty. If he had to picture a face in all those stories he had heard about the Lords, then that one would certainly belong to Raizel. Fierce and powerful to the point that his gaze could make you tremble. The exact opposite of Lord Mendax's face.

The Lord approached Nesto, and placed his hand on his chest. "Call forth the power of the ancient Gods," he ordered him. "I must see which of them favour you, before our training begins."

That was not necessary. Nesto already knew the answer to that. "None," he told him and, for some reason, he felt embarrassed admitting that to the White Lord.

"Don't talk nonsense, child. That's not possible. No Lord in his right frame of mind would have let you take part in the ritual and, even if someone did, you would be a pile of ash trapped in the baths hall right now."

"But that's what the Lords of the castle told me."

"Then, probably these Lords were fools that didn't know how to perform their duties. Most likely, you are favoured by all three of the ancient Gods, and those impotent Lords must have been confused as they had never had the chance to see such a Lord Candidate." However, when Nesto revealed the Mark, Lord Raizel immediately changed his mind. "That's unprecedented," he said without hiding his disappointment. "You will be the weakest Lord in the history of the Order if you manage to obtain the title."

Nesto erased the Mark. He didn't turn to look at Daemon, but he was sure his face was adorned with that arrogant smile, or he was trying to stifle a laugh. And he didn't have to tell him; he could almost hear the noble's thought. "You see, I told you that you were really, really weak, commoner," it was saying to him.

"If that was true, I wouldn't be standing here, alive," he said, trying to defend himself. He would say more, but he stopped because, now that he was thinking about it, he didn't actually care about how strong he would be. His main and sole purpose was to survive and reach the top of the Tower of the Lords. Everything else didn't really matter.

When it was Daemon's turn, Lord Raizel gave him a scrutinising look for quite some time, before he placed his palm on the noble's chest. "You look awfully familiar," stated the White Lord, but he didn't get any response. That was quite weird, considering the fact that what the noble needed was something that would trigger a ironic remark.

This procedure lasted longer than in Nesto's case and, when the White Lord finally removed his hand, he remained silent, his nostrils twitching and the muscles of his body tightening. "The only God that favours you is the initial ruler of the skies," he told him. But something was definitely wrong, he could feel it, he could see it. Nesto's instinct was right as he heard the Lord's teeth gritting and, then, in the blink of an eye, a kick landed on Daemon's head, sending him hurtling out of the stream, his legs dragging along the ground, and crashing into a rock, which began to crack. Instantly, dust picked up, and that obstructed his view: he couldn't see what state the noble was in.

The dagger was in his hand, without even realising it, while the Mark of the ancient Gods began to scorch his chest, as it appeared. *Why did he do that? Did he somehow find out that*

Daemon is a noble, or is he simply a half-lunatic and ruthless? It was of little importance. Daemon was in danger, and maybe it would soon be his turn. After all, it was time to pay the noble back for all his assistance. He only managed a tentative step before Lord Raizel's voice froze his body. "You are his son, aren't you?" he asked Daemon in a voice tinged with hatred. Nesto could clearly see him trying to restrain his anger.

He loosened his grip, and the dagger made of glass dropped, when he heard the White Lord tell him: "There is no point in hiding it from me. You are the son of Jenon, admit it. Son of the Demon!"

CHAPTER 12

"Well, I'm not his daughter, that's for sure." The dust began to clear up, and Nesto could make out Daemon's figure. When it was gone completely, he could see the wound across his forehead, and the blood trickling down his face. What was most alarming, though, was his smile. It was a cross between arrogance and madness.

"It's not only your appearance. You are cocky and disrespectful, too. Just like your father was," said the old man, walking towards Daemon. Every step he took made him look like a predator.

"I have nothing to do with that demon. I'm not like him!" screamed the noble, and snapped his body off the rock. At first, Nesto thought that the blood coming out of Daemon's wound was over his eyes, dyeing them red, but he was wrong. The noble's hair had turned silver grey and, coupled with his bloodthirsty red eyes, he looked like a creature that did not belong to that world.

A demon!

Lord Raizel covered the distance between them with a leap. He grabbed Daemon by the throat with his left hand, and pressed him against the rock again, while in his right hand a sword began to materialise, which shone like the sun. The tip of the blade aimed between Daemon's eyes. "Oh, but you are…you are just like him in every way," he said. Tension on Raizel's body was obvious. It seemed like he desperately wanted to pierce through the noble's skull, but he was restraining himself. More likely, he was waiting for him to make a move. The wrong move, and then the noble would find himself with a burning sword stuck into his forehead. "The worst thing of all is that his fiendish blood is running through your veins. A blood thirsty for battle. I'm sure that right now you are feeling the urge to kill, to destroy. A demon's only desire is to wreak havoc."

Thankfully, Daemon didn't try to attack; he didn't even try to resist. His hands were loose by his sides. "I'm not like that. I can control my desires…I can control the demon inside me," he claimed. He was probably telling the truth because his hair turned back to their normal colour, so did his eyes.

"If only it were that easy." The Lord stopped choking him, but his sword was still pointed dangerously close to him.

"It is for me."

The old man snorted. "You must be really naive to believe something like that," he said. "Don't you know what your father did? Hasn't he told you what that demon inside you is capable of doing? All my friends, my family, all those that bore the title of the White Lord lost their lives to that monster."

Instant relief coursed through Nesto's body as he knew what came next. Maybe it was thanks to the stories he had heard from his village storyteller, and those from Lord Cornius in the Black Castle, but he was able to tell when a story was about to be told. And now was one of those times. The sword disappeared from Raizel's hands just as quickly as it had materialised. The Lord started his story, while Nesto and Daemon listened, standing still, the one with his feet dipped into the stream, and the other with his back pressed against the rock. Threat still lingering in the air.

The White Lords were formed more than fifty years ago, and only those who were favoured by all three ancient Gods had the privilege to bear that title. They had a single duty. To hunt down all the remaining dragons.

That came as a shock to Nesto. "All the remaining dragons?" he asked. "Weren't all the dragons killed by…the Lords centuries ago?" The dragons were actually eliminated due to the magic of the elves, but he wasn't sure if that was the right time to reveal that knowledge he possessed.

"The Order is insisting on keeping a lot of secrets, I see. No, the last dragon was killed by me almost twenty years ago, I believe, and this scar is a reminder he left behind," said the White Lord, showing the scar in his throat.

Lord Raizel went on to tell them about Jenon, Daemon's father. "He was a disciple of mine," the old man admitted bitterly.

He had loved him like he was his own son. His skills were unparalleled as a Lord Candidate, the most promising of them all. But, when he obtained the title, even though as a Lord he was favoured by all three of the ancient Gods, he refused to join the White Lords. According to Raizel, Jenon became by far the strongest Lord in the history of the Order of the Lords. His swordsmanship was said to have been envied even by the ancient Gods. That was what caused his downfall. He became arrogant, overconfident. The reason why he didn't join the White Lords was because he wanted to hunt down the dragons by himself.

A demon breaking the barrier that separated the two worlds had only occurred once before, when the dragons still ruled the skies, so when another demon broke the barrier again, there was turmoil in the Order. The White Lords waited for their orders, but Jenon, blinded by the glory he would receive, tried to eliminate the threat of the demon all by himself, and he was victorious. The only problem was that he had decided to accept the demon inside his body. He had gone mad, he wanted a power far greater than the Mark of the ancient Gods. He wanted to become equal to a god.

"He swore to me that he could control it, and then he killed almost half the ruling class. Rumours have it that he even wounded the previous King. In the end, he escaped, hiding away from the nobles' rage. But the Order couldn't let him get away with it. They tracked him down, and ordered us, the White Lords, to eliminate him. I was the only one to refuse. I still cared about my disciple, but I regret it now. If I had joined them, perhaps we would have managed to kill Jenon and the demon that he accepted inside his body, and my fellow Lords and friends would still be alive now.

"Most of them were his friends, too, and one of them, Lord Commander Ousen, was his father…He slaughtered his own father, while he had sworn to me that he could control it!" He paused only to look Daemon in the eyes. "Do you still think that you can control it, too?"

Daemon did not respond; he didn't say a word, and that was probably the best thing to do, for it was clear that the Lord could barely keep his anger in check. Nesto followed the same policy, so the old man stood looking at them in silence, not sure how he should react. Finally, he walked into the cave, cursing himself, the Order of the Lords, and that ominous day the demon managed to break the barrier.

Nesto expected Daemon to ask him to leave as fast as possible, and go back to Lord Asaer to ask her to open the Gate to the second island, before the old man changed his mind and resolved to let his rage run wild. However, all the noble did was sit on the ground, his back leaning against the rock, and his stare blank, lost in thought, making a gloomy face. Could he not sense the danger he was in?

Everything sank in, amid that hush that fell on them. What Daemon was, the story of Lord Raizel about Jenon. Nesto even remembered Lord Mendax telling him the story about the demon that wiped out the White Lords. "The demon is back," he had said. Could it be that he had returned because he was searching for his son? The noble had mentioned that he had run away from his father, so that was a possibility. Or maybe what Lord Mendax and the old man had said was true, and the demon was just seeking a bloody battle.

Nevertheless, the Lord Commander was on the move, too. Lord Ereina was one of the Lords that he had recruited in order to stop Tzenon, and surely there ought to be a lot more Lords like Lord Ereina that had been summoned for the specific mission.

The sun had set, and the air had grown chilly. It seemed they would spend another night out there. After he retrieved the dagger, Nesto picked up some dry twigs from the wood, making sure he wouldn't stray too far away from the cave, so as not to be attacked by any wild beasts, and started a fire close to Daemon. He sat next to him, not knowing what he was supposed to do. This was the first time he had had a friend, let alone a noble friend in whose veins ran a demon's blood. His mind pictured a scene where Daemon, having lost control, was covered in blood, not his own, trying to kill everyone that dared approach him, even Nesto. He tried to shake it off, though, as such thoughts wouldn't be particularly useful right now. After all, he had constantly been under the threat of death ever since he set foot in the Black Castle. There shouldn't be anything too scary for him anymore, not even a demon.

What he needed now was to find a way to console Daemon, like he had when Nesto was feeling guilty about killing that girl Lord Candidate. "Not sure what's worse," he said in order to strike up a conversation. "Being a commoner or a demon?"

"I'm quite sure we both know the answer to that," the noble replied almost indifferently, his eyes staring at the fire.

"Yes, nobody in their right mind would want to be born a commoner."

"Exactly."

"Actually, I still think being a noble is far worse." Making jokes seemed to work. Daemon smiled; he even let out a snort of laughter.

"Don't be ridiculous, commoner."

The fire danced, reflected in Daemon's eyes, making them look almost red and just as scary as Nesto had seen them that morning. For fear of being caught staring at them, he raised his eyes to the wound. "The wound on your forehead has almost healed," Nesto noted.

"That's one of the good things about having the blood of a demon. My wounds tend to heal a lot faster than normal. The one on my hand is already gone." He showed him. "However, just like Lord Raizel said, one of the bad things is that we feel the urge to kill and, apparently, that urge grows stronger towards our fathers. I didn't know that he had killed my grandfather," the noble admitted. "I didn't even know about his battle against the White Lords. I only thought he was a ruthless man, who had somehow managed to get a demon's power in his hands.

"I can see now why our housekeeper insisted on my entering the Tower of the Lords. Because of the previous incidents, my father wouldn't dare search for me here. For me, this is the safest place I could be if no one knew about my connection to Jenon."

Nesto was tempted to tell him that demon Jenon was on the move—he might even be on his way there—, but he couldn't be absolutely sure of such a thing. Perhaps, it would be better not to upset the noble, especially now.

He had gone without food for more than a day, so it didn't strike him as odd when his stomach began growling. Hunting, though, with his injured hand was out of the question, despite the protection the fiery power of the ancient Gods gave him. Instead, he was content with imagining the food he would eat if he were in the Black Castle. His thoughts filled with fried eggs, sausages, and meat from deer and wild boar. In the end, he pictured gorging himself on pastes for the sweet taste that lingered afterwards. *I had no idea I would miss the Black Castle so much…well, their food, actually.*

When Daemon managed to close his eyes, the fire was almost out, so Nesto went gathering some more dry twigs to maintain it. On his way back, the smell of burning meat assailed his nostrils. It came from within the cave. The old man was surely about to taste all that crunchy meat from the morning kill.

He was wondering if it was safe to spend the whole night outside the cave, while Raizel had clearly shown them his intention of killing whoever was associated with Jenon and the demon he had accepted inside of him, when the White Lord got out and went closer, with a face that Nesto couldn't read.

He shook Daemon to snap him out of sleep, and prepared for the worst. He placed his hand close to his glassy dagger, and forced the fiery force of the ancient Gods to engulf his body by making the Mark appear.

"Did you come to take your revenge?" the noble smilingly asked, and he sounded almost happy about it, as if he had been expecting it all day.

The old man's inscrutable face didn't change, and he said: "I don't blame you for your father's sins, and I don't hate you for being his son. It's only him I want to kill. But you also share the same demon blood, and this, I cannot ignore. I will train you for two months, as I promised Lord Asaer, but if you ever dare show, even once, the demon's face you hide inside of you, then I will kill you without a second thought."

To be honest, I wasn't expecting something like that. He was even kind enough to throw them each a piece of meat. *It almost made me trust him…almost.*

CHAPTER 13

The next morning, he was awakened by a bucket of cold water. Although the sun was strong, and it was a hot day, Nesto's body immediately began to shake as he recalled the frozen waters of the baths hall. Lord Raizel stood above him again, holding the bucket in one hand, and carrying one of the forest beasts on his shoulder. The words he didn't say were written all over his face. "You can count yourself dead again." The old man headed towards the cave to leave his morning kill, while Nesto went by the stream to wash, just like Daemon.

The previous night, Nesto had a wild thought. What if the mark across his ribs meant that he had the blood of a demon inside of him, just like Daemon? *It could be. I mean, it explains why the Lords would want me dead. They wouldn't like the same incident that happened to the White Lords. The sooner they get rid of me, the better.* But this thought was gone when he saw the noble washing himself. Except for the scars on Daemon's chest, inflicted that day in the baths hall, all the other wounds had already healed, even that on his forehead, while Nesto's arm still ached every time he abruptly moved it.

That most probably indicated that he was no demon.

The White Lord decided to make some things clear before he commenced training. The first thing was that they would have to call him "master," from now on. Secondly, he decided to name Daemon "number one," and Nesto "number two." He had asked what their names were, and they told him, but apparently they weren't to his liking. He even threatened to kill them if, by any chance, they used their real names or if they failed to call Raizel "master." And he really meant it because the first time Daemon disobeyed him, he got a kick in the ribs as a warning. And he made it clear that there wouldn't be another one.

Unlike the Black Castle, here, no breakfast waited for them on the platter. They would simply have to settle for a piece of meat at night, when the Lord was to cook his prey. So, they embarked on their training on an empty stomach.

Because of the lack of ancient Gods favouring him, even the White Lord wasn't sure if Nesto could perform the basics of what a normal Lord was capable of. So, when the old man asked him to materialise a weapon of his choice in his hands, and he did it at his first attempt, all three of them were flabbergasted. Nesto only had to picture the frame of the weapon, as Raizel told him, and then he felt the ancient Gods' flame run through his right hand, taking the form of a dagger similar to the glassy one he carried on him.

His joy was short-lived as Master Raizel told him off for his choice of weapon, saying that all Lords worth their salt chose to use swords, and only rarely did the Lords opt for spears. Anything beyond these two choices was deemed to be useless or second-rate in a battle. And, when Nesto showed him the glassy dagger and told him there were surely some Lords who used it, thinking of his father, the old man adamantly refused it. "That's a weapon of the ones we refer to as the Cursed Ones," he said scornfully. "No Lord would ever use that kind of weapon." Then, he grabbed the glassy dagger from Nesto's hands, and threw it away.

Under the Lord's orders, Nesto materialised a sword that shone, its tip almost going up in flames, and he began to train. Daemon, unfortunately, was as impressive as Nesto in materialising weapons and, apart from this, he had one of the ancient Gods, the initial ruler of the skies, favouring him, which meant that, with a lot of practice, he could shoot bolts out of his hands.

After some training and lots of sweat, the Mark of the ancient Gods on their chests vanished by itself and, despite their efforts to call it forth again, nothing happened. When they informed master Raizel of the incident—he had cut off ten small twigs, and was now placing them along the stream—, he explained that overusing the power of the Gods would lead to the Mark getting erased. They would need to rest at least half a day to be able to make it reappear.

All the days flew by, with all three of them doing the same things. Every morning, Nesto and Daemon would practise the sword, while Lord Raizel would put town twigs along the stream, setting them on fire. Usually, by midday, their bodies were exhausted, and the Mark erased itself, and then the old man had them climb up the rocks next to the cave or run through the forest. That was always the worst part of their training, and also the most dangerous.

You don't know how fast you really are until you are forced to run through a forest that is filled with wild beasts, without any sort of weapons or the power of the ancient Gods.

Mastering the skill of the ancient God that favoured him seemed quite easy for Daemon. He was shooting bolts out of his hands as early as the first week. He was good, no matter what he applied himself to, and he always attributed that to the fact that he was born a noble. *So irritating.* Even master Raizel praised him for his dexterity with the sword. He was constantly comparing him to his father, and that was something Daemon didn't like.

His humiliating remarks on Nesto's performance was a permanent fixture but, thanks to the White Lord, Nesto had found a way to pay him back. So, when the noble saw him practising the sword and made a remark, like: "I see that you are as bad as ever, number two," Nesto would reply: "Yes, and you are almost as good as your father, number one." That made the noble gnash his teeth and flash him a vengeful smile. The truth was, Nesto felt satisfied and, at the same time, guilty for making the noble suffer this way…but, mostly, satisfaction.

Beyond the noble's irritable behaviour and his display of swordsmanship, which made him seem unbearable, there were times when Nesto felt sorry for him. Out of the blue, Master Raizel tended to hit him on an everyday basis, probably venting his spleen on him for all the hatred he felt for Jenon, for he hardly ever hit Nesto. On one occasion, he hit Daemon so hard, who was protected by the power of the ancient Gods, that Nesto thought he was going to die. The noble's clothes were covered in blood, while he sustained some broken bones. The Lord had seen Nesto's worry painted over his face. "Don't worry, number two. He won't die from anything like this. Demons are quite resilient, I think," he had told him. And, for some reason, Daemon didn't complain even once.

Days flew by more quickly and calmly than ever. Even though Nesto had to deal with someone that carried the blood of a demon inside him, and might have lost control whenever they practised and fought together, and a half-lunatic that threatened to kill them if they didn't call him "master," he felt more secure here than back in the Black Castle. Perhaps, this had to do with the fact that master Raizel was focused on the Lord Candidate who was the son of Jenon, and not on Nesto, a weak Lord Candidate that no God favoured.

After almost two months, they had consolidated all the techniques the Lord had shown them in the sword. The only thing they lacked now was experience of real battle. Besides, they were able to master a skill that normally only the ones favoured by all three Gods could learn. Within short distances, they could talk to each other only through thought. That made the old man suspicious. While he usually didn't pay much attention to Nesto, when they sat around the fire to fill their stomachs, master Raizel began to ask him about his ancestors and his father. Questions that Nesto couldn't answer truthfully. But, thankfully, he didn't know the entire truth, so telling the Lord that he never knew his father and that he was raised by his uncle, Garon, was partially, if not entirely, true.

"For an instant, I thought you were going to reveal to the old man all the things you once told me about your father and the mark across the ribs," said the noble, when Lord Raizel walked into the cave, and left them alone. "If we consider the fact that he didn't kill me, although I'm the son of the odious demon, Jenon, then I think it's safe to assume that he wouldn't kill you, either, if you showed him the Mark. Don't get me wrong. I'm not saying that the Order of the Lords wouldn't kill you…us. I'm only saying that master Raizel seems different from the other Lords. He has a sense of pride and morality that all the Lords at the Black Castle lacked. He resembles more of a noble than a Lord in that matter."

It was such words that sometimes made Nesto doubt about Daemon's judgement. For some reason, he believed that nobles were paragons of gallantry and morality. And from the stories Nesto had heard, that was most certainly not true.

The fire they had lit sizzled, and some howls were heard coming from the dark forest, so it was highly unlikely that their conversation would reach the old man's ears. "I can't trust anyone so easily. It's against my instincts," Nesto told him, making sure his tone was low, despite the noise. *I barely trusted you.* He had to admit, though, that it would have been easier for him to trust Daemon from the start if he had known that a demon's blood was running through his veins. Knowing that there was someone the Lords would definitely want dead, perhaps more than himself, would probably have broken the barrier between them far more easily.

"What a pity! Maybe, Raizel could tell us what will happen when you reach the age of sixteen. He seems knowledgeable. Certainly more than Lord Cornius."

"I don't need Lord Raizel," declared Nesto. "I'll learn that by myself soon."

In two days' time. *That* soon.

The last night they would spend outside the White Lord's cave, under the countless stars and the two moons that were almost fused together, Nesto couldn't sleep. At first, it was because he had turned sixteen a few hours before, then it was the howls of the night predators and the same cold, strong wind that surrounded them every night. Later, he was no longer feeling cold, and the reason why he wouldn't go to sleep was that his body grew so hot, he felt the fiery force of the ancient Gods was trying to scorch him. He was wrong. It wasn't the Mark of the ancient Gods. He figured that out when all that warm sensation was concentrated at one single spot…

Where the smaller mark was.

The burning sensation there was unbearable. He had to bite his lips to keep himself from screaming. And he wanted to scream so badly and hit something so hard that even the pain would go away. But he couldn't let Lord Raizel know, that's why he swallowed his howls, and forced himself to take it silently. When the burning sensation eventually subsided, he lifted his top to check the mark. The three lines that looked like scratches were bright blue and cold to the touch, although, deep within, he still felt warm, as if someone had lit a fire there.

As that flame gradually went out, he felt weak, his consciousness slipping away, and his eyelids growing heavy. There was immediate need for sleep.

Several repeated sounds awakened him. It was as if Daemon was exercising with his bolts, but that couldn't be right. It was still early in the morning, the sun hadn't come out. That was the time when master Raizel usually went hunting. "What's going on, Daemon?" he asked. When he turned over, he only saw his back. Black bolts bounced off his left hand, and a sword was forming on his right one. But why?

He saw why, a moment later. Someone was standing opposite him, and they were aggressive. Nesto saw the black clothes flapping in the wind, and the white mask that hid any facial characteristics. *A Cursed One! What's the masked man doing here?*

He didn't have the chance to ask him as the noble started shooting bolts out of his left hand, while the Cursed One was desperately trying to fend them off. Then, Daemon charged at him. His hand moved incredibly fast, and the masked man was barely able to follow his movements. If Daemon were a normal Lord Candidate, he would be dead by now, just like Lord Mendax had warned them the first time they saw a cursed one. But now, things were different. The noble had cornered his opponent with countless attacks in a row and, finally, dealt a blow to the man's face, breaking the mask in two. Yet, it wasn't meant to be the final blow as green smoke came out of the glassy dagger that the masked man wielded, forming a weird four-legged monster with sharp fangs that made the noble step back.

The monster vanished as fast as it had turned up. That was probably some kind of magic.

The female face that was revealed when the pieces of the mask fell off was majestic. As the faint moonlight shone on her, her skin looked as dark as the night sky. Her hair was pitch-black, held back, while her green eyes glistened, almost as bright as the two moons, making Nesto's heart beat faster.

He didn't realise how and why but, when he saw Daemon tighten his grip on his sword, ready to attack again, he ran as fast as he could to prevent the noble from harming her, putting the girl behind his back. *Why am I doing this? Is it perhaps because of that girl candidate that I killed?* No, that wasn't it. It was something else, something deeper. He felt the burning desire to protect her, no matter what.

"What are you doing, you foolish commoner?" Daemon demanded to know. "She wants to kill you. Get away from that thing immediately."

"I don't wish to kill him," claimed the Cursed One, while she threw the glassy dagger as proof.

"I guess I was wrong, then. Wasn't it you standing over his head a few moments ago, sticking your sharp weapon into his throat? It must have been another Cursed One," said the noble, his ironic tone more than obvious.

"It's true, I won't deny it. For a moment, I was tempted to kill him. However, the true reason why I am here, believe it or not, is to keep him alive."

While the girl was telling them about Lord Mendax's big mouth that finally led her to Nesto, he didn't stir from his seat as Daemon kept on giving her that black look he flashed at Nesto every time they practised. A piercing gaze, just like a blade that promised a swift death.

While pacing the corridors, the Cursed One had heard Lord Mendax—on one of the countless conversations he had had with just himself—speak of a glassy dagger he had seen under the mattress of one of the Lord Candidates. At the first opportunity, she scoured all the rooms, until she found it. The dagger was, obviously, the same as those used by the Cursed Ones. A normal Lord Candidate shouldn't be able to obtain something like that, that's why she decided to silently follow the candidate it belonged to to learn more about him and how he had come by the specific weapon.

"The next evening, I overheard the secret that you confided to the noble," said the girl. "I was so taken aback that I almost revealed my presence when you two started fighting. Who could have imagined that someone who bore the mark still existed?"

"So, you know what the mark means? Tell me," Nesto asked her.

"The Cursed Ones know what it means better than anyone else. I will tell you the meaning of it, but first there is one thing that is a matter of urgency. Your blood has awakened, and now all the Cursed Ones are aware of your presence. I must use a word of magic on you in order to make it harder for them to find you. Please, trust me," she told him, as she bent over to pick up her dagger.

It was almost disturbing how easy and natural it felt trusting her. Trusting her every word like he had known her forever, while he hadn't yet trusted the noble, even if he had saved his life, when the fire of the ancient Gods almost turned him to ashes. The girl picked up her dagger, and then put it in its side case on Nesto's chest, after asking for his permission. "That's what I was trying to do when you suddenly began to attack me," she said, looking at Daemon out of the corner of her bright green eye, while he gave her a look of doubt.

"Isihir Occultus," she whispered, and Nesto saw a puff of green smoke come out of the dagger, which surrounded him, before it vanished again. "That will make it harder for the other Cursed Ones to track you down. The Lords must have already given them orders to run after you. They definitely want you dead."

"We already know that," said Daemon. "What we want to learn is why."

"Because the mark shows that he has the bloodline of the Gods. He is what the Order of the Lords fears the most." She turned towards Nesto, her eyes carefully lowered, avoiding any eye contact. "The Lords have disguised their fear into a trophy, and they do not miss the opportunity to show it to the whole world. You have seen it in the Black Castle. You have heard it in their stories. They even made you believe that you could easily kill it."

Nesto stood there, puzzled. What she was implying, what she was saying actually was…what was it?

The Cursed One knelt before him, and said in her soft voice what Nesto couldn't fathom: "You are a descendant of the almighty dragons, Lord Candidate Nesto."

CHAPTER 14

He could hear a faint nervous laugh from somewhere, but it didn't come from Daemon or the Cursed One. Most probably, it came from his own mouth. He imagined himself through the girl's eyes. A look of disbelief, his mouth wide open, while blood must have oozed away from his face, just as it happened with the noble every time he heard of his father. His mind couldn't fully apprehend what those words meant, so Nesto instead tried to focus on the next words that came out of the Cursed One.

"Soon enough, there will be a phenomenon that occurs every thousand years, more or less. The alignment of the planets and the two moons. If you, in whose veins runs the blood of the dragons, are still alive when that happens, all the dragons will rise from their graves, and the era of the dragons will start once again."

Suddenly, he remembered Lord Mendax saying, after the story of the White Tower, *"There is a legend, though, that one of the dragons survived. It took a human form and still wanders our world, waiting for the right moment to reclaim the skies. But that's just silly."* And he started laughing again, nervously. Nesto tried to focus, but his head kept spinning. He felt like a leaf that was about to be blown by the wind.

Well, here it was. The secret of the mark was revealed to him. There was a moment he had desperately wanted to know and, now that he did, all he wished for was to somehow forget about it. Pretend like he had never heard it, as if that would somehow change the truth of things. What was he supposed to do now? Panic? Would that help him in any way? *Probably not. Now, I understand why my brother wanted to keep that secret.*

His mind went blank, and he barely remembered the rest. What he retained in his memory was that the girl and all the Cursed Ones were, in fact, elves that, because of their betrayal, received a divine curse, which cost them their immortality and almost all their magic power, and had them wander throughout their lives like treacherous beings. At some point during the day, he thought he had caught a glimpse of White Lord Raizel and Lord Asaer, but he wasn't absolutely sure.

He must have spent at least an entire day remaining silent, and hearing strange noises that couldn't reach him, when his mind started working again. It was probably the sensation of falling that woke him up, then he abruptly plumped to the hard ground. He had the taste of mud in his mouth.

"Do you like the mud so much that you're thinking of lying in it all day, commoner?" Daemon sounded annoyed.

Nesto tried to get up, but it was harder than usual. He felt heavy, as if carrying someone on his back. After his shock, he wasn't sure of his whereabouts. "What happened?" he asked, while he stood up with difficulty. His legs almost trembled under his weight. "Where are we?" Fortunately, he still possessed the survival instinct, which was pushing him to get hold of himself. He looked around, and saw there was fog, like it was dawn and the sun rays would soon come out. All around, he could see some strange black trees with dozens of thick leafless branches, while their trunks were thick as five persons standing side by side.

"Finally, you were able to utter some words. For the remainder of the day, you were lost in thought. Every time I spoke to you, all you did was nod unceasingly," the noble complained.

"How would you react if you were in my place?" Nesto almost shouted. He didn't want to raise his voice at Daemon, but he felt the need to take it out on someone, to blame someone, even if they had nothing to do with all those things that troubled Nesto's mind.

"But I am in your place...I have the same mark as you, and I'm also the son of Demon Jenon," he said inside his thought.

Probably, the Cursed One didn't know about Daemon's mark, and the noble must have wanted to keep it under wraps. "We've just got on the second island," he said softly after a small pause, acting like he wasn't really affected by Nesto's shouting. "And, according to Silan-te here," he cast a glance at the Cursed One, "we have to survive for the first seven days without the fiery power of the ancient Gods. Unlike the other three islands, this particular one has a lot of magic on it, and this affects—not in a positive way—all the Lord Candidates who set foot on it for the first time. Until our body gets used to it, it is almost forbidden to use the Mark, unless we want to suffer the side effects. But you should not worry. Because Silan-te has promised to protect us from the wild monsters of this island, and from the other Cursed Ones that will be hunting us down." The noble smiled, almost ironically, at this statement.

"I only serve, Lord Candidate Nesto," Silan-te said brusquely, "not you."

Daemon's smile was wiped off his face. "Why not me?" he asked.

"Because my kind was created for serving the sons of the ancient Gods, and the only way to remove the curse placed on me is to do exactly that, and only that. Besides, Lord Candidate Nesto also tried to protect me, while you, on the other hand, tried to kill me."

"I thought we'd gone over that, when I agreed to let you serve me."

"I never agreed to that"

They continued to bicker, showing that they weren't fond of each other's company, until Daemon suddenly said, "Shh, I hear footsteps. Follow me quickly." And he quickly strode towards a tree trunk. Nesto called forth the Mark, and followed the noble. Clearly, right now wasn't the time to worry about the side effects his body would have to face for using the power of the Gods.

"Is it the Cursed Ones?" asked Nesto.

Silan-te stood a few steps ahead of the noble, away from the tree foliage, looking far beyond with her bright green eyes. "It's a herd of lygars," she said in a calm voice. "Dangerous creatures, but they never attack members of my race."

"Yes, but I'm sure they attack members of my race." Daemon held Silan-te's hand, and pulled her back, so that the monsters wouldn't see her. That pull was so strong, he lifted her up in the air, hurtling her between himself and Nesto. Almost by reflex, Nesto kept her waist from hitting the trunk, and then felt her black hair stroke his face. As he held her tight to protect her, his lips softly touched her neck, while the enticing scent of her hair assailed his nostrils.

She was beautiful, he had to admit that. It wasn't the kind of beauty that Lirel had. It was somewhat different, stronger in a way. He was attracted to her smell, her melodious voice, her facial lines, and her sparkling eyes. They promised him safety and peace of mind. Nothing would be able to reach him. No threat, no Cursed One, no monster, no irksome thought, no voice…*"Commoner, you are drooling."* No. Voices aren't gone, after all.

He wiped his mouth, but there was no spit; it was just one of the noble's jokes. *I'm glad he, at least, is able to retain his irritating, trying-to-be-funny, personality.* When the herd of monsters went away, so did the girl, apologising for daring touch him without his permission. *Why?* Nesto was about to ask, but he didn't. The answer he would get would probably not be very pleasant. *"Because you are the descendant of the dragons"* wasn't what he would want to hear right now.

They started moving. Staying in one place for a long time could be fatal. By now, all the Lords of the islands must have been informed about the Lord Candidate carrying the mark across his ribs. Passing their trials in order to enter the portal for the next island wasn't an option anymore. They would have to steal the crystal that opened the portal somehow. Besides, they had to watch out for the Cursed Ones that would be on all four levels. The only good thing, according to Silan-te, was that they would have to worry only about a bunch of Lords as the reappearance of the demon kept busy the Lord Commander and many other Lords. The noble's father, without knowing it, had made their struggle for survival somewhat easier. Not easy, but easier.

On the other hand, though, the magic concentrated on the second island was bearing down on them. Nesto's body was extremely heavy, and his gait looked weird, tiring, and clumsy without the help of the Mark. Daemon too seemed to have the same symptoms; only Silan-te walked normally, but she was already a creature of magic, so she couldn't be particularly affected. They had been walking for only an hour before they were forced to stop for a break.

They found a place covered by thick trees and several big stones, and they sat there to get some rest. They didn't light a fire as this would betray their presence. Fortunately, the Cursed One had a small bag full of cooked food she had taken from Lord Asaer's kitchen, so they needn't worry about that, for the time being. For sure, they wouldn't have to care about water, either. The fog and the muddy ground indicated that there was a large supply of it somewhere on the island. Apart from meat, Silan-te also had some fruit and bread. This must have cooled down, but it was still better than nothing.

They ate in silence, always listening out for various noises that might give their pursuers away. When they were done, Daemon spoke first. "We have to find a place to hide, until our bodies adapt," he said. "Then, we'll think of a way to steal the crystal from the Lord of the island."

"There's no point in trying to steal the crystal right now," the girl agreed. "Passing the portal, without adapting to the island's magic, would cause serious side effects to your human bodies."

"I only hope we'll find your father and brother at the top of the Tower, as you said, otherwise I don't know how we're going to avoid this," said the noble to Nesto. "I hope I'm wrong but, even when the alignment's done, I don't think they'll let us live, after all the trouble they went to. I bet our struggle for survival will carry on even outside the Tower of the Lords."

I don't know, he wanted to say. *How can I be absolutely sure? There's nothing I can be sure of right now.* But instead, he said in a firm voice: "They will be there. I trust my brother."

"They won't be able to harm you that easily if you reach the top. If you earn the title of Lord, the Order will need the King's permission to sentence you to death," said Silan-te, trying to reassure them. But she didn't make it. It was more than certain that the Lords would easily get that permission. No one in their right frame of mind would deny it. *I know I wouldn't.*

The noble and the girl began to talk, ignoring Nesto. Daemon wanted to know as much as he could about the Cursed Ones. Was there a way for them to sense them before they were too close? Was their sight better than humans'? What spell should they be more aware of? What was the easiest way to kill them?

The last part made her flinch for a moment but, in the end, she revealed to him everything that he wanted to know, proving to both of them that she meant it when she said that her desire was to keep Nesto alive. Their talk went on for a while, and they kept ignoring Nesto the whole time.

He couldn't blame them for that. After his reaction when he learnt what the mark meant, he must have seemed weak to them. A mere boy that needed their protection. He didn't like that, nor did he fancy trusting the girl. Why didn't he doubt any of her words? He had been trusting her from the start, without once being suspicious. That wasn't like him. His normal self would be totally different. He had only made it so far because he hadn't trusted anyone. Well, he trusted Daemon now, but only because he was in the same situation as Nesto—running for his life.

And he had the same mark, the bloodline of the Gods. Of course, he wasn't a descendant of the dragons; he was the descendant of Jenon. A man that had accepted a demon inside him. He wondered if the Lords would also need him to be dead when the alignment was over. He had the mark...

He rubbed his head with his hands, trying to relieve the tension. All this thinking made him feel lost, unsure, and afraid. *I should just focus only on one thing. My survival...and not trusting anyone.*

"How did you manage to find me before the rest of the Cursed Ones?" he wanted to know in an aggressive voice, showing Silan-te that he didn't trust her.

"There is a spell that allows me to locate the previous owner of the dagger," she said in a gentle and submissive voice, taking the green dagger out of her waist case. "I was meaning to return it yesterday, but you weren't in a position to take it." She wouldn't look him in the eyes, and she seemed so fragile. That made him want to protect her. *Was it this protecting feeling that made my brother risk his own life for me?* Nesto gave the dagger a careful look before taking it. It looked like the one Lord Asaer had given him but, somehow, he knew it was the one he was carrying when he entered the Black Castle.

She had even brought back his brother's dagger. He sighed and put the dagger behind his belt. It would be a difficult task trying not to trust her.

"She has already told you that, but you were lost in thought," the noble declared. "I'm sure you don't remember even the look of the old..." The noble's face almost froze, and he gulped. "I mean MASTER Raizel...when he learnt you were a descendant of the dragons, and he searched for the mark across your ribs. I kind of feel sorry for him. The shock he received was almost equivalent to yours."

Yes, but I bet his mind didn't freeze for an entire day. The White Lord had learnt about Nesto's secret, and he already knew Daemon's, yet he let them go. Maybe, the noble was right. Maybe, master Raizel was different from the other Lords, after all.

Silan-te stood on guard for at least an hour, so that the two of them could rest their eyes and, once they were well-rested, they started walking again, in an attempt to find a suitable place that would keep them well hidden from any threat. The naked trees did not cover them, but the fog compensated for that and, coupled with the lack of sunshine, it was enough for them to move like they were almost invisible. They never let their guard down, though, even after several hours, when both Lord Candidates' bodies were drenched in sweat, and Nesto's breathing was short and heavy.

A Cursed One could pop out of nowhere, or at least that was what Silan-te warned them about. At times, some branches snapped off, or footsteps were heard on the muddy ground, and roars, which made Nesto suddenly turn around, but no masked men appeared.

So far, the only thing they had encountered were more packs of lygars. And now, they seemed a bigger threat than the Cursed Ones. They were the size of a bear, with pointed horns, sharp jaws, and a red fur. *I hope their meat will be tasty.* They would spend at least a week on that island and, no matter how dangerous it might look, they would have to find a way to feed themselves.

His body couldn't take it anymore, and he was slightly bleeding from his mouth, so he slowed down. He had to rest again, but the other two kept going at it. They wouldn't stop, until they found a suitable place. He didn't want to complain or look weak, that's why he gritted his teeth, and kept on walking, no matter how heavy his legs felt.

Maybe, it was tiredness or what Lord Mendax had said was true—that the Cursed Ones moved like shadows—, but Nesto never saw the hand dressed in black coming from behind, closing his mouth and nose, pinning him down…stealing his life.

CHAPTER 15

The Cursed One's moves were so quick and silent that they caught Daemon and Silan-te unawares. Nesto's half face was plunged into the mud, with the masked man's hand gagging him. He could feel a knee pressing him down, while the man's other foot stepped on Nesto's left arm. Both of them had one free hand, but for Nesto it was useless; that of the Cursed One, though, must have been wielding a dagger made of glass, ready to taste his flesh.

Breaking free was too hard. Screaming, impossible. And death probably inevitable, but he could still warn the others. "Daemon!" he shouted in his thought.

The noble turned around abruptly, then Silan-te. It was the girl, though, that made the first move to save him. And Daemon placed his hand on her shoulder and stopped her…STOPPED HER! Was he already beyond saving?

Something weird happened then. Both of them lay in the mud, near the tree trunk next to them, and no longer paid any attention to Nesto or the masked man standing over him. Their eyes looked up slantwise. When Nesto followed their gaze, he saw through the fog two dark figures flit by, silent and noiseless, like shadows. Nesto thought the masked man would call them for reinforcements, but he didn't. All he did was tighten his grip on Nesto's face to block his breathing.

He was almost out of breath, and the figures had gone, when the Cursed One suddenly set him free, "Did you have to breathe so hard? They almost noticed you," he said in a soft voice, and stood up.

Nesto's mouth opened wide open as his lungs gasped for air, bringing back the blood on his face. When his muscles loosened up, he turned to look at the man he thought would steal his life. It was obvious now that this man had probably saved them from an encounter with the two Cursed Ones he had just seen flit by. On the face of it, he seemed to be dressed in black, but Nesto noticed the scarlet colour of the uniform he wore under the black mantle. His beardless face, with the thin nose and the considerably long black hair, seemed familiar to Nesto. However, he couldn't tell with certainty if he had met him before or not, until that man introduced himself as Lord Zoloc, the Lord of the second island.

It wasn't the first time he had heard that name. Maybe, they hadn't met before, after all, but he had seen him in that weird dream-memory, when Lord Asaer had thrown him her glassy dagger. It was the man he had thought looked like his father, Nestal. Now that he saw him up close, he realised that he didn't bear such a strong resemblance to his father. Only his green eyes were almost alike.

When Nesto stood up, he wiped the mud off his face and hair, and saw Silan-te jump in front of him. She moved him away, and stuck her dagger in the man's throat. "If you belong to the Order of the Lords, then why have you chosen to help us?" She wanted to know. Her words were carefully chosen, not wanting to reveal so easily the secret of the mark that Nesto bore.

The Lord wasn't frightened or, at least, he didn't let it show. He touched the tip of the dagger with his index, and made a futile attempt to remove it, cutting his finger. "You mean even though I am aware of what this boy is?" he said and looked at Nesto smilingly. A strange smile that made him seem like he was enjoying that knowledge of his, or even maybe the whole situation. "I was asked by his Lord father to help him. Almost all the Lords of the islands have promised to do so. Including myself, of course. Now, if you please, remove this dagger from my throat. It's quite sharp, and we wouldn't want an accident to happen, would we now?"

"And why would a Lord agree to a request like that?" Daemon asked. Under normal circumstances, Nesto would be the first to ask such a thing. He was the one that didn't even trust his own shadow. But he was taken aback by what the man had said. That was the first solid clue he had found that proved what his brother had told him. They were really waiting for him at the top of the Tower.

"That's none of your business…noble." The Lord's tone of voice betrayed irritation, if not aversion, so did his wince. It shouldn't strike him as odd that Lord Zoloc knew of Daemon's noble origins; after all, everything about him—his stance, expressions, and tone of voice—betrayed exactly this thing. The real question was, if he knew about Nesto, did that mean that he also knew about the mark on Daemon's body, about demon Jenon?

"If you don't wish to tell me, I can order my little servant to give that throat of yours a kiss with her green knife," Daemon threatened, mimicking the same grimace.

Silan-te gave Daemon an irritated look, but she didn't complain about being called a servant. *I guess having a common enemy has united them.*

The Lord carefully scanned the place, and then said: "Now is not the right time to be arguing. I will explain everything that needs explaining, eventually. But, first, I will have to hide you somewhere where the Cursed Ones and the Lords that have settled on my island will not be able to find you. When your bodies are ready, I will open the portal to go on to the next level."

"Silan-te, put away your weapon," Nesto urged her. "It's evident that he is not an enemy. If he were, he would have informed the Cursed Ones." It was useless threatening him, one way or another, if he remembered correctly what he had seen in that dream. The girl obeyed almost immediately, and unwillingly put the dagger back in her waist case. "Where are you going to hide us?" he wanted to know.

"Plain sight is always the best hideout. Back in my fortress, with the other Lord Candidates that have, by chance, yet to pass my trial. Even though it's full of Cursed Ones and Lords, I can guarantee your safety there. Staying in the woods is dangerous. There is an order to kill anyone that is found outside of the fortress." The Lord sucked the blood oozing out of his finger, and then addressed Silan-te. "I trust that you know where my fortress is located."

"Yes, but why?"

"Good. Pick some plants, and kill some monster. I will go and inform the guards at the gate that I sent for three persons to hunt for my needs," he told them, then vanished into thin air, leaving behind a puzzled noble and an astonished Cursed One. Nesto couldn't blame them, in contrast to himself. It was the first time they had ever seen such a thing.

"I don't like the way he was looking at me, or his scent. It reminds me of a specific, disgusting Lord," said the noble after a while. "Do we trust him?"

There must be something wrong with me because I can't believe I'm going to say this and mean it. "Yes, let's trust him, for now."

They followed Silan-te towards the path that led to the fortress, and picked whatever kind of plant they ran into without caring if it was eatable or not. The guards wouldn't probably care, either. They had to hunt, too, and that part would be a lot more difficult. Trying to spot a wild beast while keeping an eye out for the Cursed Ones wasn't an easy task. But they were lucky enough to come across a pack of lygars. Those packs seemed to be everywhere. Silan-te managed to make a lygar stray away from its pack, using a word of magic. The rest wasn't that difficult. A joint attack was enough to kill it. Then, they removed the head, and cut the body in three, so that they would split its weight.

When they got out of the forest, the half-hidden sun appeared; it was about to set and its red rays spread across the clouds. They looked like burning ropes that pulled the orange clouds closer. In fact, they hadn't stepped out of the woods. It's just that someone had cut off the trees, almost down to their roots, and had made out of the trunks what Lord Zoloc had called a fortress. A gigantic outer wall that didn't let anyone peek inside. Undoubtedly, it seemed more than enough to protect you from any external threat.

"Once we get inside that, we will be trapped. There won't be an easy way getting out of that thing," said Daemon when he saw it.

Silan-te, who walked ahead of them, stopped short, and turned in their direction. "We should not trust that Lord," she suddenly said, with an expression betraying she had been mulling over that thought for some time.

The noble agreed. "I will have to agree with our cursed servant on that score," he said. "Of course, it's ironic that these words come from someone who claims almost the same thing as Lord Zoloc. But still, trusting a Lord is the worst possible decision."

"You trusted Lord Raizel, didn't you?" Nesto demurred.

"I told you: he seems different…"

"I didn't hear it," said the girl, interrupting the noble, "but I'm sure the Lord used a word of magic. And it must have been a very powerful one to make him disappear like that. No man or Lord should be able to use the words of magic. Even for us, the Cursed Ones, it is impossible without using these daggers. They were created by the elves, and only the elves can use them. He is hiding a lot of things. And what is more disturbing is that he didn't flinch while my dagger was stuck on his throat. I don't think it would be wise to trust that man."

Why were they acting like this now? *It must be the sight of the fortress. It's not like we have any other choice.* Surviving for a week out in the woods with their sick bodies having the constant threat of monsters and the Cursed Ones was probably impossible. "I heard in a…dream of mine that those who use the words of magic can never use a word of lie. Is that true?" Nesto asked Silan-te, hoping that he would convince them that way.

"It's true, Lord Candidate Nesto. But only for the elves. And, even then, there are a lot of ways to deceive someone without having to lie. That's how my ancestors killed…yours." The girl never looked him in the eye whenever she spoke, while she had no such problem with Daemon. "What's more…I'm sorry, but those who have the bloodline of a God cannot dream. What you saw must have been a memory of another person or even an object. And, if you have seen a dream in your life, it must probably have belonged to someone sleeping next to you."

"Does this mean that none of the dreams I have seen were actually…mine?" he said and this realisation left a void inside of him, as if someone had taken away a part of his body. A part that, obviously, wasn't his own. Nesto recalled some of the dreams he had seen ever since he was a child. Dreams full of wolves, deer, bears, and hunting. Those belonged to his uncle, Garon. Those with their father and the fires must surely have belonged to his brother. He also remembered the dream where he was still in the Black Castle. His father had referred to him as Almar, not Nesto. That must have been a memory of his brother hidden in the dagger. *Not even one of them belonged to me.*

Eventually, they all agreed that they would enter the fortress, on condition they did not trust the Lord's words, and they tried to obtain the crystal at all costs. So, if the worst came to the worst and the mark was revealed, they would use the crystal to open the portal, even if their bodies had still not adapted.

The masked men guarding the small wooden gate did not suspect them, and it stood to reason that they wouldn't bother them if it weren't for Silan-te. "Why have you chosen to reveal your eyes?" one of them demanded. The excuse that her mask had fallen while hunting wasn't enough. Fortunately, though, Lord Zoloc turned up with an angry face, ordering them to let them in. He had waited quite a long time for those plants, and now they were making him wait even more? His serious tone of voice, and probably the power he wielded on the second level, made them obey at once.

The first obstacle was cleared. Yet, no matter how insistent the Lord was, they didn't really feel safe in there. It looked like a small village, with slipshod houses built in a row, with their small, almost inexistent, yards, and the wells that dotted the landscape, but the tall wall that surrounded everything gave them the impression that they were inside a huge cell. They saw no other Lord, as they followed Lord Zoloc into his quarters, and there were very few Cursed Ones. However, there must have been at least a hundred Lord Candidates wandering along the muddy roads. Although they did not yet have the title of Lord, they still posed a threat.

"You will be safe here," the Lord assured them again, while they were entering his house. It was a beautiful two-storey building, much bigger than the rest, built meticulously. It had a fireplace, a chimney, and a balcony. It even featured some windows. The bad thing was, it was farther away from the gate than the other houses. "The Lords and the Cursed Ones have focused on searching the woods as all the other Lord Candidates residing in my fortress have already been checked to find out whether they bear a mark across their ribs. And there are lots of them. I am sure that, if you keep a low profile, no one will ever suspect that you've just arrived on the island."

They threw the meat and plants in a corner, and Lord Zoloc promised to give them as many explanations as they required, at dinner time. He had prepared some hot water for them to wash themselves, but only Nesto accepted his polite gesture. The other two preferred to stay in the living room, along with the Lord, showing him they did not trust him, from the word go.

The water was lukewarm when Nesto got into the wooden bathtub. Still, even cold water would be welcome right now as his mark across the ribs was burning him again, just like it did the previous night, when he came of age. His body was sore, while the taste of blood lingered in his mouth. The stronger he felt when calling the power of the ancient Gods, the weaker he was now, under the influence of the island's magic. He didn't want to admit it, but without Silan-te's help he would be already dead. *And regardless of whether I trust him or not, it's obvious that Lord Zoloc's help is just as important and valuable...*

He waited until his burning abated, then he put on his muddy clothes. He almost dragged his worn-out body into the living room, where he found the others eating. Silan-te nibbled at her food without tearing her eyes away from their host, while the noble and Lord Zoloc were exchanging bitter remarks and threats, feigning smiles. That was a relief.

To be honest, I was expecting something worse. For instance, they could be pointing blades at each other's throats.

Food here, on the second island, looked more like that at the Black Castle, less like that on the first level. On the table there were fried eggs, sausages, mushrooms, wild boar meat, and several pastes. There was also some red wine, which Daemon eagerly savoured, but Nesto preferred to steer clear of it. Same with the meat. He had already tasted enough of it over the last couple of months, so he settled for some fried eggs and pastes.

"Enough with the pleasantries," said the noble after Nesto's couple of mouthfuls, and he placed the glass of wine on the table. "You said you were going to give us the explanations we need. We're all ears, then. Speak up!"

But the Lord didn't have time to do so as there was a loud knock on the door, and a raspy voice said: "My apologies for disturbing you, Lord Zoloc. But I was instructed by the other Lords to inform you that, tomorrow at noon, there will be another check for the mark. We request your permission to gather all the Lord Candidates in our headquarters."

Lord Zoloc seemed unfazed by these words. "Make no sound," he only whispered to them, then he stood up and walked towards the door. Seeing a Cursed One and two Lord Candidates dining with the Lord of the island would seem suspicious, to say the least. Only a glance at Nesto's or Daemon's ribs would be more than enough to make at least a hundred people run after them. Still, the Lord seemed oddly composed, just like he had been some hours before, when the Cursed One had stuck her dagger on his throat. While the look on Silan-te's and Daemon's face told him they were thinking exactly the same thing.

So much for being safe…

CHAPTER 16

All three of them exchanged quick looks, forming a plan. It was easy to figure it out by just one glance. *Kill. Don't get killed.* If only it were that easy to execute it. Especially the second part.

Silan-te prepared her dagger and, under the table, Nesto could hear black bolts dancing in the noble's hands. He didn't summon the power of the ancient Gods, but his hand stroked the handle of his dagger made of glass. Behind his back, the Lord of the island had opened the door, and greeted the man. "Of course, you have my permission," he told him. "And you can tell Lord Doral to skip these kind of formalities. I have already given him full authority on my island and on my Lord Candidates, as well. Is that all?"

"Yes, Lord Zoloc."

"Please forgive me. I have a dinner to attend."

Nesto felt a sense of relief in the pit of his stomach, when Lord Zoloc closed the door and went back to his seat. "Is this what you meant when you said that we would be safe here?" Daemon asked him in a noble-like tone. There were no bolts flashing in his hands, but Nesto couldn't be sure about his eyes.

"I must admit it—that was…unexpected," said Zoloc. "But it's something that I can deal with. You are still safe. However, it would be a lie if I said that I didn't expect you to be so easily scared. You are a despicable noble, after all."

"You, on the other hand, act like you have never feared anything in your entire life. Do you want to have a taste of what it feels like?" asked the noble.

"I doubt that you can accomplish that."

"Well, if you insist…"

"Daemon, stop it!" said Nesto. "Both of you. Lord Zoloc, we are grateful for your help, but we would feel safer if you handed over the crystal to us. In this way, you would gain our trust."

The Lord snorted. "I'm glad that I'm not as terrible a liar as you are, descendant of the dragons," he said. "Otherwise, I'd be dead now, and so would you, probably. None of you is going to trust me completely, and I don't expect such a thing. All I wish for is to keep you alive until you manage to reach the top of the Tower, and see your father. As for the crystal, even if I wanted to, I wouldn't be able to give it to you right now. I have already given it to Lord Doral. He is the one that leads the Cursed Ones on this level. He belongs to the guard of Lord Commander Legris, and bears the title of Deathlord. A powerful Lord that is used for disposing all threats. I strictly advise you to avoid engaging in a fight with him, by the way, no matter the case."

"You were right. Now that we are trapped in here without a method to escape, I feel…safe," said Daemon ironically.

"There is no need to worry. I will think of a way to retrieve the crystal when your bodies have adjusted. The only reason why I handed it over to the Deathlord was that I wanted to gain his trust. The Order of the Lords suspects everyone, since they learnt about the existence of a descendant of the dragons. Even us, the Lords of the islands. I had to blind them with actions like that. They wouldn't hesitate to kill half of the Lords, just to make sure that no dragon would remain alive."

"You are one of them. You belong with the Order of the Lords, so why are you risking your life by helping Lord Candidate Nesto?" Silan-te wanted to know.

"And you are one of the Cursed Ones. The ones that betrayed the dragons in the first place, and yet you have chosen to help him," the Lord of the island demurred. "You have your own reason for helping him, and I have mine. You are probably asking for forgiveness, while what I seek is to avenge myself on the Order."

Lord Zoloc wasn't clear about the reason why he was seeking revenge, but he gave them all the explanations they needed, convincing the Cursed One and making the noble less hostile against him. As for Nesto…He still couldn't trust the Lord the way he trusted Daemon, or the unexplainable way he trusted Silan-te, but it was enough to convince him. Honestly, it was enough, since he had said he was a friend of his father's. He could tell that these words were real because, if he weren't Nestal's friend, then how come he knew he was waiting for him, along with his brother, at the top?

The only explanation left that the Lord had to give was how they would manage to go through the mark control that would be held the next day in the Lords' headquarters. Unfortunately, this explanation wasn't so convincing as the others. He just said in a relaxed manner: "I've been practising my painting skills." As if a brush and some paint would be enough to fool the Lords. However, none of them raised any objection to Lord Zoloc's plan. Mostly because they had nothing better to propose. And, if Nesto had managed to hide his mark from the Lords at the Black Castle with no paint, while standing naked in front of them, then the Lord's plan might be successful, after all.

When they finished their meal, the Lord led them through a secret door to the adjacent house, where they would stay for the next days, until their bodies managed to adapt. Staying in the Lord's house wasn't really an option as it would grab attention.

Nesto lay on the wooden floorboard, and wrapped up in the woollen blankets that must have been made of lygar's wool. There were two beds in their new abode, but Silan-te took one of them, at Nesto's bidding, although she insisted that the descendant of the dragons should sleep on a soft mattress. The other one…well, he was a noble—of course he wouldn't deign to sleep on the floor. His butt must have been used to sleeping on silk sheets and soft beds.

After all this fatigue and hardship, he should have dozed off as soon as he shut his eyes, but worry and fear of what was to happen the following day kept him awake. Maybe, if he lay next to Silan-te, he would sleep without fear. He could still remember that feeling that seized his body when Daemon had accidentally shoved the girl all over Nesto. It was more than just a feeling of safety. He felt free, as if all the shackles that weighed heavily on him and trapped him were gone. A unique sensation that he wanted to taste again.

If he asked her to lie by her side, she might obey. She seemed to be obedient, no matter what Nesto asked her to do. Just like when she was with Lord Zoloc, when she thought that some Cursed One had attacked him, Silan-te didn't hesitate to run to his rescue…unlike the noble. Eventually, he slept on his own.

Silan-te woke him up the next morning to repeat the word of magic, so that the Cursed Ones wouldn't be able to sense the dragon's blood running through his veins. *But for this spell, the masked men and the Lords would have already spilt my blood all over the island.*

"Is there anything else I should know about the dragon's blood, now that it has awakened?" Nesto asked her, while Silan-te put her green dagger back into her waist case.

"I'm sorry, Lord Candidate Nesto," she said, "but I don't know much about your blood. However, there are ancient books, thousands of pages long, written on dragons, back in the Tree of Life, where my tribe has chosen to hide from the outer world. There, you can find all kinds of knowledge. Unfortunately, mine is limited, and most of what I know, you already know." Her bright green eyes never met Nesto's. When he asked her about this, Silan-te said: "Your bloodline is that of a God, and my creation was meant to serve you. But the magic that still lingers inside my eyes served only to deceive you."

Just then, Lord Zoloc turned up out of the blue, with a brush in his mouth, holding containers of paint. He said something and left them on the floor, but his words didn't make much sense, with the brush still in his mouth. "What are you waiting for?" he then said, after releasing his tongue. "I told you to stand up and take off your top. We don't have much time ahead of us, and the paint will take some time to dry."

Nesto removed his sweater, just as he was told, and the Lord began painting him, while the Cursed One stood there watching, almost admiring, the mark that had turned blue ever since the day his blood awakened. Lord Zoloc was painting the mark and the surrounding area meticulously, starting with a white colour, and then adding some darker layers, until he got the right shade.

"What's my uncle's name?" Nesto asked him, while the Lord seemed engrossed in his task. Such questions were almost pointless, now that they were already involved in this condition, where they had to trust the Lord of the island. Yet, in this way, he might elicit some answers, even for a moment, so that he would get rid of that knot in his stomach.

"Garon. And your brother's name is Almar. Is there anything else?"

"No."

"Good." The Lord raised his gaze and looked into Nesto's eyes. "There is no need to worry. I have already killed two Candidates that look almost like you, so that we'll have the same number of them when they count you, and I'll be in the hall during the check. I know I keep saying it, but you are safe. Both of you," he said, and continued his diligent task.

"Both," he heard, not "all of you." *Because only two of us are in danger. He definitely knows about Daemon.* And, somehow, he probably knew that they, meaning Daemon, had kept it secret from Silan-te.

By the time the Lord completed painting across Nesto's ribs, the noble had come out of his room to find them in the living room. Zoloc must have already covered Daemon's mark, for the noble moved more carefully, and avoided bringing his hand close to his ribs. The Lord of the island had also found a mask for Silan-te. All this attention to detail and his constant use of the word 'safe' gave the impression that his plan would work. But Nesto didn't fool himself. Most probably, that check would end up in a bloody battle.

"Why don't you just reveal your mark to the Cursed One?" Nesto asked him, while the Lord and the girl had left earlier to get their positions in the building that the other Lords used as headquarters. Both of them had lain on the lygar's leather, waiting for the sun to reach above their heads. Or, rather, above the roof.

"I can't trust anyone that easily. It's against my instincts," Daemon replied. That was Nesto's reply when the noble once posed the same question. Only, back then, master Raizel was in Silan-te's place.

Nesto too could play the same game. "Typical nobles," he said and snorted. "You are going to be annoying till the end. You know that Zoloc's plan isn't exactly brilliant. We might not make it till the end of the day."

"Speak for yourself, descendant of the dragons," said Daemon, and the way he stressed 'descendant of the dragons' sounded more diminishing than 'commoner'. *Well, at least, I'm not just a commoner anymore.* "I'm not going to die. I have my own plan. I'm going to steal the crystal from the Deathlord, and escape to the next level."

"That's not a brilliant plan, either. You heard what Lord Zoloc said about the Deathlord," said Nesto.

This time, it was the noble that snorted. "I'm not afraid of him. I'm only afraid of one man…Besides, I might even use you as a decoy. Don't look at me like that, commoner. Weren't you the one saying that one's own survival always comes first?"

He did it earlier, and he was doing it now. He was just using Nesto's own words against him. *He is probably joking...or not.* He couldn't be sure. Daemon was a noble, and claimed to have a kind of honour that Lords and commoners lacked. *But again, when the time comes, as I had said: one's own survival always comes first.*

They knew it was time to go, when they heard some noise, voices, and footsteps wading through the muddy ground. They got out and saw the Lord Candidates moving towards a big wooden building next to the gate. Before the Lords' arrival, it was used as a training hall to keep all those fools busy, as Zoloc had said. While they were headed for the Lords' headquarters, the Cursed Ones were scouring the empty houses and the wells, in a last-ditch attempt to find the descendant of the dragons.

Maybe, it was due to fear but, when they walked into the hall teeming with Lord Candidates, Cursed Ones, and Lords, the mark across his ribs began to burn again. The good thing was, it was somewhat bearable.

The Candidates were split in two rows, and at the top of each row, there were two Lords dressed in grey mantles, seated in chairs on a pedestal; they were the ones that made the checks. In every single corner stood masked men, with their impersonal masks glowing in the light of the dozens of torches placed across the walls. He couldn't recognise Silan-te, with all those masks around him. He even found it hard to make out Lord Zoloc among that crowd, but he saw the Deathlord at the end of the hall standing on the pedestal, supervising everyone. He stood out from the rest of the Lords. He was dressed in black, with a heavy mantle covering his shoulders, while on his chest was engraved in golden colour the Mark of the ancient Gods.

One of the Cursed Ones separated him from Daemon, and put them in the two long rows. He didn't realise it was Silan-te until she held on to his elbow tight, and her black hair coming down on his shoulder with a jerk. She must have seen the way he nervously moved his fingers, and she must have wanted to remind him that she was here, by his side, to protect him. As for Lord Zoloc, he was nowhere to be found.

He hadn't seen him even when he reached the pedestal, and he was only ten persons away from the check. That wasn't a good sign. If something went wrong, he would need the Lord's power to steal the crystal.

Unlike Nesto, the other Lord Candidates were completely relaxed, and most of them were telling jokes. From the conversations he had overheard, they had the impression this was yet another strange trial of Lord Zoloc, which almost no Lord Candidate was able to pass. There was one of them stuck on the second level for two years.

His heart was ready to burst, when only one Candidate stood in front of him, while the mark was still burning. The noble was a few metres ways, second in the row, as well, but he didn't look worried. His gaze was fixed on the Deathlord.

He is probably thinking of a way to steal the crystal.

"Lord Doral," said the Lord from Daemon's row, "I might have found what we're looking for." The Deathlord slowly walked towards him, and then the Lord showed him the ribs of the Candidate standing in front of him. Nesto couldn't rule out the possibility of there being another one with the same mark, apart from Daemon and himself, but he was sure that the particular Candidate didn't bear the bloodline of a God. What could initially be characterised as a mark looked more like a bruise. Besides, it was in the wrong place, over the heart, while Nesto's and Daemon's mark was hidden under their right hand.

"I got that a few days ago during training," the Lord Candidate said to account for it, after being asked by Lord Doral. From up close, the Lord looked as intimidating as master Raizel.

"Yes, indeed. It seems to have been caused by a blow." The Deathlord groped it with his fingers, until his hand tightened up and a sword materialised in his grip. The fiery blade pierced through the Lord Candidate's heart, and jutted out at the other end. Exactly where the mark should be. Blood trickled down on the wooden floor, like raindrops, which soon formed a red rivulet. "But still, we'd better be absolutely sure."

CHAPTER 17

The atmosphere froze solid as more than a hundred people were stunned. All the hum and talk ceased just as suddenly. Some of them must have stopped breathing too. Nesto was one of them. The burning mark made him break out in a cold sweat, and whole beads trickled down his body.

A Cursed One removed the soulless body with the glassiest eyes, so that the check carry on. "Next" said the two Lords in unison, and now it was his turn.

He hesitated. Fear had taken on the form of stone hands keeping his legs still. He had to see Daemon get on the pedestal to pluck up courage. All he needed to do was take off his sweater and show the Lord his bare—free from the mark—skin. If that didn't work out, then he would probably discover how strong he had become thanks to his training with White Lord Raizel. He stepped onto the pedestal, removed his garment, and stood, his hands behind his waist, while the previous Candidate's blood had encircled his shoes.

The Lord's hand instantly made for his ribs and, when he lowered his eyes, he knew the reason why. The mark's blue colour had seeped through the layers of the paint, and now looked blurry like a bruise. *It must be due to the fire still burning inside of me.* There was no other choice now. He knew what was coming next. He witnessed it a few moments ago. A blade with a fiery kiss. Another flame started to burn in his chest, and the Mark of the ancient Gods turned up. At least, he wouldn't die without a fight, like the other Lord Candidate.

Although Zoloc had advised them not to mess with the Deathlord, Nesto's first target was Lord Doral. Maybe, after that turmoil, Daemon would be able to steal the crystal, and escape to the third level. There would be tremendous side effects, but it was preferable to death.

He waited for the Lord to call the Deathlord but, strangely enough, he didn't. His hand had covered the mark and, when Nesto looked into his green eyes, the Lord made a slight motion with his eyebrows. As if he were telling him to erase the Mark on his chest. Like he knew what Nesto was thinking about, and warned him about the result; like he was...another ally of his father.

Zoloc hadn't mentioned any other ally, apart from the Lords of the islands, but what other explanation could there be? With a single thought, Nesto's flame on his chest stopped burning, while the Lord pretended to be examining his body thoroughly. When he felt he had pretended long enough, he sent him next to the pedestal to wait with the rest of the Candidates who had already been checked.

Daemon too was sent next to the pedestal shortly afterwards. *"I can't believe it worked. Now I have to apologise to that obnoxious Lord for doubting him,"* he said to Nesto through his thought.

"You won't have to. It didn't work. Actually, it half-worked. My mark was almost visible. But the Lord didn't reveal it, even though he saw it."

"An ally?"

"What else?"

"Your father must really care about you. He's left allies everywhere."

He hadn't really thought of that possibility at all. The sudden realisation came as a shock to him. *My father really cares about me?* He didn't know what to feel. It was so much simpler just hating him. Apart from his will to survive, another reason he wanted to reach the top of the Tower was his desire to punch his father as hard as he could. And, in a way, that had strengthened his will. What was he supposed to feel about him now? Love? No, that definitely wasn't the right feeling. Not even gratitude felt right. And…and, obviously, this wasn't exactly the right time to be thinking about it. He was surrounded by people that wanted him dead.

Still, that thought racked his mind, when the check was over, and they went back to their house, safe and sound. He tried to remember his father, but no memory of him came out of his head. He even found it hard to remember his characteristics. Apart from his look and eyes, everything else was fuzzy. The only recollection he had was the dream, but that was Almar's dream, not his own. A weird one, with the orange flames turning an entire house to ashes, and a baby's cry louder than the wind. A baby's cry…

A baby!

Why hadn't he realised all this earlier? It was one of Almar's childhood memory, and the baby that was crying was surely Nesto. That's why he had no recollection of his father.

"I bet Lord Zoloc was scared, and crawled back to his quarters," said Daemon, as they got to the Lord's beautiful abode, and their own scanty house. Yet, when they walked in through the secret door, they didn't find him there. They took some food from the kitchen, and returned.

Silan-te came back after sunset, when she found the chance to stray from the other Cursed Ones. Still, she didn't know Lord Zoloc's whereabouts. They weren't worried, though. There was no way Zoloc would be in danger. It shouldn't be easy harming someone that could pop out of nowhere in the blink of an eye, and disappear just as easily, especially if that someone was a Lord.

That night, before turning in—on the floor again—, he decided to place his brother's dagger next to his head, hoping to see that memory hidden inside it, and try to retain his father's characteristics. It would feel weird reaching the top and seeing a man of whom he had no recollection. A total stranger. And now, he wasn't so sure about punching him, either.

Much to his chagrin, the following morning came with no dreams or memories. He didn't lose hope, though. Maybe, next time.

The sound of splashing water came from next door, where their well was. Silan-te or Daemon must have been having their bath. Most probably, it was the noble as he was the only one in the habit of washing once or twice a day, whenever the opportunity presented itself. He cared more about his personal hygiene than the risk of his mark being revealed.

"Make sure you don't wash away all the hard work of Lord Zoloc put on you, noble." Nesto said, trying to mimic Daemon's tone of voice. It felt quite good calling him 'noble' in a demeaning way. It helped with all the nervousness. *I should have done this from the start.*

"You are awake, Lord Candidate Nesto?" said Silan-te.

"Oh, I thought you were…" Nesto was at a loss for words, when the girl appeared before him. Her dark moist hair had straggled all over her breast, and beads of water trickled down her belly, dancing around her curvy legs, before they dropped on the floor. She was naked, as Nesto found out, his mouth wide open. A knot suddenly formed in his stomach, and dissipated just as quickly, taking the form of a wave, which swept through his body and flustered his face.

"Well, I guess that's one way to serve Lord Candidate Nesto," said Daemon, who had descended from his room.

"No! We didn't…I mean she…I was just…" Nesto huffed, giving up any attempt to explain what the situation was.

The girl didn't seem to understand. "I need to use a word of magic on you," she said, holding the dagger.

"No, you need to put something on first," the noble told her. "While you, commoner, should be ashamed of yourself. You still don't know how to treat a lady." Daemon took the pelt of a lygar, and covered Silan-te, while the girl was using a word of magic on Nesto.

"It was only for a single moment, but I saw you call the power of the ancient Gods while on the pedestal," the Cursed One told him, sheathing her dagger. Most of her skin was covered, but still some beads were seen trickling between her breasts. "Your body already exerts itself under the magic of the island, and my words of magic, calling forth the Mark of the ancient Gods, can only make it worse. Please, refrain from doing so. How do you feel now? Does it hurt somewhere?"

"I'm fine," he said, only to find out that he wasn't. Unfortunately, she was right. As soon as the girl completed her word of magic, Nesto felt the taste of blood in his mouth. He assumed that the dizziness, the excruciating headache, and his rambling legs must have been related to his exertion. "I'm fine," he repeated, more to himself than to the others, but just one step was enough to make him fall and smash his face on the hard floor.

When Nesto regained some of his consciousness, he could tell that he was lying on a soft mattress. The pain was still there. His eyelids were heavy, and he couldn't open his eyes. After several times of drifting off and waking up again, he eventually managed to wake up for good. Next to him was a platter of fruit, fried hare, and bread. It smelled good. There was another smell in his nostrils, a sweeter one. He sat up and rubbed his eyes, realising that he lay on Silan-te's bed. That sweet smell belonged to her.

First, he took a hot slice of bread, and then tried the crunchy meat. With all those things on his mind, he had almost forgotten how good it felt eating. He left the fruit last.

When the noble came, there were only a few bones on the platter. "Will you stop being so weak, passing out all the time?

You are embarrassing yourself," he told him. There was still a hint of headache and dizziness, but it tended to subside. It struck him as odd that Daemon wasn't in the same condition—after all, he used the fire of the ancient Gods just as often—, until Nesto remembered that he was the son of a demon. With a body that could heal its injuries within a single day. "Can you walk?"

"I think so."

"Lord Zoloc did us the honour of turning up. He wants to see you."

"What for?"

Daemon made a face. Nesto knew that face. "I'm not sure. He wants to tell you a story about your father or something like that." Nesto had the same face when he saw the other kids with their fathers. A face full of envy. Which was utterly absurd. Demon or not, Jenon had been there for his son. At least, he had managed to have some memories of him. But that was not something he could discuss with the noble. He didn't react very well to discussions that concerned his father. *That probably makes two of us.*

"Did the Lord, by any chance, mention why he wasn't there during the check?" Nesto asked.

His usual arrogant look came back on his face. "Believe it or not, he was there. Right before our eyes. You saw him. We both did."

"No, I didn't," Nesto said with confidence.

"Oh, yes, you did. He just had a…different face. Lord Zoloc is capable of using a kind of magic that even your little servant cannot comprehend. He, somehow, assumed the appearance of one of the subordinates of the Deathlord."

"You mean to tell me that the one who inspected me about the mark was actually Lord Zoloc?"

"I'm impressed," said the noble ironically. "You are quite smart for a commoner. Guess whose else's face he did borrow. I will give you a small clue. I hate him."

That wasn't much of a clue. He hated all the Lords, except maybe Lord Raizel. But, if there was someone he really detested, that was… "Lord Mendax," exclaimed Nesto.

"Apparently, he had been helping us all along, while we were at that castle. Of course, it was no accident that the Cursed One learnt about your mark."

Nesto stood up and walked towards Lord Zoloc with difficulty. He found him in the living room, seated in a wooden chair, savouring his red wine. The afternoon sun rays piercing through the windows were of much the same colour as the wine. He must have lost consciousness for almost a day. "You can call me Lord Mendax if that makes you feel more comfortable," the Lord told him, moving his glass in a controlled motion, making sure he didn't spill his wine.

"What about the real one, the acquaintance of my uncle?"

"Dead. I killed him," he said almost indifferently. "I can't take the form of someone who is still alive. I'm able to bend the truth of magic, but not break it."

For some reason, the death of Garon's acquaintance did not really touch him, nor did the fact that Zoloc had been Lord Mendax all along. After hearing about him being a descendant of the dragons, everything else seemed so…trivial. That aside, he felt a little bit angry. *And by a little, I obviously mean a lot!* "If you knew about my secret all along, why didn't you tell me? I had a need for an ally. For as long as I was at the Black Castle, I would see even my own shadow as a threat. I felt, as if I were inside a pit full of dragons."

"Then, it must have felt like home to you."

"Ha! Very funny! You know I didn't mean it that way."

"I know." The Lord stood up and walked towards him. "It wasn't safe to reveal it to you, then. I couldn't predict how you would react. One wrong step, and both of us would have revealed our secrets to the Order of the Lords. We wouldn't want that, would we? I'm sure that it's still hard to sink in that the blood of Gods is running through your veins. But, like it or not, that blood is part of you, and you have to accept that, sooner or later. That said, I'm going to need a small portion of that part."

"What do you mean?"

"Your blood. I need it. It has power in it, and I'm going to use it to mislead Lord Doral, and take back the crystal." The glass slipped through his fingers, more like he dropped it, and smashed into pieces, splattering his wine all over the place. Zoloc bent over to pick up the broken glass. "Show me your hand," he ordered him, then the wet glass cut his flesh.

It happened again. Out of the blue. A memory. *Was it mine or Lord Zoloc's?* Or was it the glass that caused it, or even the wine? It could be anything, really. This time, some stone grey walls encircled him, and he found himself in a huge hall illuminated by a lighted fireplace and torches hanging from the walls. A man in a black-and-red coat stood before him, his silvery white hair almost hiding his eyes. Something about him curdled Nesto's blood. His young face was pallid, but there was something dark and unapproachable to it.

The man's look pierced through Nesto, like he didn't exist. When he turned back, he saw about ten men dressed in white mantles, stabbing him with their eyes, and then it dawned on him which memory that was. The slaughter of the White Lords. The fair-haired man was, without a doubt, Daemon's father, Demon Jenon.

Lord Commander Ousen was a step ahead of the rest. He stood out in his silver uniform, with his thick grey hair, and the purple Mark across his chest. His face was hardened, and Nesto was sure that fear and hesitation tried to hide away in his eyes. "Come with us in peace, son. No more blood has to be shed," he said.

"You must be mistaken," said the demon in a voice that didn't resemble that of a human being. He ran his fingers through his hair, and lifted it up, revealing his bright red eyes. "I'm no longer your son. I'm a God. And no one is going anywhere. You will all meet your end here."

Silence came only to warn them, prepare them, and equip them with fiery spears and swords, which seemed to be hiding the sun in them. Then, one of the White Lords made a lunge at Jenon.

One small step and one fast swing of the demon were enough to turn the Lord's white uniform into a dark red piece of cloth. The blood oozed away, and the slaughter began. The Lords charged like wild beasts, full of power and agility. Their weapons pierced through Nesto's body, and sought to find Jenon's flesh. They surrounded him and attacked him on all sides. Spears wanted to be stuck into his chest, blades into the ribs. Some of them wanted to cut his back, while one of them tried to give him a fiery kiss on the neck from above. But none of them managed to touch him. Not even the tips of their blades were able to graze him.

A God walking among the mortals. That's how the demon's moves looked to Nesto. *A terrifying God.*

Nesto saw two White Lords, behind Jenon, open up an oaken door, and beat a hasty retreat. After a while, yet another one followed. The rest were frantically trying to spill the blood of the demon.

A second sword materialised in Jenon's hands, and then the Lords began falling on one another. The first one lost his head, the second one his heart, while the third one was found with a blade stuck deep into his belly. All the demon's attacks were merciless. None of them aimed to injure, but only to kill.

Jenon's thirst for blood was painted across his face, except for his eyes. In the end, soulless, gory, and mangled bodies were scattered around the stone hall. Only Lord Commander Ousen was still alive, but seriously wounded. Before killing the last White Lord, the demon had grabbed the Lord Commander and hurled him on the oaken door, smashing it. He left his father in the adjoining hall, with a blade jutting out of his chest, and stuck a spear into the White Lord's eye.

Nesto followed the demon, who stepped on the pieces of the broken oaken door. In that smaller hall, he saw the Lord Commander stand up with difficulty, while before him stood one of the White Lords that had fled the fight earlier on. He held a weeping baby in a protective way, while his own uniform was full of blood. The baby was surely Daemon, and there was no other explanation, apart from the fact that this White Lord had killed the previous two in order to protect him.

The Lord Commander reached the same conclusion. "What have you done, White Lord…?" Another blade was stuck into the old man's back, and he dropped dead on the floor. Jenon stood over him. Wisps of his silvery hair had been dyed red, while his pale face was splashed with blood. The demon had just killed his father in front of his son, but there was a dark sense of satisfaction in his eyes.

Daemon's sobbing suddenly ceased, but his tears were still trickling down his innocent face. And Nesto couldn't help but wonder. Was this the kind of memories the noble had obtained from his father that he was so envious of?

CHAPTER 18

"Are you feeling alright? You collapsed for a moment." Lord Zoloc stood over him, holding a small vessel made of glass that contained some drops of blood, probably Nesto's, since his palm was still bleeding. He helped him up and had him sit on a chair. "The burden must have been too much for your body. Don't worry you're not weak. It's perfectly understandable. You've had too much: learning that you are a descendant of the dragons, your exertion due to the island's magic, the mark check and, of course, learning that I have been keeping track of you from the very beginning. Your head must be boiling."

I don't know why everybody thinks that I'm weak, but it makes me furious. It's like they have made a secret agreement with the noble to make fun of me. It was true that all those things that the Lord mentioned had taken their toll on his body. And he had passed out earlier, but this time he hadn't collapsed. *It was a dream that I saw, a memory!*

A really sad and scary memory that gave a hint as to the reason why Daemon's blood kept disappearing from his face whenever his father was mentioned. He wondered what the outcome would have been if White Lord Raizel had finally followed the rest of the White Lords. Would they have been able to slay the demon with master Raizel's aid?

"Apart from the need for your blood," the Lord kept saying, after he drew up a chair and sat opposite him, "I thought that you would like to know some things about…"

"My father," Nesto interjected.

"Not exactly. I wanted to talk to you about your ancestors, not your father. About your godly blood, not the human. I have a vast knowledge of ancient creatures and forgotten stories. It might ease your burden. I'm sure you'll learn as much as you should about your father from his own mouth, when you reach the top."

"I don't want to hear about the dragons," Nesto insisted. "I want to know more about my father. Even a small characteristic of his would be enough. I just want to have a clearer picture of him."

Zoloc didn't seem enthusiastic. Perhaps because he enjoyed narrating these forgotten stories. He did that quite often, when he was at the Black Castle, in the form of Lord Mendax. *And I have to admit, his stories are a lot more interesting than those of Lord Cornius.* "Your father is a very foolish man," he declared. "And foolishness is usually accompanied by bravery. He is brave enough to mess with the Order of the Lords on his own. He is the first Lord, after demon Jenon, to do such a thing. I almost admire him. Does that cover you?"

"Yes." *Foolish and brave.* His father seemed like an older version of Almar. It was without a doubt foolish of him to risk his own life, just to show that acquiring the title of the Lord wasn't impossible. But, apart from that, he might also have wanted to obtain more power in order to be able to protect him. Nesto would have done the same thing if he had been in his place.

He remembered that it was Lord Zoloc who had mentioned the story of the White Lords and the demon, and he had a wild thought. "Have you seen Jenon up close?" he asked him. The memory he had seen could have easily been his.

"Of course. Most of the Lords have. He used to be a Lord, too. The only ones who haven't seen him up close were probably the three Lords who were at the Black Castle. That must have been the reason why Lord Cornius and Lord Ereina didn't recognise Daemon as his son. This and their hatred for the nobles. He is both a demon and a noble. I almost feel sorry for him."

"So, the Order does not yet acknowledge that the demon's son has entered the Tower of the Lords. They're hunting down only me."

"They will soon know. It can't be kept a secret much longer, now that Jenon got out of his hideout. And when they do know, Daemon will be in deep water. There's no one waiting for him at the top." As soon as he blurted out these words, he gave Nesto a sudden look, his green eyes narrowing dangerously, his tone strict. "If you are thinking of taking the noble with you, with your father, then don't. You don't know the stories, but dragons and demons don't get along well. You both have divine blood in your veins, but it's from different Gods that hate each other. After the alignment, hatred will gradually start to suffocate you and, eventually, Daemon will kill you."

Nesto couldn't believe that. "I can't abandon him. He saved my life," he said. "Besides, when we were training under White Lord Raizel, he proved to us that he could control his urge to kill. You can't know for sure that he will try to kill me."

"Neither can you." He sighed. "Alright, if you care about him that much, then after you reach the top and the alignment is complete, I will find a place to hide him. I promise to protect him. I guess that it won't be that difficult, since the Order of the Lords will have their hands full with the dragons coming out of their graves." He saw hesitation on Nesto's face. "Don't worry. I can't lie," he insisted. "No one who uses magic can."

The Lord urged him to stay in bed for the following days, whereas he would fill the void of Lord Mendax and the subordinate of Lord Doral, so as not to arouse any suspicions.

And Nesto did just that. He kicked Daemon out of his room, and lay in bed. Silan-te insisted on offering him her own room, but it felt wrong letting the girl sleep on the hard floor. *If he is going to kill me eventually, then the least he could do is give me his soft bed.* It might seem like a joke to him now, but the very thought vexed him. Not because he feared that the noble would really kill him, but because, in the end, he might end up losing his first and only friend. And it was extremely hard to get one, especially for him.

He placed the glassy dagger next to the table, hoping that one of those days it would give him the memory it carried of his father, and he tried to relax, sorting everything out in his head. One of the things that he mulled over was his divine blood, but even now, he was too afraid to touch on that subject. Or what would happen when the dragons returned. The Order would surely lose its power, or it could even be completely destroyed...then, all humankind would be in danger. He wondered if the dragons were really as cruel and merciless as they were described in all the stories. Surely, they couldn't be so ferocious. It was the Lords that had made up these stories. It could possibly be yet another one of their lies. It wasn't true that the Lords had killed all the dragons; why should that one be true, after all?

He tried to think of Lord Mendax, or better say Lord Zoloc disguised as Lord Mendax. How he had mentioned the dragon that had taken a human form and waiting for the right moment to reclaim the skies. Nesto also remembered him saying, a few seconds before going through the Portal leading to the first island: "Now is the hard part, but rest assured: in this part, you will be able to get assistance openly." *He had been trying to help me from the beginning.*

In the end, he decided to trust one more person. The list of those he trusted was growing longer, and he couldn't tell for sure that he liked it. *I feel like a fish out of water.* The first one he trusted was his elder brother, who didn't hesitate to enter the Tower for his sake. Then, the arrogant noble, who had been keeping the same secret. Then, Silan-te, whom he trusted for some reason from the word go, and now Lord Zoloc, who had kept him alive, for as long as he was at the Black Castle, without revealing his presence. *I can't say I trust my father, but it wouldn't be fair, or even true, if I claimed the opposite.*

And Garon! He had almost forgotten about his uncle. The one he had actually trusted the most, the one that took care of him. *He is first on the list.* He wondered if his uncle, or even Lirelle, missed him. He wasn't sure about her, but Nesto had surely missed his uncle.

Almost three days had passed. *Just four more.* He spent the fourth day lying in bed, waiting. The Cursed One attended to all his needs as well as she could, whenever Daemon left her alone. Maybe, it was because Lord Zoloc was gone, and the noble felt bored, but he began to fight with her again. They didn't shout loud enough to be heard upstairs, where Nesto lay, but he could see it on her upset face. A sort of irritation only Daemon could inflict.

The evening of the fifth day, he decided to stand up and walk as he felt much better and lighter. A cool bath would rejuvenate him. He stretched out and went down those miserable, slipshod wooden stairs. He didn't see either of them, but he supposed they would be in the Lord's abode for supplies. At the touch of cold water, his muscles tightened up. After that couple of months he spent with master Raizel, his body had become more muscular. It had transformed from the small boy's skinny body to that of an adult, with plenty of scars. The spot Lord Zoloc had painted now looked more like a dark smudge and, although the layers of paint hid the mark, it was completely useless. It was supposed to conceal the mark, not draw all attention to it. Nesto rubbed it hard, until its blue glow finally appeared. Maybe, it was just Nesto's idea, but the more he looked at it, the more the mark resembled the head of a dragon.

Daemon was already siting in the parlour, when Nesto finished his bath. He was holding some juicy grapes, and he was waiting patiently, just like Nesto, just like all of them, so that the days would fly away and they would move on to the next level. Then, things were expected to be easier as the Order of the Lords was focused, and gathered the best part of their force, on Lord Zoloc's island. Most Lord Candidates, almost all of them, were on the second island, so that was to be expected.

"So, did you finally get bored with my bed?" asked the noble, while sticking a grape into his mouth.

"Oh, no, no. It's perfect, and soft. I really enjoy sleeping on it. It doesn't compare to sleeping on the floor," said Nesto. Daemon would surely use that against him. But it was worth it. Wiping that smug look off the noble's face was one of the very few things that cheered him up. These chances were rare, so he didn't want to miss any of them.

This time, though, he didn't succeed. "Yeah, I know. I feel almost sorry that Silan-te is forced to sleep on the hard floor."

He should have expected that. He claimed to be well-mannered, due to his noble descent, but Daemon never put anyone above his own comfort. Maybe, that's why they were fighting all the time. The noble had occupied her bed. "Where is she? I haven't seen her all day."

"She wanted to spy on the other Cursed Ones and the Lords. She didn't feel comfortable sitting and doing nothing but wait. And, for some reason, I don't think that she feels comfortable being around me, either. I honestly don't understand why. I'm quite charming," said the noble, and he ate yet another seed.

Nesto flew his eyes open. "Yes, you really are. That's certainly one of the traits of your noble blood. Like modesty, I imagine."

"Modesty is for the commoners," he stated.

His empty stomach didn't allow him to dwell on that. He made a beeline for the Lord's kitchen, which was always full of cooked food, pastes, a wide array of sweets, and a lot of fruit hard to come by on the island. Zoloc must have been stealing them from the kitchen of the Black Castle. Just like his red wine. He gorged himself on the food, and stopped eating only when his stomach was swollen, and could take no more.

Silan-te came back late at night, her look alarmed. "They have grown restless," she told them. The Order asked the Lords for results as soon as possible, since the alignment was on the cards. She didn't learn any details, but the Deathlord was up to something drastic, no doubt. They had also begun to notice the long absence of the Lord that Zoloc had killed. Lord Doral was now suspicious of everyone and everything. He summoned all the Cursed Ones that had been searching night and day for the descendant of the dragons outside the fortress and, after placing another five persons at their gate, he ordered to forbid exit to Lords and Lord Candidates, alike.

That night, none of them slept a wink. They couldn't risk it. Not that agony and stress would let them sleep. They all gathered in the parlour, and sometimes sneaked a peek outside, hoping that, no matter what the Lords were up to, they would find a way to deal with it as they wouldn't be caught unawares. That was naive thinking, he knew that. But there was really not much that they could do.

The stars were still shining in the deep blue sky, when Lord Zoloc turned up before them—out of the blue, as usual. *Clearly, he doesn't know the meaning of doors.* He wore Lord Mendax's clothes, but not his form. It was a scarlet uniform, with a purple mantle hanging from his shoulders. His news was as bad as Silan-te's, if not worse.

"My days as Lord Mendax are officially over," he told them. "Lord Cornius entered Lord Mendax's room, while I was away, and discovered the dead body of his dear friend. That can't have been very sightly. He had been dead for over two months. The Order of the Lords must have surely been informed by now. Unfortunately, they're not too daft to realise that the appearance of the descendant of the dragons and the Lord's death are connected. They must have already concluded that Nesto is aided by someone belonging to their circle."

"So, what are we supposed to do now? Do we remain hidden, or do we try stealing the crystal that you so willingly gave away?" Daemon asked.

"You are leaving for the next level immediately, of course."

"But their bodies haven't adjusted, yet. They need at least another couple of days," the Cursed One demurred.

"I'm sure they will be fine," said the Lord. "Their bodies must have considerably adjusted. The side effects can't possibly be that bad. After all, I don't think we have any other choice. The Order won't just sit and watch. Most probably, they will have ordered to wipe out all the Lord Candidates."

If they were to judge by the Deathlord's actions, then that was probably true. Why else would Lord Doral gather all his forces inside the fortress? For once in his life, Lord Zoloc decided to use the door to go to his quarters. When he got back, he wore his black mantle, instead of the purple one, and held a flask of red wine in one hand, and in the other a bag full of food. He put the flask in his pocket, and gave the bag to Silan-te.

"What's the plan? What do we do now?" Nesto demanded. They had to steal the crystal somehow, that was for sure.

"My plan is already in motion. Now, we just have to wait," said the Lord, while walking towards the door. He opened it, and looked up. Then, he got back with a small smile on his lips.

Wait? Wait for what exactly?

He found out soon enough. At first, a loud bang was heard that sounded like a thunderbolt. That very moment, the earth began to shake. Dust seeped through the cracks, then a piercing, scary roar was heard that made Nesto's hair stand on end. His heart began to beat fast, while the flame of the mark scorched him again, like it warned him about the danger.

"What…what was that?" asked the Cursed One in a quivering voice.

It was more than just weird that there was no worry or fear across Lord Zoloc's face. It was as if that man were immune to such emotions. "Oh, it's nothing you should really be worried about," he replied nonchalantly, and took the flask of wine to sip a few drops. "It's just a dragon."

CHAPTER 19

All three of them reacted in exactly the same way. "What?" exclaimed Silan-te, and then Daemon and Nesto. "What?"

His words, so calm and ridiculous, sounded like a lie. They ran towards the door and, when they opened it up, they saw a small cloud of dust wafting in the air. It began to dissolve, giving way to some loud panicky voices and noises that sounded like snapped twigs. "It fell from the sky," a voice was heard amidst the din. What fell from the sky soon appeared. It looked like a huge shadow in the light of the two moons that had almost fused together. It was only a few blocks away. The shadow spread its wings, stretched, and roared, leaving its blue flame sear the sky. A flame similar to the one that had stolen the lives of so many Lord Candidates in the Black Castle.

A divine flame.

"How can...how can it be?" asked the Cursed One. "I thought Lord Candidate Nesto was the only one left." Fear was etched in her green magic eyes.

"He is," the Lord replied. He came closer to take a look outside. "That's not alive. Not the way it would be after the alignment, at least. I brought it up from its grave to keep the Deathlord and the others preoccupied." The dragon's roars were successive, and were now creepier than himself. "I didn't expect it to be so infuriated, though. It might have something to do with the fact that it was the first dragon to be killed. Slain by the Dragonslayer."

"First the painting thing, now this. Your plans are horrible," complained the noble.

"Just stay away from its jaws, and you will be fine. I would also try to avoid that blue flame if I were you. Anyway, try not to die, until I manage to retrieve the crystal from Lord Doral."

He turned his gaze on Daemon. "Not you. You can die if you please," he said in the end, assuming the same look whenever he fought with the noble, and vanished.

The dragon had burnt alive around a dozen Lord Candidates who didn't have the foresight to steer clear of this creature—some of them were so daft as to try to attack it. Then, Silan-te suggested keeping a safe distance as the dragon was dangerously closing in. Nesto suddenly remembered that something was missing. "My brother's dagger! I have to get it," he said and ran back, clambering up the stairs to his room.

He could hear the dragon's fierce clapping of wings rend the sky, wood break, and houses get burnt down to the ground. He wondered how Lord Zoloc had managed to bring the dragon back to an early life. Nesto's blood must have surely played a role. But was that enough, or was magic involved, too? He found the dagger next to the bed, where he had left it, and he grabbed it. Yet, just as he was about to leave, the floorboard collapsed with a loud bang, and he found himself buried under the debris.

That couldn't harm him. He thrust it aside, as soon as he called forth the Mark of the ancient Gods, and was set free. But the heavy hot breath he heard behind him could. What was the right thing to do now? *Run as fast as I can?* No, no. That would probably be the worst choice. *Any sudden movement would definitely invite it to attack me.* He turned slowly, too scared to even breathe. Nesto swallowed hard, when he saw its blue eyes burning like bright flames right before his. Its black horns stuck out a few metres behind its head in a slightly spiral fashion, while its hard nostrils gave off a puff of bluish smoke with every breath it took. The dragon's gaze was more than enough to freeze his whole body.

Nesto was holding the dagger in his right hand, but the dragon was holding Nesto's life in his terrifying jaws. Even if he could, pointing that dagger at it would be just plain stupid. He let it smell him, take his presence in, hoping that his being the descendant of the dragons would somehow get him out of this unscathed. Nesto understood the flaw in his thinking when the dragon groaned and opened its jaws wide to devour him, identifying him only as potential prey.

It was the ones that wanted him dead the most that actually saved him. A Lord accompanied by some Cursed Ones attacked the dragon with blades and magic, dragging it away from Nesto. The creature spread its perforated black wings, and flew high in the sky, clapping them loudly. A vortex of fire was enough to sear the ground, along with half the Cursed Ones that had attacked it.

"Stop staring at it, and run, you fool!" Daemon grabbed him by his top, and pulled him away. The encounter with the dragon made all his courage disappear. And he ran desperately, following the noble and the girl. It didn't matter where. Running away from the dragon, away from the flames was enough. The fire spread fast, swallowing all the houses in its path, while the dragon was flying from one place to another, gulping down whoever it laid its jaws on. The Lord who had saved him had surely fallen prey to the creature, proving that a Lord wasn't capable of slaying a dragon, after all. It was just one of their many lies. There was one thing, one story that wasn't a lie, though. Dragons were as ferocious and merciless as all the stories presented them.

They were running away from the fire, but their main problem was that there was smoke everywhere. It made breathing difficult, scorching their nose and throat. Tears trickled down Nesto's eyes, and made them itchy. They stopped at a well, which the fire hadn't yet reached, and the noble splashed some cool water over them. The tingle subsided, but there was still a burning sensation whenever he tried to take a deep breath. And it would certainly keep getting worse. The wooden peripheral wall kept the smoke inside, as well as them. The threat was equally dangerous for everyone. Lord Zoloc had managed to put the Lord Candidates, the Cursed Ones, and the Deathlord in the same difficult position as Nesto. They were all running for dear life now. Everyone, except the dragon, that is. He was probably the only one to enjoy this.

"The Lord of the island was right," said Silan-te, pointing to a Cursed One killing two terrified Lord Candidates. He came behind them without being seen and, with no hesitation, stabbed them with his dagger. "Lord Doral has ordered to execute all the Lord Candidates. They must already be aware that the descendant of the dragons is hiding inside the fortress."

The Deathlord could also be aware that this was a distraction for the descendant to get away. "We can't stay here," Nesto decided, although the fire hadn't reached them yet. "We have to head for the headquarters, next to the gate. Lord Zoloc might not be able to retrieve the crystal on his own. We have to make sure he succeeds."

No one argued with that. They poured some cold water over them again, pulled the top of their shirts up over their noses, and started running. This time, not away from the fire, but in it. The damp clothes promised to offer some protection from the smoke, while the Mark kept their bodies from getting seriously burnt, at least for Daemon and Nesto. They put the girl between them to protect her from the flames as much as they could. Burnt debris hurtled overhead, out of nowhere, while they were running, and several Lord Candidates turned up just as suddenly, but these posed no serious threat. The real danger was on all fours and it had wings on its back, with such a hot breath, it could scorch you in no time.

They had just taken a turn to avoid two Cursed Ones, when he heard Daemon say: "Duck!" The noble pulled the girl to the ground. When Nesto saw the black bony tail moving like a whip, it was too late. He only had time to place his left arm in front of his face, before the thrust lifted him up in the air, and sent him hurtling backwards. He heard a loud cracking noise coming from his body, then he hit against a wooden wall. He plumped, almost slid, to the ground, letting out a scream of pain.

He gritted his teeth to muffle a second scream. This wasn't the time to let pain take over. He had to move again—and fast. He only gave himself some time to assess the damage his body had suffered. Something told him that the crack he had heard came from his ribs—not the ones with the Mark. His arm, he wasn't sure whether it was broken or not, but he could barely move it. As for the other parts of his body, they seemed to be intact. *I will know for sure when I start moving again.* If it weren't for the Mark, it would have been a lot worse than some broken bones.

He stood up on his feet with difficulty, supported by his right arm. His legs were a bit shaky and, when he tried to take the first step, he lost balance and fell, but not before he felt a slash on his back. He turned over to see a Cursed One standing above him, holding a green dagger. The masked man moved to finish him without a trace of remorse. Nesto raised his uninjured hand, a gesture that made him look like he was begging for his life. Yet, when the Cursed One got closer, a sword materialised in Nesto's hand, and pierced through his enemy's flesh, eliminating the threat. The face behind the white mask must have really been startled. *I know I would be.* No Lord Candidate should be able to materialise a weapon.

The cut on his back gave the impression of being pretty shallow, yet standing back up seemed impossible. All his energy was drained from that last effort to stay alive. He wanted to run back to Daemon and Silan-te to make sure they were safe, but even focusing on that thought alone was too much of a strain. He remained motionless, hearing the screams fade away one by one.

The only sound that remained was the dragon's roar, and the crackling voice of the flame. The need for rest overshadowed the desire for survival.

Before he lost his senses, he came to the conclusion that he didn't like this plan of Lord Zoloc's any more than the noble did.

A hard slap across his face was enough to bring him back to consciousness. "Stop hitting him. He's already hurt from the blow and the fall." He recognised Silan-te's voice.

"I'm not fond of taking orders from servants." Another hard slap hit his face. When he opened his eyes, he saw Daemon and the Cursed One over his head. The girl looked unharmed, but the noble wasn't. A deep wide cut started from his throat and covered half his face, all the way to his eye. Dark blood oozed out of his wound, and it didn't seem to clot. There was no doubt that the dragon was behind it.

"New scar?" said Nesto, forcing a smile. "It looks good on you."

"Yes, I'm thinking of keeping it," said Daemon. "To remind me that I hate Lord Zoloc almost as much as I hate my father." He looked around. "I have to admit it, though, that, despite the fire, the Order of the Lords after us and the frenzied dragon doesn't feel as bad as it would if I were back at my father's castle. At least, I know that there is no way he could ever reach me here."

The noble began to check Nesto's wounds, while the Cursed Ones stood on guard. The sky was still dark, so that meant that he hadn't passed out for long. Some buildings were still burning, but a big part of the Fortress had already been reduced to ashes, and the fire had somehow abated. The best part was that the black smoke seemed to want to escape upwards. Still, his mind had barely been put at ease, when he saw the dragon, on the opposite side, climbing up a wooden wall with his sharp claws, then setting fire on it with his fiery breath. The specific fire wouldn't be able to harm them, but the increasing smoke would make their survival an ordeal. "A couple of your ribs are surely broken. Your arm…" Daemon lifted it up to check it, giving it a light squeeze.

"Ouch! Ouch!"

"Judging by the pain, I think it's safe to assume that it's not broken. It'll probably heal in a couple of days."

"No, it won't," said Nesto. "It will take a lot more than that. I'm not you. My wounds need more time to heal." His dragon blood hadn't given him this kind of powers. In fact, it hadn't given him anything at all. Only trouble. His only gift, discovering the memories that were hidden inside objects or dreams, wasn't exactly much help. In this kind of situations, Nesto considered it to be even less than useless.

"You wouldn't be in this mess, commoner, if you had ducked when I told you to," Daemon told him off.

"No. I wouldn't be in this mess if it weren't for Lord Zoloc's plan, in the first place." The noble nodded in agreement, then he tried to help him up, but the acute pain in Nesto's arm and the rest of his body threw him back to the ground. After several attempts, Daemon gave up.

"Oh, get up, you weakling!" he shouted at him. That had Nesto standing on his own two feet in the blink of an eye. His will wasn't strong enough to endure the pain, but apparently his ego was. He felt more exhausted than ever and, when he checked his chest, he didn't see the Mark of the ancient Gods. The only flame burning inside him was the one on the mark across his ribs, which seemed as useless as the powers his dragon blood had given him, if not less. "We are close. Try not to be too much of a burden, until we get there."

He tried, he honestly did, but in the end he had to use the noble's shoulder to support himself. The pain was too much to bear alone. They let the girl stand on guard for any possible attacks, while they tried at the same time to move as stealthily as possible. They found ashes, debris, and lots of dead bodies on their way. Most of them suffered deadly blows from blades, rather than from jaws or the fire. They reached their destination exhausted and drenched in sweat.

The plan was to help Zoloc steal the crystal, or if that wasn't possible, then to at least escape from the fortress before the smoke choked them to death. However, they didn't find Lord Doral at the Lords' headquarters, and the gate was still protected by half a dozen Cursed Ones. They hid next the building, which was still intact, as far away from the masked men as possible, to get some rest and think of their next move.

They hadn't yet made up their minds if they would stay there and wait for Lord Zoloc, or if they would take their chances against the Cursed Ones, when a wave of fire sent a body hurtling towards them. They barely managed to jump out of its way, and fell on the ground. The man was engulfed in flames, while one arm was missing, eaten by the dragon, as Nesto judged by the looks of it.

"I remember someone saying that my plans were horrible, that they wouldn't work. What do you have to say now, noble?" Lord Zoloc appeared through the smoke, unscathed. His black mantle was full of ashes, while some flames flickered around the edges. He was flashily wielding the crystal.

"I never claimed that they wouldn't work," Daemon admitted. "I just found them really, really horrible."

"Is this Lord Doral?" asked Silan-te, pointing to the burning man.

"What's left of him. I had to lure him into an encounter with the dragon, in order to retrieve the crystal." Yet another roar of the dragon echoed in their ears, proof that they were dangerously near. Lord Zoloc hurriedly took them to the front side of the building and, after he advised them to seek the Lord of the next island at the earliest opportunity, turned the crystal, and the portal opened behind them.

He had the Cursed One go through the Portal first. It had something to do with the side effects, the Lord explained to them. But, when it was their turn to enter, Zoloc placed his hand on the noble's shoulder, and stopped him abruptly. Nesto stopped short, too, alarmed by that gesture. There was that strange smile upon the Lord's face.

"I almost forgot," he said in his usual tone, despite the threat of the dragon. "Daemon, Jenon sends his love." Then, startled as they were, he pushed them gently into the vast darkness of the portal.

CHAPTER 20

Again, there was a falling sensation, and then cold waters welcomed them. The darkness of the bottom beckoned to them, and Nesto couldn't turn down its offer. He couldn't move his body. His stomach was killing him, as if a cold metal blade had pierced through it, his lungs were about to burst from the lack of oxygen and, no matter how hard he tried, the Mark of the ancient Gods wouldn't appear on his chest. All he could do was observe the air gush out of his mouth, forming bubbles that showed him the way to the surface. Yet, try as he might, he was unable to follow them. His body was almost touching the bottom, and his senses were fading away, when he felt something wrap around him and pull him upwards.

As soon as his head stuck out of the water, he desperately gasped for as much oxygen as he could, then he exhaled with difficulty. Even this was painful. A hand came from behind and ran over his chest, pulling him backwards. He would have recognised that hand, even if he were blind.

Without realising it, he found himself lying on solid ground. *What happened? Why can't I call the fiery power of the ancient Gods?* he wanted to ask Silan-te, but he didn't have the strength. The only thing he could do was watch her looking worriedly at the water surface. Finally, she dipped in again.

Only when he heard him cough did Nesto recall Daemon. He had just got out of the frozen water, and was standing up. His hair was stuck on one side of his skull, and his face featured another deep cut, a reminder of his encounter with the dragon. Blood gushed from his nose, and was instantly washed away by the raindrops. He hadn't noticed earlier, but it was raining, and the sky was grey and ominous.

"Were you looking for me, perhaps?" the noble asked, as Silan-te jumped out of the water. "I thought you served only the descendant of the dragon. I didn't know you cared so much about my safety."

Relief was painted across her face, as well as a hint of irritation. "I...your death would sadden Lord Candidate Nesto," the girl said indifferently.

"So, does this mean that, from now on, you will protect me, too?"

"No, I..."

Daemon knelt before her, coughing up blood. "I'm alright," he told her, as she gave him a scared look. But the noble was far from alright; Nesto could see that clearly. His one palm was filled with blood, just like his mouth, while his whole body was shaking, and he was sure it wasn't only the frozen water and the cold rain. He wondered how he could stand on his two feet, and talk, while Nesto himself could simply look on, impotent and motionless.

Silan-te dragged both of them under a tree. She mumbled a word of magic, and instantly the branches of the nearest trees, covered in thick wide leaves, joined together and gathered over their heads, protecting them from the fury of the rain. She lit a big fire and took off their damp clothes, leaving them with only the bare essentials on. When she tried to take off Daemon's top, he stopped her, but Silan-te insisted. The sight she saw, though, made her gulp with difficulty.

"This is just a gift from my beloved father," said the noble with a forced smile, seeing the Cursed One shocked. A huge slash ran over his heart all the way to his pelvis, and another one split his chest in two. These two scars were clear on Daemon's pallid skin, and they were so deep, a normal man would have died on the spot. Of course, the noble was far from a normal man.

Nesto mustered up the strength to speak. "These are the side effects?" he asked, trying to draw Silan-te's attention away from Daemon. The noble hated showing his scars, let alone mentioning his father and whatever had to do with him. Nesto too doubted it whether he would enjoy doing it now, after what Lord Zoloc had told them.

He hoped that the Lord had simply been trying to provoke him one last time. It certainly gave that kind of feeling. After all, the demon must have been too busy facing the Lord Commander and the rest of the Lords—sent by the Order to wipe him out—to have any contact with Zoloc. Supposing, of course, that both of them had such encounters, which Nesto really doubted. However, the memory he had seen about demon Jenon made him wonder. It could have easily been Lord Zoloc's, although the truth was, he hadn't discerned him anywhere in the specific memory.

"Yes," the Cursed One said, and lowered her eyes in front of Nesto. "Your bodies haven't had the time to adjust, and now they pay the price."

I suppose it's preferable to facing the dragon or the Deathlord. He didn't know why, but that dragon didn't look at all like those depicted in the Black Castle. He was emaciated and small. The stench of death still lingered on him. Maybe, the fact that he had risen before his time was to blame. "Do you know when these side effects will wear off? When will we be able to use the power of the ancient Gods again?"

The girl rekindled the fire that was about to die out because of the strong wind and the raindrops. "In a few days…at best."

"At worst?" Daemon asked.

The answer flashed through her face before she spoke. *Never!* "I can't tell with any certainty. It may…it may last for long." Whenever she spoke, her green eyes travelled, probably unconsciously, over the nobel's slashes. "I have to take care of your wounds, and make sure you have something to eat. I'm sorry, but I lost the bag with all the food in this turmoil. I'll go hunting. I'm sure I'll find some useful herbs. I won't be long," she said.

"Catch something with wings. I wish to eat a grilled bird today, little servant," Daemon ordered her, as she stood up to go.

Silan-te turned to look at him out of the corner of her eye. She snorted, muttered something under her breath, and then left. "Was that a 'yes' or 'no'?" he shouted behind her, as she walked away. But the Cursed One chose not to respond.

Nesto was still unable to move his body as it was sore almost everywhere. He was in pain because of the smoke he had breathed in, from the dragon's blow, from the cut the Cursed One had inflicted on him and, of course, from the side effects of the portal. The taste of blood in his mouth was surely due to these side effects. The worst thing of all, though, was that they couldn't call forth the Mark. They were utterly defenceless. They were forced to rely only on Silan-te. Which meant that making her blood boil, just like the noble did earlier, wasn't such a wise decision.

Surely, he acted like that because he couldn't stand the look of pity in Silan-te's eyes. *I mean, he can't be unaware of the dangerous situation we are in. If the Cursed One wished to, she could kill us both without even breaking a sweat. And, now that she has seen the danger, she is in for allying herself with us, chances are, she might actually do it.* But Nesto had to agree with him on this: any other emotion, even hatred, was more preferable to pity. On the other hand, he couldn't exclude the irritating trait the noble was born with. *He might not be able to help acting like that. They tend to feel superior to everyone else.*

After a while, the noble stood up, and put on the top the girl had left by the fire to dry out. There was another, deeper scar along his back. Nesto hadn't noticed that before. And it looked just as lethal as the other two. There was a time, back in the Black Castle, when Nesto envied the attention Daemon had got from his father, but now, seeing all those wounds on his body, he wasn't so sure about that anymore.

"Are you alright?" he asked the noble, as he lay down next to him.

"Shouldn't you be more worried about your own skin, commoner?" asked the noble. "You are the one who can't heal his wounds in a matter of days."

"I'm not asking about this kind of wounds. I'm referring to the ones that are inflicted by words."

Daemon leant his head on the tree trunk behind him, and shut his eyes with a wheeze. All the tiredness and pain he hid behind his smile appeared in his puffy eyes and the furrows across his face. "I doubt that his words were real," he said. It seemed he had reached the same conclusion as Nesto. "Lord Zoloc was just trying to play with my mind to infuriate me. Most likely because I insulted his brilliant plan. But, of course, we are not too fond of each other, so he probably didn't even need a reason to try and aggravate me, in the first place. He would have done it, anyway. I know I would."

If that was true, then Lord Zoloc had achieved his goal. When the Lord had pushed them through the portal, Nesto saw the noble's face reflect pain, rage, fear, and hatred. All this in a hair-raising moment. Even his eyes had turned red, showing that his emotions were out of control.

"That doesn't look like a bird," said Daemon, when he saw the Cursed One holding a small, four-legged monster. "Unless you cut off its wings, while trying to catch it." She was soaked to the bone, and was almost shaking. For a moment, he felt guilty for being dry by the fire, but he had no other choice. He could barely move his body, which was still sore.

The girl gave the noble an angry look, and Nesto noticed that, apart from her lips, her nostrils were also tight. "If you don't like it, then you might as well starve," she said through her teeth.

"I guess I will have to compromise. Anyway, if I were in Nesto's position, I would torture you every day for your lack of manners."

"Oh, don't worry, you already do," said Silan-te, and put the dead creature she had caught over the fire. The girl wasted no more time. She took out her dagger, and began to cut her clothes into long, thick straps of cloth. When she was done, she took out of her pockets the herbs she had picked, and placed them on the pieces of cloth, after she chewed them. The cut across the noble's face looked more serious, but she chose to treat the one on Nesto's back first. That was the price Daemon had to pay for enraging her.

She asked for his permission to touch him, as if he were a God. Which, apparently, wasn't all that wrong. A part of his was divine, which essentially made him a God. A very weak one, though, judging by his current condition. He gave her his permission, and felt her touch. It was so gentle and warm, it almost made his pain fade away. Silan-te bandaged his wound, just like she did with his hand and ribs. These two would mainly take time and lack of movement to heal, but the herbs helped on that score, especially as far as the swelling was concerned. Finally, she used her lips to check if he was running a fever or not.

If Nesto hadn't been running a fever, he certainly would now. For some reason, blood rushed through his head, while his mark began to sear him dangerously. It was so intense, it almost made him sweat. The burning sensation inside his chest was similar to the one caused by the fiery power of the ancient Gods, but not so painful. The girl had to move away before Nesto's colour got back to normal, and the burning sensation abated.

"Your wound seemed to be healing a lot faster," the Cursed One realised, when she began to treat the noble's wound. She pushed it with her hand, and Daemon let out a grimace of pain. She pressed it again, showing she hadn't done that by accident. "My apologies. I don't mean to torture you," she said without really meaning it. The satisfaction oozing out of her eyes showed the exact opposite. "But, since we don't have a healer with us, you will have to compromise, again." She wrapped the piece of cloth around his head in such a way that almost shut one eye. Strangely enough, the noble let her do it without complaining. *Maybe, he realised—at last!—the disadvantaged state we are in!*

She forcefully removed Daemon's top, and checked for more wounds, starting from his back. Watching her touching the noble with her warm and gentle hands gave Nesto an unpleasant feeling. He didn't like the kind of smile she was trying in vain to hide behind her lips, either. It was a different kind of pleasure, this one. It made him wonder if she had the same smile when she was treating his own wounds.

These thoughts faded away when Silan-te's hand fell on Daemon's mark. She groped it with her hands, but the corrosion due to the water hadn't washed away all the layers of paint, and it must have looked to her eyes like an innocent bruise the noble's duel with the dragon had left him with.

Until the meat was cooked, all the touching, the awkward silence, along with the weird feeling on Nesto's chest, had stopped, and Daemon had returned back to his usual irritating self. Most of the pain wore off, but Nesto was so exhausted, he dropped off after a few bites, having in his eyes the last image of the raindrops falling incessantly, while in his ears jingled the bickering between Silan-te and Daemon.

Lots of weird dreams visited him in his deep slumber. And all of them were mainly about the Cursed One. She saw her on her knees in a dark room, where a green light glimmered. Her face was pale and looked somewhat scared, while her hands were gory. Before her stood five persons dressed in black robes and white masks, who chanted loudly. "We are the Cursed Ones. We hide our shame. We seek our former glory…" One of them took a step forward and placed a white mask over Silan-te's face, hiding her bright green eyes, while the rest continued to chant. "We are the Cursed Ones. We hide our shame. We seek our former glory…"

He saw her again along the torchlit corridors of the Black Castle, blending with the shadows. Away from the Lord Candidates' unsuspicious eyes. Away from his own and the noble's eyes, while pacing towards the armoury. The unknown ancient words that adorned the stone walls revealed their meaning to Nesto's eyes now. "Beware, if you can hear them talk, then you are one of them."

He followed Silan-te, and she led him to a Lord's whispers, which weren't so indifferent, a hidden green dagger, and a secret that needed to be kept hidden from the Order of the Lords. A desperate Lord Candidate was stabbed outside the baths hall, in his attempt to enter it. Pain was painted across his face; Nesto could see it. It was so vivid, he could almost feel it.

He watched her sneak onto the second level of the castle, the forbidden one, and open the portal, making sure she didn't get caught. He saw scenes of the disputes between Daemon and Silan-te. Their mutual aversion was so clear that Nesto never saw it coming.

The soft kiss.

The noble wrapped his hand around her waist, pressed her against him, and his lips softly stroked hers, leaving her frozen. Maybe, he hadn't felt the pain of the Lord Candidate that was stabbed in the stomach with the dagger of a Cursed One, *but I think I can feel it now. Not in my stomach, but deep inside my chest. Like something is being torn apart.*

The next morning, that weird dream was still etched in his mind. After that, he had suddenly woken up, breathing with difficulty, and hadn't gone back to sleep. He only lay, drenched in sweat. He recalled the image of Daemon holding and kissing Silan-te, and he felt the stab in his chest come back again. That was just stupid, feeling that kind of pain only because of a thought. Only someone in love should be overpowered with such emotions…*Could it be? No. No, no, no. Definitely not.* Besides, it was only a dream, just a stupid dream.

Only it wasn't his own dream. Nesto himself couldn't dream…

CHAPTER 21

Five days had passed, but rain continued to fall continuously. All those days, he had been listening to the raindrops trying to pierce through the green leaves gathered over their heads, forming a makeshift roof flapping in the strong wind. Obviously, on the third level, the damn rain never stopped. After so many days, his wounds had healed to a certain degree. The deep cut across his back looked as if it had never been there, while he could freely move his injured hand without feeling any pain. His ribs, though, needed some more time.

As usual, the noble was in better condition. The cut across his face had surely healed, but Daemon still had that piece of cloth tied around his head, so that his quick recovery wouldn't arouse the suspicions of the Cursed One. Unlike Nesto, there were no side effects on his body, and now he could freely call forth the power of the ancient Gods. *It almost makes me wish I had the blood of a demon, too.*

So did the noble. "No difference, as far as the Mark is concerned?" he asked in a displeased tone. His fingers groped the cut under the bandage, and cast a furtive glance at Silan-te, who stood on guard duty. Throughout those five days, the Cursed One had been patrolling the place in the rain. She would let her guard down only when she was forced to sleep for a few hours at night. But, even then, she would suddenly wake up, wielding her dagger. The frenzied dragon had inflicted no wounds on her, but all this exertion must have brought her to a state worse than Nesto's.

"No, nothing. I'm feeling better, so I guess it won't be long till I'm able to call forth the Mark again. In any case, something tells me that it's going to take less time than the wound on your face."

He faked a smile. "It wasn't that deep. Don't be surprised if you see it's fully healed by tomorrow."

"I won't," said Nesto, returning the fake smile, and stood up to drink some water from the lake. He wasn't particularly thirsty, but he wanted to keep his distances from the noble. He couldn't bear him anymore, he couldn't stand anyone right now. *I really hate the rain.* It crushed him emotionally. It brought back emotions he had put aside. Pain and hatred, especially pain. Even though he now knew that Almar and his father hadn't exactly abandoned him out of choice, the memories, along with the horrible feelings, were still there. And the rain helped them emerge.

He carefully walked towards the lake, looking out for possible enemies. The trees and their branches kept them away from any prying eyes, but it was easier for someone to track them down around the lake. As early as the second day, Silan-te had suggested looking for the Lord of the third island, as Lord Zoloc had told them, but Daemon and Nesto were opposed to this idea.

"Not until we're able to call forth the fiery power of the ancient Gods again," the noble had said. They didn't know what risks looking for this Lord might involve, or even what was in store for them on the fourth island if they managed to go through the portal. Without the Mark, any reckless move would almost certainly lead them to their graves.

A scream of pain pierced though Nesto's ears, and then shivers went up and down his spine, while he was coming back from the lake. It was Silan-te. She was holding her right hand, shaking. Her legs were about to buckle but, before she plumped to the ground, Daemon was by her side, running his hands around her waist. "What happened? Are you hurt?" he asked.

That scene put him in mind of the dream he had seen, with the noble bringing her close to him and kissing her. Then, there followed the stabbing sensation in his chest. It was no use denying it anymore. *Maybe, I just have to admit that I like her. I don't love her, of course, but I do like her…a lot.* He wondered if Lirelle had felt the same pain when he turned her down. He hoped not. A second scream coming out of Silan-te's mouth made his thoughts go away, and Nesto ran towards her. For a moment, he thought that perhaps it was a side effect from the previous level, that she too had been affected, but no, this couldn't be true. *She is a creature of magic. She is not affected.*

Tears trickled down her face, while her teeth bit her lower lip with all their might. She looked so sensitive. "What…what is this?" Nesto asked. Her black garment was fraying at the edges in her right hand, and red flames seared her skin. It looked like some kind of magic, but Nesto didn't see an enemy, a Cursed One, anywhere around.

The flames died out before Nesto himself tried to smother them, leaving behind various marks. No, not marks. They were words.

THEY ARE ACCOMPANIED BY ONE OF OUR OWN

The Cursed One stood on her two feet, as the words disappeared off her skin, turning into green smoke. No scar was left behind. Her face looked calmer now, but her body didn't seem to have recovered yet. She held her right hand tight. "It's a secret way of communication used by the Cursed Ones," she said, obviously scared. "It's very very old, and they don't use it, unless there is something of extreme emergency."

"I don't understand. Why did they send that message to you?" asked Nesto.

"They didn't. The words appear to all the Cursed Ones, and then disappear. The thing is, the person who sent it has to bear these marks forever. This is the first time I have experienced anything like that. I didn't know it was so painful."

"So, now, they know that a Cursed One is helping us," said the noble, but it was a lot more than just that. The message read, "They," not "He." *They know I'm not alone. That Silan-te is not the only one helping me.* Lord Zoloc had told him that, sooner or later, they would find out about the demon's son. Most probably, they already knew. They must have assumed that those with the divine blood have come together, in order to survive. *And, more or less, that's exactly what we have done, even though it was by pure coincidence.* He wondered if that would make the Order focus more of their force on them. They might withdraw some of the Lords they had sent to face demon Jenon.

"They must have seen our little servant on the second level, when she went through the portal," Daemon continued. "But it's been five days since then. Why did they send it now?"

"Because something must have been preventing them, so far," said the Cursed One. "Our lack of magic energy makes it one of the hardest incantations. One that requires time and space to perform. It should have been impossible for them, given that they had a dragon over their heads. Especially, if they had Lord Zoloc pursuing them. Isn't that the very reason why he chose to stay behind?"

"Does this mean that the dragon has stopped its rampage, or that Lord Zoloc is actually…dead?" asked Nesto.

Silan-te shrugged her shoulders. "Lord Zoloc is quite cunning, and he can use the words of magic in a strange way that no Cursed One can, but his lack of fear in the end might have led to his death."

"That would be exceptionally good news for once, even though I doubt it," said the noble. "Anyway, we can't stay in this place for long. My body has fully recovered from the side effects, and I can freely call forth the Mark of the ancient Gods. I suggest waiting until tomorrow, hoping that Nesto's body will have managed to recover, then we search for the Lord of the third level."

Nesto nodded in agreement, but Silan-te seemed preoccupied with her thoughts. When Nesto asked her, she said: "It's nothing, Lord Candidate Nesto. Really. I just feel that I'm forgetting something, but I can't remember what. Maybe, it's because I haven't used the word of magic on you, yet, to conceal your presence," she concluded.

She asked him to stay still, and took the glassy dagger out of her case. As the green smoke engulfed it, a disturbing thought hit him. Nesto had his father and Almar waiting for him at the top, while Lord Zoloc had promised to secure a safe place for Daemon, although they did not get on very well with each other—on condition he was still alive, of course! What about the girl? What would he do with her? *Will she carry on following and serving me?*

"Will you still have to use a word of magic on me every single day after the alignment?" he asked, hoping that she would have to remain by his side.

"No, it won't be necessary. All the dragons will have risen from their graves by then, and your presence will no longer stand out. The Cursed Ones won't be able to track you down...Oh, no!" she suddenly exclaimed.

"What is it?" Nesto asked. Her face had gone pale.

"Quick! There's no time! Run as far away from me as you can! Now!" Her voice seemed to come out of her lungs with difficulty, and her chest went up and down at a fast pace, which was far from normal.

"I think that you're showing some side effects from the previous level's magic," said the noble in a mocking tone, however, he got closer to check up on her.

The Cursed One paid no attention to him. "Since I saw the message, there was a whisper in my head, bothering me. Warning me," she said frantically. "There's an old spell they can use to track me down. And, if they can find me…"

"…then, they can find us, too." That realisation made Nesto's blood curdle.

"You must leave immediately! Before they do find me."

"Too late. I already did." Nesto turned his head, while these words still echoed in his ears. Some metres away from them, there were two dark figures. *A Cursed One,* he thought, as soon as he saw the white mask one of them was wearing. The other one wore no mask, only a hood that covered his face. Grey smoke came out of his mouth, but Nesto had focused on the golden symbol across the chest of the dark-clad man. *The Deathlord!* Lord Doral had the same golden symbol on the second level.

The flame under his mark began to sear him again as a warning.

Everything happened so fast and so slowly, at the same time. As soon as Daemon turned to look at the Deathlord, he charged him, while there were two black bolts in his hands. But everything was in slow motion: the noble's legs jumping off the ground, hurling mud behind. The raindrops that looked like small pins piercing Silan-te's face slowly and torturously, the Cursed One charging him, seemingly rending the air, like a winged predator. He felt empty inside, as he tried to call forth the power of the ancient Gods. The Mark wouldn't turn up on his chest, no matter how badly he sought it. That flame wouldn't flare up. In all this void he felt, the only thing he could hear were his heart beats. *Ba-dum, ba-dum, ba-dum.*

Daemon's fist collided with that of the Deathlord, and black sparks came out of his hand. Nesto saw them pierce through the raindrops, as a hand pushed him over, and he was sent hurtling up in the air, his body parallel to the ground. *Ba-dum, ba-dum, ba-dum.* Silan-te had moved him away, saving him from the attack of the Cursed One. Green monstrous forms had turned up under the masked man's feet, and all of them, including him and the girl, collided. They were dragged metres behind, until they were out of Nesto's eyeshot.

Nesto could almost feel his body hovering. He was moving so slowly towards the ground that he thought someone had frozen time. The sound of the rain falling on the leaves reached his ears in a distorted way. It seemed to him that dozens of drums were playing above his head. He could see the noble exchanging fists with the Deathlord, and every time their hands touched each other, there was a loud clangour. But it was his heart beats that were clearer and louder. *Ba-dum, ba-dum, ba-dum.*

The fall to the ground and the mud that stuck in his mouth and nose seemed to wake him up. These strange sounds and everything around him moved at a normal pace. The rain sounded normal, too. *Strong, but normal.* The leaves overhead were back in their former position, now that Silan-te was away. The thought of her made him worry about her safety, but he knew that, apart from Daemon, he himself was in greater danger as he still couldn't call forth the power of the ancient Gods.

He stood on his two feet, and spat out the mud. Next to him, he saw the noble land on a tree trunk, and a pang of pain, like the sound of a branch breaking, pierced through his ears. He wished it had really been a branch, not Daemon's back. "You are too weak, son of demon Jenon," he heard the Lord say.

There was no doubt anymore. *They really know the noble.* And, just as Lord Zoloc had said, they didn't find it particularly hard to recognise him. Not that it was any difficult. Between the two, Daemon looked more like his father, Jenon, than Nesto did.

There were some black sparks glimmering in his hands, and Nesto noticed that the small finger in the noble's left hand was crooked and at an angle. He removed the bandage Silan-te had used—that blocked his vision—and said: "If I'm the weak one, then why are you the one that is bleeding?" The Deathlord's hand disappeared into his hood for an instant and, when it came out again, his fingers oozed blood.

"I'm going to enjoy killing you," said the Lord, after snorting and wiping the blood on his mantle. He turned his head towards Nesto. His eyes weren't visible, but he was sure he must have been looking him straight in the eye. "You must be the dragon that still walks among us humans. I'm pleased to say that I have some unpleasant news for you. Your kind won't be ruling the skies any time soon. I have already killed the Lord of this island, and Lord Zoloc must have been dealt with by now. Most of your allies have been eliminated. You can't escape from this island, and there is no dragon here that can save you. All who bear the divine blood are going to die today."

I am a dragon. I can save my own self, Nesto wanted to say, but he was a powerless dragon. Without the fiery power of the ancient Gods, he was a powerless Lord Candidate, too. The only positive thing was that there couldn't have been any other enemies around there. Otherwise, several Cursed Ones must have surrounded them already.

The black bolts in Daemon's hands multiplied and glowed. One of them hit a tree, ripping its trunk in two, while some others hit the ground. Finally, the noble walked towards the Deathlord. They destroyed whatever they could lay their hands on, like countless whips, before they aimed at the Lord's leg and face. The Deathlord shuffled a few steps backwards, while his hood fell and revealed his characteristics. Black smoke came out of one cheekbone, while half his face was covered in a weird tattoo made up of curved lines and various letters of an ancient language. That tattoo went all the way to the top, covering the best part of his shaven head. Maybe, it was due to the blood running through his veins, or the dream he had seen, but Nesto could understand those words.

"Even Gods tremble in fear before death," it read. *And if I'm considered to be a God, then I won't deny it. It's true. I'm shaking like a leaf.*

The Lord began walking towards them slowly but in a creepy way, his spiteful smile sending shivers up and down Nesto's body. "You don't know how to fight effectively," he said. "You're wasting your power of the ancient Gods, and you've already broken two bones. Just like I told you, you are weak!" Two spears materialised in his hands, and they shone and seared the rain. "Let me demonstrate to you the right way of fighting." The first one aimed at Daemon's heart. There was a hiss, as it rent the air, then stopped on the two hands that were placed above his chest. But the second one was stuck into his shoulder, before the noble had time to react.

Blood began to trickle down his arm when Daemon removed the spear, but most of it was being washed away by the rain before it reached the ground. In the white of his eyes, there were some red lines, and it seemed that he was finding it hard to muffle his dark smile that strove to appear across his lips. "Commoner, go away. Find Silan-te. You'll be safer there," he told him, and a sword materialised in his hand, which sparked like lightning.

With a jerk, he charged at the Lord. His blade was pushed back twice by a spear, before it managed to kiss his enemy's flesh, right above the elbow. It wasn't deep enough, though. Not enough to cut off his arm. With a move, both of them were disarmed. The spear and the blade were sent hurtling away from them. The noble managed to land one of his fists on the Lord, before he found himself on the ground, with the Deathlord's foot pressing him on the chest. It was obvious that there was a whole lot of a difference between them, power-wise.

"Death has come for you," stated the Deathlord, his smile darker than ever. Nesto tried to call forth the power of the ancient

Gods, and cursed himself when he drew a blank. But that sense came back. Time began to freeze, and his heart beats were heard louder than ever. *Ba-dum, ba-dum, ba-dum.* The wind spoke to him in a language he couldn't understand, while his hand began to burn, as if engulfed by flames. Just like his mark did. He charged the Deathlord. He couldn't let his irritating friend die. Not here, not like this. Not on another rainy day that he so much hated. The pain would be unbearable. His body moved so slowly, but he wasn't the only one; everything around moved just as slowly. He saw the Lord stand over the noble, the rain trying to obliterate the ancient letters off his face, his mantle flapping in the wind. *Ba-dum, ba-dum, ba-dum.*

He had almost covered the distance, when the Deathlord turned to tell him, "I guess death wants you first." His voice reached Nesto's ears distorted, as if the words hit the sharp raindrops. Nesto could see his own reflection in the Lord's black eyes. But his own eyes looked *blue.* Blue like the flame dancing around his hand. Before he had time to touch his burning hand on the Deathlord, he felt something sharp pierce through his chest, which made him cough. Blood splashed all over the golden symbol, and Nesto felt his heart beat slow down. *Ba-dum, ba-dum.*

He found himself hover in midair, stabbed with the Deathlord's spear. Everything got dark. His first thought was Silan-te. He wondered if she was safe, and slightly chuckled. *I'm the one dying, not her.* Then, he thought of his brother and father waiting for him at the top of the Tower of the Lords. *How much longer will they be waiting until they give up on me?* His last thought wandered off to the noble. He lowered his eyes and, before everything got dark forever, he saw Daemon's bright red eyes wake up.

Ba-dum…

CHAPTER 22

Silan-te dropped to the ground, breathing with difficulty. She was more wearied than she wanted to admit. Next to her lay the dead body of the Cursed One that accompanied the Deathlord, with his dark blood oozing from his neck. She hurriedly looked around, although she was almost sure that there were only two enemies from the start. *Only one now.* The Order of the Lords was definitely short on manpower. They were lucky on that score, at least. If they managed to kill the Deathlord, then the path to the fourth level would be clear. But she damn well knew that there was a catch in that "if."

She stood up with difficulty, placed her hand on the face of the Cursed One, and borrowed his white mask. The only way she could get close enough to the Lord, so that she would deal a deadly blow, was to pretend to be one of his allies. There was really no other way for a Cursed One or even a Lord Candidate to be able to wound someone who bore the title of a Deathlord. She was aware of the formidable power of the Lords who belonged to Lord Commander Legris' guard as all the Cursed Ones took orders directly from him.

Some of them were considered to be of equal power with the rumoured White Lords.

She put on the mask and, without a moment's rest, headed for the other two. There were more trees and bushes, as Silan-te ran as fast as she could, with the rain weighing heavily on her body, and her wounds taking their toll on her steps. There might be only a few scratches along her arms, but one of the monsters created by her opponent had stuck its sharp jaws into her leg, and every time she put it down, pain shook her body. Her fight with the other *Cursed One* had led her quite far away, but she hoped they were both safe. *Even Daemon.*

Before the Old Ones had her wear the white mask, Silan-te had been taught about death and mortality. "We are no longer immortal," those older than her used to say all the time. "We will eventually die. This is something that we need to live by." *But they hadn't prepared me for this.* It was one thing dying, and another thing killing. The hand in which she held the green dagger was still shaking, as her thought scurried back to the scene where she forced its glassy tip to kiss the throat of another *Cursed One*. She couldn't see his face under the mask when she did that, and she was grateful for that. *I had to do it,* she kept saying to herself again and again, but she found it hard to convince herself.

She looked at the overcast sky. She couldn't see it, but the two moons must have become one. The alignment might take place by the end of the day or the next one, at the latest. The day she would be free from that curse was within her grasp. It looked so near, yet so far away…

Silan-te could recall the Old Ones constantly chanting: "We are the Cursed Ones. We hide our shame. We seek our former glory…" She herself was surely cursed. She didn't need to hear it from the Old Ones; she could feel it deep inside; the wind was whispering it to her, the sea, and the trees. But she no longer wanted to hide her shame behind a white mask, just like the rest did. She had decided to break that curse that held her tied to death, misery, and isolation. It was selfish of her, she knew it, but she was intent on keeping the Oath her ancestors had taken to the dragons, even if that meant their return and the destruction of the rest. After all, the Old Ones said that. *We seek our former glory.*

When her leg failed her, she decided that it was necessary to bandage it. The signs of the monster's sharp teeth were etched on her skin. Fortunately, they weren't so serious as she had thought. If she stopped the bleeding, maybe she wouldn't have to lose part of her leg. She quickly tore off a piece of her already tattered trousers, and wrapped it around her wounds, tightening it with all her might. *That was enough, for the time being.*

The Deathlord was on his knees, and standing up bolt upright, when Silan-te found them with a hobble. He thrust back his head and wiped with his hand the blood trickling down his face from a hole under his eye. "You are stronger than I thought. I should have killed you first," said the Deathlord, and only then did she notice the dead body left a few metres away from Daemon. His head was titled to the side, and had a faint smile across the lips. He would have seemed to be sleeping if it hadn't been for his gory top and the blood all over the place. The rain was trying to wash it away in vain; that blood would not leave that body.

"Lord Candidate Nesto?" Her lips moved, but no sound reached her ears. *No, it cannot be.* She threw the white mask, ran towards him, and knelt over his head. His eyes were still open, but they were blank, looking nowhere. She didn't know what to do. What could she do? How could she fix this?

She was shivering, she noticed. She didn't know if it was the rain or the unsightly spectacle. She placed her hands on his face. It was frozen. The flame of life had died out. She turned her eyes towards the noble, tears welling up in her eyes. She wondered why she was crying. Did this have to do with the oath, or had she grown attached to him? If the last descendant of the dragons was gone, then she would never be able to liberate herself from the curse. *For the curse,* she said, trying to convince herself, but she wasn't successful. "Daemon…" Her voice crackled, before she could say anything else.

"Have you lost your sanity, son of Tzenon?" asked the Deathlord. A small hollow laugh was heard from the noble, but it was so bad and wrong that it curdled Silan-te's blood. His hand was gory, but what scared her was the sinister smile and mainly his eyes, which were bloodshot. She had never seen anything like that before. His eyes looked like they were bleeding from the inside, but no cut was visible.

"No, not son of Tzenon. Son of Demon," the noble corrected him, after he stopped laughing. His voice, though, didn't sound the way Silan-te was used to. It sounded deeper, more like a loud whisper. His blood stopped trickling down to the ground, and it turned dark. So did his flesh. A pair of sharp black wings jutted out of his back, boring more holes in his top. Two grey horns came out of his head, while his hair got longer, the colour of the moons. Some sharp lumps decorated his elbows and shoulders. Silan-te covered her mouth with her hand to stop herself from screaming, when she saw that his face was completely raw-boned. His sight was even more frightening than the black dragon she had seen on the second level. He looked more dead than alive.

*Son of the demon…*Well, that explained everything. *His appearance. My uncontrollable trembling. The cold sensation wafting in the air.* That was the first time, however, that she had heard that this unwieldy demon had a child. *Another one that carries the blood of the ancient Gods. And this is the most terrifying one.* Had it been fate that brought those two boys together? Or had it perhaps been the desire of their divine blood? Of course, that didn't count that much, now that Lord Candidate Nesto had already gone out of their reach.

"Daemon…," she said in a trembling voice, but shut her mouth again, when that creature in front of her roared, frightening even the rain.

"Nothing is going to change; you are going to die, just like the one with the dragon blood did," said the Deathlord. "Your blood isn't going to save you, monster. I already told you. All who bear the divine blood will die today…even your demon father. Lord Commander Legris and the rest of the Lords are making sure of it." Without wasting any more time, he materialised a burning spear, and immediately charged at him. His attacks rent the air, but not the noble, although he made no attempt to fend them off. The spear smashed into pieces, throwing up sparks, in its attempt to pierce through the creature's hard chest. All it could leave were a few scratches that could in no way be considered wounds.

In his frenzy, without realising it, the Lord's head was found in the grip of the demon's sharp nails. He fought tooth and nail to set himself free, but to no avail. There was a huge difference of strength. Finally, the creature set him free, only to thrust him onto a tree. The Lord's body snapped a few thick branches, and landed on top of some others.

Wait, Daemon! she wanted to tell him, as he was heading for the Deathlord, but fear stopped her. That was not the Daemon she knew. He wouldn't respond to her with an offending remark, just for the sake of teasing her, having that complacent smile across his lips, like he always did. Had she lost him, too? All the hopes, the sense of security, and the warmth she had felt by their side were gone. Her dream to get rid of her curse was long shattered. She was truly cursed. No matter what she did, death and loneliness would follow her forever.

"How can this be possible? You should be the one to tremble with fear, not me. Why won't you die, damn it! Why won't you die!" she could hear the Lord shouting, as more branches broke, and sparks were thrown up. But the creature wouldn't reply; only its roar could be heard, and that was enough to strike fear into her heart. It pierced through her and made her blood curdle, while it whispered the sweet song of despair.

The descendant of the dragons was the only one who seemed not to hear that song. Fear hadn't touched him, even when he was breathing his last; you could tell by his smile. Silante wondered which could have been his last thoughts that made him so happy. *Maybe, he thought he had reached the top of the*

Tower of the Lords, or of his father and brother, who were waiting for him there. "Do you have a family?" she recalled Nesto asking, when they were still hiding at Lord Zoloc's Fortress. He lay motionless in bed, his body trying to adjust to the magic of the island. That question had struck her as odd as the boy seldom talked to her. He may have protected her from the noble on that single occasion, but that was due to his non-human blood. He didn't trust her. And he showed it at every opportunity.

"Yes, I do, Lord Candidate Nesto," she had replied, thinking of all the Cursed Ones. These were her family. *But not now.* Not after what she had done. *I betrayed them with my choice to ally with the descendant of the dragons.*

After the fall of the dragons, the Lords and the Cursed Ones joined forces to hunt down all the remaining dragons, making sure that none of them would survive. Her own tribe worked in the shadows, while the Order of the Lords took all their glory. But that didn't really matter. As long as the tyranny of the dragons ceased to exist, they were ready to stand everything. After all, lack of recognition was nothing compared to the curse they had to bear because of their betrayal.

The ones that were born by the purity of magic were, in the end, abandoned by it, thus losing all that was pure and sacred. The name Cursed One, we deserve for sure.

She betrayed them because she wanted to change that. To feel the purity her ancestors possessed. She had promised herself to grasp the glory they once had, but now she was still there, on the third level, with the rain blaming her for her failure.

After howls, curses, and broken branches, the Deathlord's body dragged itself across the muddy ground, and stopped next to her. "I do not fear you…I do not." His face was furrowed, so was his body, while one hand had been cut off. She wanted so badly to take out her dagger and stick it into his heart. *He stole my dreams, he deserves this!* She was that close to doing it, but she stopped her hand, when she heard his delirium. "Why won't you die? Why won't you die...," he kept saying. Death would only relieve him from his pain. He deserved to suffer even more. It if weren't for him, everything would be different. *No, it's my fault. If I had remembered the existence of that spell sooner, they wouldn't have found us.* Both of them would have escaped to the fourth level. There can't have been any other enemies, except the Lord and the Cursed One, otherwise they would have turned up by now.

A black monstrous hand came from behind her, and Silan-te was forced to muffle a howl. The hand gripped the Deathlord's head with its nails. The pressure was so great, one ear was cut off in two, while there were some sounds, while his skull was being smashed into pieces. He lifted him up in the air, and the blood started to gush from the joint where there used to be the hand and the shoulder, dyeing the ground red. He dropped him headlong. He repeated this again and again, while in her mind reeled the words the Deathlord had blurted out, "Why won't you die! Why won't you die!" *He won't die, but you will,* she thought.

Silan-te gulped with difficulty, as Daemon's bloodshot eyes silently scrutinised her, after he stopped pounding the Deathlord's dead body. He had thrown his carcass aside, and now it was time for her to receive the monster's frenzy. It moved towards her. But she didn't step back, nor did she think of running away. It would be futile. *I will leave my last breath here,* she said to herself. *We are the Cursed Ones, we hide our shame, we seek our former glory...but we will never taste it.*

If she had a choice, she would rather see Daemon's real face, not that of the demon, as her last image, but maybe that was too much for a Cursed One to ask. She had accepted the idea of her own death, when suddenly a strange net, which looked like a piece of rag, was thrown around the noble, and then stuck into the ground, bringing him down on his knees. She took a step backwards, having Nesto's soulless body in her hands, and watched that creature, which used to have the noble's face, roar and try in vain to set itself free.

Surprised, she looked around to see a man with a furrowed face getting closer. He wore no top, only a pair of trousers full of holes, so she could see the wounds that studded his body—new and old. His long grey, wet hair covered his face, and Silan-te couldn't tell who he was, although his gait seemed familiar and frightening. A white sword began to materialise in his hand—first the handle, then the blade—, shining like gold for an instant and, when he stood before her, he turned it against Daemon.

"Number one," he said, his tone of voice wearied, rather than exasperated. "I thought I had warned you. If you ever dared show that dark side of yours in front of me, I would kill you…"

CHAPTER 23

"NOOOO!" she cried. She had seen the Deathlord's spear smash into pieces, in his attempt to pierce through the creature, that's why she couldn't believe that White Lord Raizel could harm him, but the black blood that began to gush out of Daemon's chest gave the lie to her assumption. "Please, stop! Don't hurt him!" Even though that old man didn't quite belong to the Order of the Lords anymore—he proved that when he spared Nesto's life, although he knew about the mark across his ribs—, trying to stop him still meant treason. Death.

But she didn't care. In her mind reeled only the memory of the noble saying to her: "So, does this mean that, from now on, you will protect me, too?" and the only thing she wanted to do was cry, *"Yes! Yes, I will!"*

The White Lord looked exhausted, just like his body. An old scar studded his neck, and came all the way down to his chest, while some new ones were still bleeding on the opposite side and his belly. "Silence, Cursed One," he said, and Silan-te could now see hesitation in his eyes. "There is no turning back for him. The demon has devoured his soul and mind. The only thing he desires now is massacre and death. He is no longer the boy you knew. He has to be killed."

She knew she couldn't let that happen, but she didn't expect her body to move on its own and threaten the old man by sticking the dagger into his throat, whispering to him the song of death. "I have nothing left, and I don't fear death," she said. Her hand was shaking, but she hoped that the cold would hide her terror. "If you value your life, then please put that sword back in its place."

The White Lord shooed the glassy dagger, like it was an annoying fly. "You are too young to be making threats, Cursed One," he stated. Strangely enough, though, the sword disappeared from his hand, then the old man suddenly sat on the ground, sighing and swearing. His wounds seemed to be sore. "I have to admit, for a certain amount of time, I truly believed that he could control his tainted blood. While he was training under me, I made sure I broke him to the point where his only desire would be to kill me. Not just because of his blood. Even a normal human being would burst, in the end, and try or even think of killing me. But, to my surprise, number one never did."

"Then, why? Why did it happen now?"

"Would you be able to stop your blood from boiling if a friend of yours were to be killed in front of your eyes? This was the line, the limit that he couldn't surpass. No one ever can. And I have to stop him now, otherwise the twigs I burn every day in honour of the Lords that perished because of my decision will be over ten."

"No, please. There has to be a way to bring him back." Her throat burnt, and she couldn't tell for sure if she was crying or if the hot raindrops were trickling down her face.

"I only know of one way. By killing the initial ruler of the skies, one of the ancient three. The God that created the abominable world of demons. Do you think that you are up for the task, Cursed One?" he asked in a mocking tone.

She was getting cold, feeling her strength ooze away, and the world reeling around her. She wasn't sure if this was because of the White Lord's words that left her bereft of hope. It could be the emotional pain, or those last sleepless nights that she stood on guard duty, making sure that those two were safe. It could also be her wound that seemed to be bleeding, despite the makeshift bandage—maybe, it was all this together.

She bit her lower lip, in an attempt to keep herself from fainting. It seemed pointless. Her eyelashes were unbearably heavy and, much as she tried, she couldn't stop her eyes from closing, or her body from falling. Silan-te knew what to expect when she opened her eyes again. The noble's soulless body lying in the rain, just like Nesto's. There was no doubt that the Lord would kill him as quickly as possible, and she wouldn't be able to do anything about it. *If that's the way it is, then I hope never to open my eyes again.*

Cursed as she was, the Gods didn't make her wish come true. She ought to have known better as it was the Gods themselves that had cursed her tribe, in the first place. She opened her eyes and, instinctively, tried to run towards the noble, but a hand held her pinned to the ground. "Sit still, or else you will reopen your wound." The Lord had gone to the trouble of treating and binding her wound. This act of kindness held no meaning. She would be dead soon. A Cursed One, most probably, or even a Lord would come, seeking to steal her life.

She couldn't feel any pain coming from her leg. The old man must have put on it various herbs, otherwise he wouldn't have managed to staunch the flow, let alone allay the pain. She wondered if he had carried them on him all along, or if he had collected them for as long as she was unconscious, after killing Daemon, of course. The roasted meat he was holding pointed to the latter. She must have been unconscious for too long. Lord Raizel had had enough time to slay the demon, pick up the herbs, and hunt for food.

The creature's roar startled her. "You didn't kill him," she realised.

"Yes. It's not an easy task killing your own disciple. No easier than killing a God," the old man said, almost ashamedly. "Right now, I need to keep you alive, so don't make any rush movements."

Right now, I need to keep HIM alive. She looked at the creature, which ran his claws over the strange white net, trying in vain to set himself free. Somewhere behind his emaciated mask and those bloodshot eyes lay Daemon's face. She could almost see his arrogant smile. She never expected to miss it so much.

Killing a God... Well, she had nothing left to lose.

"Why didn't you kill Nesto when you found out about the mark?" she asked. "Why didn't you kill Daemon…or me? I'm sure you knew about him from the beginning. Don't you oppose the Order of the Lords with these actions?"

"I do as I please. And I have stopped taking orders from them for a long time. They think I am insane, that's why they leave me alone. Maybe, I am…" He looked at the demon, then at Nesto's body lying next to her. "Maybe, I am…because they remind me so much of the family I once had."

"Then, help me kill the ancient God." It sounded crazy to her eyes, but so what? White Lord Raizel himself admitted to his own insanity.

The old man snorted with laughter. His wounds must have been serious as his laughter turned to cough and blood, which oozed out of his mouth. "He has captured your heart, hasn't he?" he said, wiping his lips with the back of his palm.

"No, I…," Silan-te started to speak, but the words wouldn't come out.

"No you what? You can't lie, Cursed One. The pure magic in your eyes isn't letting you."

It was true. She could feel her throat choking, not allowing her to speak any words of lie. Which was so bizarre. Of course, she didn't want the noble to die, but him capturing his heart… "I care about them both," she finally said.

"Then, you should focus your energy on number two. He is the only one you have a slim hope of saving."

"What do you mean? How?" Warmth returned to her frozen body. It was hope now that was warming her.

"I will make a deal with you, Cursed One. I will tell you how to bring number two back to life and, in return, you will convince me that killing that demon is for the best for us and, especially, for him. What do you say? Remember, you can't lie."

"I will try," she said almost immediately. That wasn't exactly a lie, even though she wouldn't really try that hard.

The old man shook his head. "That's not enough. Trying to deceive me won't do you any good. Won't do any of us any good."

Silan-te looked at Daemon again. If only she had been given that choice on the first day she met them. She wouldn't have hesitated for a moment. Back then, he was just an obnoxious Lord Candidate, he wasn't a noble, he didn't have a name. He was a stranger, someone she could use as a shield to protect the descendant of the dragons. Dead meat. The only thing that mattered to her was lifting her curse.

And lift the curse, I will. If what the White Lord said was true, then she was given another chance. It would be foolish of her not to take it, grab it. Besides, the noble may have gone forever, unlike Lord Candidate Nesto. Killing one and saving the other was the best decision…*But I can't do it.* In her mind reeled Daemon's words. *"So, does this mean that, from now on, you will protect me, too?"* The picture of him coughing up blood still haunted her. *And what if the Lord is lying?*

But he obviously wasn't. He had no reason to. She took a deep breath, and gave herself some time to relax, physically and mentally. To make a decision. *To convince myself, I should better say.* She knew what she had to do, what the right choice was. She could no longer fight herself. There was no way she could prevent this from happening…—at least, not her.

"So, what do you say? Do you agree with my proposal, Cursed One?" asked the old Lord.

"I do. I agree," said Silan-te in a firm voice. She would honestly help him, convince him that killing Daemon was for the best, for all of them, even for the noble. Of course, this didn't mean that Nesto would be agreed. If she managed to bring him back to life, then he would surely stop them. *Definitely!*

The Lord gave her the piece of meat he was holding. "Good," he said. "Eat up now. You're going to need all your energy."

For as long as Silan-te was eating her roasted thigh, Raizel—obviously tired—was narrating the way in which she would be able to breathe life into Nesto's soulless body. The dragons, and surely their descendants, needed just a trigger to defy death. For the divines, death was something temporary. And a part of Nesto, the one running through his veins, was godly, so bringing him back to life was not an infeasible task. The alignment of the planets was that trigger. That was well known to many, but only a few knew about a second trigger. One that wasn't so distant, so rare.

Her tribe had burnt all the books mentioning such a thing as the Old Ones and the rest wished to sever all their bonds with the dragons once and for all, and eradicate the temptation. However, in the library of the King of Humans, there were still such books. And the White Lord had come across one in his youth, when he had just acquired the title of a Lord. His position as personal guard of the King allowed him to visit the library whenever he saw fit, and he had not let that chance slip by. His days began by the King's side, and ended over big, heavy, and ancient books. "It would be no exaggeration to say that all the world's knowledge resided in those books. Things that even the ancient Gods might have forgotten," the old man stated.

One of those books revealed the second trigger to him. "It is you," said the Lord, and that made her heart skip a beat for an instant. "Your tribe, the Cursed Ones. Their green eyes," he carried on. The pure magic that still lingered inside them, more precisely. The very eyes with which she didn't dare look Lord

Candidate Nesto in the eye. When Raizel's story came to an end, she realised that his knowledge was somewhat patchy.

"Pure magic is the trigger to make Lord Candidate Nesto's heart beat again. It will cost me the magic of my eyes, I understand that. But how exactly am I supposed to do it?" she asked.

"That, I do not know. You have to find out for yourself. I suppose you use a word of magic or something like that. Isn't that what your cursed race does?"

She knew that, on the third level, rain would never stop, but she hoped the sun would come out, even for a while. She couldn't take the ruthless patter of the rain anymore. Most branches were broken in the aftermath of the fight between the demon and the Deathlord, so she couldn't use them to cover them. She thought of moving to another tree that had remained intact, but she didn't want to stray away from Daemon. *He is worriedly calm,* she thought when she gazed at him. He was no longer fighting; he seemed to have given up all effort.

She carefully sat up, so as not to open her wound, and leant towards Nesto. She held his hands. They were frozen. She had shut his eyes. She couldn't bear his blank stare, with the raindrops falling on them, but they still wouldn't close. She held her weapon, and bent over him. She didn't know exactly what she had to do, although it was certain that a word of magic would be necessary. That was the only way to call and activate the magic hidden inside her eyes. That's what her tribe did, that's what all those who wanted to use magic did. *Except for Lord Zoloc.* She was almost sure that, even in the library of the King, she wouldn't find an explanation for it.

She placed her glassy dagger on top of the boy's wound, with her one hand holding the handle, and with the other the green blade. *Words of magic, words of magic...,* she kept repeating in her mind. *But which word?* Finally, she decided to use the word *"life."* She took some time but, finally, remembered the word in her ancestors' language. *Zivor.* She took a deep breath and shut her eyes, while whispering "Isihir Zivor," focusing all her magic energy on her dagger. She repeated "Isihir Zivor, Isihir Zivor…"

After several attempts, while her stomach was in knots due to the doubt that had gripped her, she heard the White Lord's voice saying: "Use your eyes, foolish Cursed One. Don't keep them closed."

She opened her eyes, just like the old man said, and kept saying the magic words. "Isihir Zivor, Isihir Zivor…" To no avail. She wanted to blame the rain and the wind, but she ended up blaming herself. She was aware of the risk they ran. She had to be more careful; she had to remember that spell; she should have run away as fast as she could. She should have. But she hadn't done anything of the sort. Tears trickled down her cheeks. It was then that she felt the pure magic power of her eyes waking up.

Everything around her was dyed a beautiful green colour. Nesto's face, the tree trunks, the cloudy sky, even the raindrops. Her tears didn't burn her anymore. She could see them glistening like thousands of small crystals that resembled distant stars. As the bright green colour began to fade behind a huge, dull grey expanse, she knew that the magic of her eyes abandoned her to enter the lungs of the descendant of the dragons, granting him the gift of life.

She allowed herself a single moment to take a deep breath of relief and elation….And now was time for the hard part. Killing the noble.

CHAPTER 24

Am I dead? Is this the afterlife? Nesto wondered, as he fingered that spot on his chest where he remembered there was a hole from the Deathlord's spear. The hole was gone. He didn't feel the pain in his broken ribs either. *That means I'm dead.* But why did he feel like he was dreaming again? The place where he now was had black clouds, darker and more ferocious than those on the third island, which hid the sun or the two moons. He couldn't see if it was day or night. He lay on some grey stones and, when he stood up, he noticed that he was stepping on top of a tower. Another two grey towers loomed ahead. These three towers were connected through three stone broad bridges on their tops, and just as many in their middle.

He heard waves roar behind him and, when he turned his head, he saw a small battered body bound hand and foot with thick chains, on a wooden pole, forcing it to form the letter Y. "Daemon?" he shouted, as he got closer. It was the noble, but he looked four or five years younger, almost a child. *Daemon, are you alright? What happened?* he wanted to ask him, but he didn't. *This must be a dream, a memory of his,* he thought. The noble wouldn't talk to him, no matter how loud his yells. Nesto was no part of this memory.

Under the tower were some rocks eroded by the sea, and waves that were trying to reach that small boy, setting him free. Little raindrops were falling on his emaciated, worn-out body. There was no trace of fat on him, only skin, bones, and almost no muscles. He must have gone without food for weeks. There were many scars on his body. Obviously recent ones, otherwise his demon's blood would have already healed them.

No matter how hard he tried to find those marks he recalled over his heart and on his chest, Nesto drew a blank. Obviously, he hadn't sustained them yet. Suddenly, the sound of the waves was gone, and the wind abated, whispering in his ear, warning him about what was to come. Noiseless thunderclaps began to illuminate the towers and the mountainside, when he turned up behind Daemon. His father, Tzenon. The demon.

He wore black trousers and an elegant blue coat over his white top. His hair was white and gold, his eyes dark like the abyss, while three slashes were visible on the right side of his jaw. They jarred with his fair complexion. They bore a remarkable resemblance to the mark they both bore across their ribs.

"Is it over so soon, or is it time for the bolts to come out?" the noble asked, his stare inscrutable. Yet, no matter how expressionless his face, his voice was vivid and tinged with irony.

"You are strong enough to speak in such a tone, so I suppose Velmar's worry and entreaties were purposeless." Tzenon's face looked just as expressionless as his son's. His hands grabbed the chains that held Daemon captive and, with no further ado, these were pried open. Daemon plumped to the ground, his legs shaking, but he soon stood up and stretched hands and body. The small noble seemed to be trying not to show any signs of pain or fatigue in front of his father. *Perhaps, he doesn't want him to take delight in his pain.*

"Oh, if it's not the bolts, then it must be our little sparring. Good, sparring is the one I enjoy the most," he said, while trying to loosen up his numb wrists, preparing them for battle.

This took place on the stone bridge, which had no protective rails. A small slip, a thoughtless move, and you fell off, meeting your death.

The thunderbolts didn't stop illuminating the castle, even for a moment. The demon must have been responsible for that. It was as if they obeyed his orders. The wind was blowing, especially up there, on the bridge, where father and son stood. Tzenon was as hard as nails, but his coat was at the mercy of the wind. Daemon's body, on the other hand, was so light, he had to be on the defensive, like a wild animal, ready to attack its prey, so that it wouldn't be blown away. "Are you ready to die, son of mine?" Tzenon asked, as he threw a sharp sword to him. He picked up another one he found in a corner of the bridge.

The boy grabbed it with his left hand, then passed it into his right. He held on to the handle contentedly. "No, but I'm ready to kill you," he replied and, with a growl under his breath, charged at him like a cat. Three strides brought him close to Tzenon and, holding the sword with both hands, brought it down with force. His father, the demon, fended it off rather effortlessly. He kicked Daemon in the chest, sending the small noble hurtling back.

"This is not what I have shown you," said Tzenon in a cautionary voice.

"Shut your mouth, and just die." He charged him again, just as strongly and thoughtlessly. This time, the demon just turned to one side to ward off the attack, then pulled Daemon's hand, throwing him off the bridge, where there were only rocks and waves.

"You rely too much on your brute force, and you have no balance. You don't pay much attention to your surroundings, either. That will get you killed," he said in a calm voice, as his son's body fell off the cliff.

"NOOO! Daemon!" He knew it was just a memory, but Nesto couldn't keep himself from shouting. He ran to the edge of the bridge. His heart beat fast, when his eyes fell on the sea and the rocks, which seemed to form the huge jaws of a horrible monster. But, much to his surprise, the noble was suspended in mid-air, as if tied with a rope. He held on to his sword, and his face looked at the void beneath him in fear. Tzenon's face was tranquil, almost as tranquil as that of Lord Zoloc. Like fear had never visited them.

In his left hand, the fingers were intertwined and, as he lifted it, he hoisted the boy's body. "I have told you before. Do not disobey me," he said, then immediately turned his palm to his side and moved his fingers in Daemon's direction. His son's suspended body charged him again. With a jerk on Tzenon's part, a rivulet of blood was splashed all over the noble, who was thrown onto the bridge wall.

This is how he got one of his scars, Nesto assumed, as he saw the huge cut along Daemon's body. The demon silently approached his son. "Now, embrace the pain because it will follow you forever," he said, and left him suffering.

In the past or, more specifically, until recently, he thought he had every reason to be hating his father. *I was wrong! I was just an ignorant child.* It was Daemon's hatred towards his father that was completely, beyond any doubt, justified. *Not mine.* They were father and son, indeed, but he shouldn't be deluding himself. There was a reason why everybody wanted Tzenon dead. It was his cruelty. *And I'm not entirely sure that this cruelty has anything to do with the demon blood in his veins.*

Fortunately for the noble, a while later, an old man came to take care of him. Judging by his clothes, he can't have been a noble; he was rather a servant. He helped him up tenderly, and carried him from the one tower to the other, until they got to his room. A warm, neat place with a fireplace and a big bed, overlooking the wild sea. The servant had him lie on the soft mattress, and left, only to come back later.

A damp piece of cloth, a little stroke, and a sad smile was all it took for the man to treat the little boy's wound, and allay his pain. The bandages and various herbs would come to nothing; they wouldn't make much of a difference, nor would the dampened cloth. The demon's blood was more than enough to heal his wound. Then, he placed a platter of food by his side, and left again. This time, Nesto followed him.

The servant went down some steps, and crossed one of the bridges that led him to two big oaken doors hiding a spacious library. Countless books were scattered all around, while in a corner there was a long wooden counter with a pile of tattered books on it. He found the demon—on the opposite side of the counter—searching through the shelves lining the walls.

That was not what Nesto expected to see. To be precise, it was the last thing he expected to see in that tower where the demon resided. A torture chamber would be more than predictable, a bloody hall of dead, butchered bodies almost…understandable, since, according to White Lord Raizel, demons were beings baying for blood and slaughter. Killing was their calling. So, how come there was a library in a demon's house? It was surely part of his human side.

"Any luck finding a way, Master Tzenon?" the servant asked.

"I have, Velmar. But it is not to my liking," said Tzenon with subdued rage. He failed to keep it in check, though, as his hand came down on the books like a thunderbolt, sending the whole shelf hurtling to the ground, along with the rest. "It requires my death. There must be another way hidden in these books."

"And I suppose that, by throwing these books all over the place, will somehow help you find it. You should try and be more patient with…"

"I don't need your preaching, Velmar," he cut in abruptly, raising his palm. "It is wasted on me. I'm good at killing, not reading. And, whenever I have to read in an ancient language that my human mind cannot comprehend, I thirst for more blood. I might be able to use the gifts given to me by the godly power of a demon, but I also have to tolerate its curses."

The demon picked up a book off the floor, walked towards the counter, and drew up a chair to sit on. "Now, tell me quickly what you really wanted to tell me, before I start reading again. I'm sure it has to do with Daemon once again."

The servant didn't seem to hesitate in the least. "Don't you think you are being too harsh on him?"

Tzenon shook his head. "Not at all. On the contrary, I think I'm being too lenient. He might not be able to overcome his demon blood if I continue to be so…affectionate to him."

Affectionate? Really? Did he have any idea what the word 'affectionate' meant, or did it have a different meaning for the nobles? He wouldn't be surprised if it was the latter. The world of the nobles never stopped surprising and amazing him. Not in a good way…at all times. Obviously, it had nothing to do with the world of the commoners. Nesto had already given up any hope of understanding them.

That memory carried on with Tzenon showing his son how affectionate he was every day. And Daemon, whenever he could, showed his father a few signs of affection, as well. Mainly in words, while sometimes he used his sword, fist, nails, and spit.

Such a caring family.

When the noble didn't fight with his father, or wasn't forced to suffer any other tortures, he spent the rest of his time recovering from his wounds, reading the books the old servant would bring him. The only occasions when Nesto saw him smile was when he was alone with Velmar, as the demon called the servant. That man, he never threatened by telling him how much he wanted to steal his life. Their conversations were somewhat normal.

"Does my beloved father know you bring me books to read?" Daemon asked Velmar on one occasion.

"It depends. If he does, will you still continue to read them, young master?"

"Probably not."

"Then, no, he has absolutely no knowledge of it," the servant smiling stressed, shaking his head. "I bring them on the sly. I fear that, if he learns about it, he will punish us both. Is that enough to make you want to keep reading the books?"

"Oh, I want to read them more than anything else now," said the young noble, returning the smile.

If only his demon father was as kind and caring as this old man was. Honestly, it was no surprise to see Daemon making an escape attempt. It would be irrational if someone didn't try to escape this nightmare that tormented him. He slipped out in the dark, through the small window of his room. He climbed down the tower with dexterity that resembled a squirrel, then ran towards the wood that sprawled on the opposite side. Away from the frenzied sea and his affectionate father. Unfortunately for him, his attempt was a complete failure. His escape led him to one of the cramped and dirty cells on the basement of the tower.

It seemed that it was no easy task escaping the demon's vigilant eyes, or those of the guards placed in the castle and across the wood. Why they carried out a demon's orders was anybody's guess. There was no other punishment, though, apart from his confinement to that tiny cell. On the other hand, what worse could he have thought of doing to him that he hadn't already done?

Nesto didn't quite have a sense of time in that memory, but Daemon must have spent a long time in that cell. His father never bothered to pay him a visit. Velmar only brought him a metal platter of fruit and cooked meat every day. He kept him company, and discussed with him for a few minutes, then went back to his duties.

The noble's belly was full of pork and onions the day the servant came to get him out of the cell. He opened the door, and gave him a sharp sword.

"So sweet of him to start the first day of my freedom with my favourite lesson," the boy said ironically.

"You know very well what your father is like, young master," stated the servant with a sad smile. He took a pleading tone. "I beg you, try not to disobey him so much."

Tzenon was already standing on the stone bridge, like he hadn't budged an inch since their last duel, when Daemon arrived. He wore almost the same clothes again: dark trousers and a blue coat; only his white top had been replaced with a dark one. It was probably morning, but the dark clouds that surrounded them hid the sun. The wind didn't seem to be particularly strong, but it must have been quite cold as he could see the little noble shivering.

"I hope you enjoyed your small break, son of mine," his father greeted him. "You have Velmar to thank for that."

"Don't you worry. I will thank him by killing you."

"Very good. Shall we begin?" said the demon and, without waiting for a reply, rushed headlong onto the small boy, who only wore a robe full of holes to protect him from the cold. Daemon fended off the attack, just like his father had shown him. His moves were no longer hasty or angry. There was more technique to them, rather than brute force or feelings that prevented him from thinking. But that didn't last long. He quickly lost his calm—a knee strike in his stomach was enough to cause this—, and he tried to pierce through his father's heart with his sharp blade. That brought him down on the hard wall, boring another hole in his already ripped robe, and sustaining a wound in his body.

Tzenon threw his gory sword, and turned his back on his son, untouched. He took a few steps, when a voice suddenly made him stop short.

"Not so soon. Our sparring hasn't come to its end. I have yet to kill you." That voice didn't sound like the noble's; it was different. It was heavier, and sounded as if someone were whispering in his ears. The boy stood on his two feet, ignoring his wound, holding the blade, his eyes bloodshot and creepy.

A black puff of smoke came out of the demon's shoulders and head. Nesto saw him clench his fists and, when he finally turned his head to look at the little boy, the black abyss of his eyes turned into some red, bloody flames simmering at every glance. A fiendish smile studded his lips, with the dark clouds having formed a vortex over his head.

"So, you finally decided to show yourself…son of Demon," he said. He went closer and picked up his sword to compete with his son. But he suddenly stopped, and averted his eyes, as if he had realised something. An intruder. Nesto!

He looked him in the eye, his glance killing him in a thousand different ways. *He can't see me, it's just a dream, it's just several memories of Daemon's. I don't exist in this dark world,* he said to reassure himself. The demon took a few steps forward, and Nesto instantly felt the need to take a few steps backwards. But behind him was only the void. When the demon came before him, Nesto gulped with difficulty, and lowered his eyes, in hopes that, this way, he wouldn't be perceivable.

It didn't work. His heart started racing and banging against his chest. Even the flame under the mark flared up as a warning. "This is the Nest of the Demons," said Tzenon in a voice that made the hair on the back of his neck stand on end. "You don't belong here, descendant of the dragons." He raised his free hand, and placed it on Nesto's chest. With a soft, slow, and torturous move, the demon pushed him off the stone bridge, while Nesto felt the wild, frozen waves devouring him.

CHAPTER 25

The ancient Gods smiled at her. Probably for the first time. Nesto's wound started to heal, and his heart beat again. A while later, everything got even better. Silan-te kept her promise, and convinced the White Lord to kill Daemon but, as he went about doing so, the noble's body got back to normal. Whatever fiendish had gripped him was gone, and the old man fell to the ground; he couldn't believe his eyes. "He was telling the truth. He can actually restrain his demon blood," he exclaimed.

In the end, Raizel stood up with difficulty, and grabbed the net that had trapped Daemon. It suddenly turned into a tattered sweater, and the old man put it on. Silan-te could barely keep herself from running to him to check every inch of his body for wounds and fractures. She only checked his pulses with a soft touch on his throat.

She regained what precious she had lost. Both of them. The need to keep them safe took over her body and, in an instant, they were all under branches and leaves, defying her wounds. She was so elated that she even whispered a word of magic to bring the leaves together, forgetting that no magic lingered in her eyes anymore. Then, something weird happened. Almost unexplainable. She felt all her body respond to her will, and the branches obeyed her voice. Magic gushed from her cursed body. There was such harmony inside of her and, for the first time in her life, she didn't feel cursed, but blessed.

She turned to the White Lord, and gave him a look that sought an explanation, which he furnished. "You proved your loyalty to that boy's godly blood," he said. "Rejoice, little girl, your curse is no more. No one will refer to you as a Cursed One anymore."

Words weren't enough to describe her joy. *I made the right choice.* She had followed the words of disguised Lord

Zoloc, and she had been rewarded for it. The risk was incredible, but it was worth it. The days—especially the nights—that had followed after finding out about the hidden knowledge of the mark were an ordeal. During the day, she was consumed with guilt and a sense of betrayal, while at nights, her heart leapt for hope that the Lord's whispers gave her. They were so enticing that obeying Lord Candidate Nesto was her only choice.

And this is my reward. My curse has been lifted. My wish came true!

Of course, she was well aware now that her hearing those words and serving the descendant of the dragons had been from the beginning a plan of Lord Zoloc's, so that he could lead that boy to the summit of the Tower. He needed her to keep Lord Candidate Nesto's presence secret from the rest of the Cursed Ones. It looked insane to her, but this act of hers of bringing back to life the descendant of the dragons could have been a plan of the Lord. However, she quickly ruled out that possibility. No matter how hard she thought about it, chances were slim, almost nil.

She had to admit it: she didn't trust that Lord. But she was still thankful to him.

"Do you feel any difference between this and your previous self, or have your magic powers increased?" the White Lord asked her.

"I do," stated Silan-te. "There's no comparison between this and my previous self." Nature used to curse her or, at best, ignore her. But now, things were different. The trees kept whispering it to her, the wind was singing about it, while the rain was shouting it. *YOU ARE FREE!* She could feel their approval and love. Her wound had completely healed, while the colours came back to her eyes, more vivid than ever. Nothing remained hidden from her sight.

The descendant of the dragons and the demon's son lay next to each other. Silan-te got closer and clearly saw the two blue flames hidden behind Lord Candidate Nesto's wet eyelids, and a third one simmering under his Mark. Daemon's eyes, on the other hand, were red as blood, while in his chest lay the dark abyss.

She checked the wound on Nesto's chest, and it seemed to have healed. She hesitated to approach the noble, let alone touch him. It had nothing to do with his demon blood or the scary looks he had had earlier on. It was just…Every time her gaze fell on him, she felt the old man's penetrating eyes pierce through her, and she almost heard his words: *"He has captured your heart, hasn't he?"* And, for some reason, she couldn't deny it. Her body, even her thoughts, wouldn't let her.

Lord Raizel's words weren't exactly true. Yes, there was a certain strange emotion that gripped her every time she saw Daemon. And, no, that emotion wasn't just unbearable irritation. But this was surely due to that kiss they had exchanged when they were still in Lord Zoloc's Fortress. "Exchanged" wasn't the right verb. That rude noble had stolen it from her.

Lord Candidate Nesto had kicked Daemon out of his room, and he had asked her to share her room. To be precise, her bed. She refused without a second thought, of course. But the noble, instead of giving one of his usual speeches on how she should serve him too, he just leant close to her and, out of the blue, placed his lips on hers.

"I will have either you or your soft bed. You choose," he told her with that irritating smile of his.

The kiss startled her, and she gave him her room without demur. But the worst thing was that his soft lips kept haunting her in her dreams. Because of that moment, she had this weird feeling, which she clearly shouldn't. She was supposed to serve the descendant of the dragons, not have this kind of emotions, these unexplainable desires. In a way, it felt like she was betraying him. *And betrayal was what caused the downfall of my race.*

She finally chose to keep her distances from Daemon, from that dangerous emotion. He was alive and breathing; she didn't have to approach him to see that. She started a fire, using a word of magic, to keep them warm, and she told the old man that she would go hunting. Those two were surely ravenous. Their bodies needed as much energy as possible, after all they'd been through. After all, at the moment, she needed to be left alone for some time to clear her thoughts about the noble and the descendant of the dragons.

She made sure not to stray too far away. She had a strange hunch, leaving them alone. Last time she did, one of them lost his life, the other one his mind, and Silan-te her hope. Clearly, this ominous feeling was somewhat justified. But now, the White Lord was with them; he would keep them safe.

Some fat four-legged creatures were boring holes in the ground, and climbing up the trees, but they would have to wait. So would Nature's call. As her curse had been lifted, she felt the need to set herself free to become one with nature and the pristine side of magic. But not yet. Time was not propitious. Her priority was to convince herself, then fill the others' stomach, along with her own. It was a task she always did whenever her heart wavered. When a decision had to be made. And it had never failed her so far. She just had to convince herself out of this dangerous emotion.

She leant against the trunk of a tall tree and, taking a few deep breaths, she ordered herself to follow three simple commands:

Do not touch him!
Do not think of him!
Do not return his gaze!

She added a fourth one, just to make sure:
Do not dream of his kiss!

There was no way she would risk losing what she had fought so hard to obtain. Salvation from this curse. Her former glory. This emotion, that kiss, she denied herself.

When she finished making her resolve, she caught two of those four-legged creatures with no particular difficulty. She got back quickly as she still had that knot in her stomach, and she found Raizel standing bolt upright with difficulty, wielding a sword that seared the rain. The other two were safe. The Lord had turned it, so that it faced him, while his face was convulsed with pain.

"My wounds are still bleeding," he replied when he saw her puzzled expression. "No matter how many herbs I applied, they came to nothing. The only solution is to sear them." He placed his searing blade on the wound in his throat, and the smell of burning skin instantly assailed her nostrils.

"Were you forced to fight with another Lord or Cursed One, before you managed to track us down?" she asked him, while the old man did the same to the other wound close to his shoulder. The sudden thought that there could be more enemies on the third level started to alarm her.

He simply laughed, gritting his teeth with pain. "Even Lord Commander's personal guard would find it hard to inflict such wounds, my little girl. Let alone a Lord or some Cursed Ones."

"Then, who?" she asked, then immediately remembered the dragon on the second level. "The dragon," she exclaimed.

"Lord Asaer informed me of a frenzied dragon on the second island," he said, ready to treat his next wound. "For an instant, I feared it was number two. Can you tell me which of these two jerks awakened that monster, and how? I doubt whether you could have."

"It was Lord Zoloc, but I don't know how."

"No doubt, I never liked that man."

"He did it, so that we could escape the Deathlord," said Silan-te, trying to justify him. She didn't want to put the blame on him after all he had done for them.

"Very witty of him. The only thing is, that half-dead creature flew all the way here, following you. It would have killed you if I hadn't been quick enough."

After that process of searing his wounds, the last drop of energy seemed to have oozed away from the old man. He lay on the ground, not very close to the fire that was still burning, and shut his eyes.

His wounds were large, and his body now weak. There was still another question Silan-te wanted to ask and, now that the Lord was almost unconscious, it was the right moment. The old man wouldn't have the strength to change his mind now. "Why did you help me bring back to life the descendant of the dragons?" she asked. "The alignment will take place one of these days, you know that. Then, the dragons will come back to life."

"They are meant to come back to life," murmured the White Lord. His voice could barely be heard. "Just like I'm meant to slay them."

Just like I'm meant to serve them... She could kill him. Right here, right now. He was too weak now, probably already passed out. As their servant, wasn't she supposed to eliminate anyone that threatened them? But, instead, she made sure she took care of his wounds. The old man had already done too much for them. The least she could do was spare his life, this time. This was probably what Lord Candidate Nesto would have wanted.

Silan-te bandaged Raizel's wounds, using pieces of cloth made of the rag the Lord had for a sweater, after she first anointed them with the leftovers of the herbs. Then, she pierced the prey with two sharp twigs, and stuck them into the ground by the fire. Only then did she decide to respond to Nature's murmured call.

She got closer to the lake, and removed what was left of her clothes. She didn't feel cold, and the raindrops were no longer piercing her like pins. Their touch looked like a soft touch. She dipped in, the cool water immediately embracing her. The swim looked like dance, and her heart gave the rhythm. Only one breath was enough for her to dance in the depths of the lake all day. Down there, all her thoughts ceased to exist, and what lingered was a tender, fulfilling emotion.

So beautiful, she thought as, through her hazy vision, an explosion of colours took place. Vivid blue and purple colours appeared from the depths of the lake. Blends of green and yellow adorned the trees and the grass, while some shades of red and orange sprang from the ground. Everything had a touch of perfection.

If only those two searing eyes hadn't turned up outside the lake that scorched her skin. Silan-te turned to the other side, hoping that it wouldn't bother her, and she repeated the commands. *Do not touch him. Do not think of him. Do not return his gaze. Do not dream of his…*

Her skin froze. And it wasn't the cold water. She felt Daemon's touch on her leg, and saw him suddenly appear from underneath her. As he emerged, his hand stroked her whole body, until it touched her face and lips. He kissed her, again! Softly at first, but then more passionately. He ran his other hand around her waist, and pressed her against his body, his heartbeat banging alongside hers. She tried to pull back. She shouldn't surrender to his kiss, his touch, to this desire.

But her body didn't obey her will. Desire was burning her. She wrapped her legs around him, while her hands ran all over his body, asking for more. She ordered her body to stop, but it clung to him more tightly, returning his forbidden kisses.

So much for convincing myself.

She didn't know how, but after a while she finally managed to find the strength to let go of his lips. "Why do you always do this?"

"Do what?"

"Steal my kisses."

"Oh, that. I thought master Raizel had mentioned it to you. My father is a demon. I can't control the urges of my tainted blood. To be absolutely honest, I don't really enjoy kissing you…that much. Not that I'm complaining about it, though. It seems you don't, either."

"I…I…"

"You…You…You can't lie, right?" he said with a smile of contentment.

I can't, but now I really wish I could. Just so she could wipe out that smug look off his face.

He leant again and kissed her. So suddenly that Silan-te didn't have time to react. She broke free, and then slapped him just as suddenly, and turned to the other side, swimming out of the lake.

Aaaaah! The slap she gave him was so satisfying, but she also liked his kisses. *What's wrong with me?*

When she got out, she realised she was on the wrong side. That unbearable noble and his kisses had distracted her. Her clothes were on the opposite shore. But Daemon was already behind her, with his own damp clothes sticking to his body. "Why don't you just admit you like me?" he said in a tone of voice full of self-confidence.

"Why didn't you tell me that you are also a descendant of a God?" She didn't really care, but she couldn't answer his question. Her body wouldn't let her lie. And, no matter what, she wouldn't give him that satisfaction.

"I didn't want you to serve me because you were obliged to."

"I wouldn't. I don't have to. My race only serves the dragons, not just anyone who bore the divine blood. Our Oath concerns only them."

"I didn't know that," admitted the noble.

"And why do you want me to serve you so badly? Is this also one of those urges that you can't control because of your demon blood?" She got closer. So close, she could almost taste his breath.

He didn't budge an inch. "Well, I wouldn't blame my demon blood for this one," he admitted. "This urge is due to my noble blood, I would say. As you can see, I'm a victim of my own blood." He came closer, too. His lips almost touched hers.

"Yes, I almost pity you." If all this carried on much longer, she would give in, and kiss him, she knew it. She placed her lips on his ear. "I have a different proposal for you. Why don't you serve me, instead?" she asked him, then abruptly pushed him into the lake. His surprised look, as he fell, was so funny, she could barely muffle a laugh.

Daemon stuck his head out of the water, and thrust it back. "It's an understandable request," he said, while he lifted his hair. The raindrops were softly kissing his face. "Very well. Let's compromise, then. How about serving each other?"

"Hmmm, that's a tempting offer. Still no, though."

"Why not?"

Silan-te had almost forgotten the reason why, until she happened to lift her eyes. Through the dark she was plunging into, she saw two bright blue flames on the opposite side of the lake staring at her. Accusing her of betrayal.

That's why...

CHAPTER 26

The wound in Nesto's chest had somehow healed, but the sight of their kiss made him feel like another spear had pierced through his flesh. This one stuck right into his heart. He averted his eyes, and went back where the small fire was burning, trying to convince himself that he was in no particular pain. The two pieces of prey had been cooked, but he didn't bother to remove them from the fire. The only one who would hate to have his meat overdone was the noble. And that was more than just welcome right now.

After that grim memory he had seen with Daemon and his demon father, he feared that, every time he looked at him, his eyes would be full of pity. Somehow, he doubted whether that would pose a problem anymore. Thinking of the noble no longer caused him that feeling; only annoyance and a little bit of jealousy. *As always.* He wondered what kind of emotion he would be gripped by when he looked at Silan-te. Would it be silent torment, or would it still be a joy hard to hide?

Master Raizel lay unconscious on the ground, feverish, his body full of burns. Nesto could find no explanation for that. His own wounds had all healed. What was most important, he wasn't dead. Nor were Silan-te and Daemon. Only the Deathlord had been killed. He saw his lifeless body dumped in the rain. He could find no explanation for that, either.

The girl was the first to get back, then the noble, after a while. "You look too gloomy, even for someone who, a while ago, had joined his dead ancestors in their eternal sleep," he remarked, before he sat by the fire to dry. He looked somewhat annoyed, but he was smiling.

Nesto wanted to say something smart and, if possible, demeaning and offensive, but he didn't. Not out of superiority, of course. He just couldn't think of anything. There were so many things, thoughts, and emotions distracting him. So, he just gave him a smile that would probably look quite murderous.

"Yes, about that 'had joined my dead ancestors' part," he said and looked at Silan-te, looking for an explanation. He hadn't made it out from the start but, as the flames lit up her face, he noticed that her hair was of a lighter colour. Yellow, almost whitish. And her skin was no longer dark, while her eyes had lost their green sheen, turning grey. So much had changed about her, but her beauty was the same.

She narrated to him in her sweet voice about the soulless body she had found when she got back, about the uncontrollable demon that had seized Daemon's body, and almost tore the Deathlord's body to pieces. About master Raizel, who slew the dragon and almost beheaded the demon. In that part, the noble's eyes were wide open in fear, perhaps remembering the old man who had warned him that he would kill him if he ever let that dark side show. Finally, she told him about her teardrops and the magic of her eyes that had brought him back to life. "My curse is no more," she added.

She only skipped the kisses she had exchanged with Daemon. *But that, I suppose I already know.*

"Does that mean that you don't need to serve me anymore?" he asked her.

"No. My oath is eternal," she said, taken by storm. "And my desire is to keep serving you."

That heartened him more than he wanted to admit. "That leaves only one question. What do we do with master Raizel?" he said, addressing both of them. "Obviously, we can't take him with us. And we can't stay here any longer. It's too dangerous." Besides, his father and brother were awaiting him at the top of the Tower. Every single moment that flew by put them in a more dangerous position. They had to move as fast as they could.

"I'll stay with him," Silan-te declared.

"No!" said Nesto. The word came out of his mouth spontaneously, almost immediately. "That's too dangerous...for both of you."

"They won't be any safer with us," said Daemon, and unfortunately he was right.

"I'll make sure I protect him and stay well hidden," said the girl to reassure him.

But it wasn't the old man he was worried about. It was her. But there was no better choice. He only hoped there weren't many enemies left. That's what the fact that only the Lord and a Cursed One attacked them on the third island went to show.

The last meal together, and probably the last meal they would have at the Tower of the Lords was overcooked, if not completely burnt. He had come to regret his earlier decision. He should have removed the meat from the fire. They ate mostly in silence. The girl spoke only once to give them some information about the fourth island. The portal to the last level was always open, so they wouldn't need any crystal, and it was in a gigantic head of a stone dragon. Because of its size, it would be really hard to miss it, she told them. If the Order had sent other Cursed Ones or Lords, then that's where they would be waiting for them.

When they finished their meal, she retrieved the crystal from the Deathlord's dead body, and opened the portal for them. She just waved them goodbye with no words. Yet, as a gift perhaps, for the first time, she looked Nesto in the eye without lowering hers. At that brief moment, he realised he couldn't have asked for a better gift.

A joy hard to hide. That's the emotion she made him feel.

The darkness of the portal covered him, and Silan-te snapped out of his eyeshot. He didn't hold on to that emotion for long, as the portal shoved him onto a hard, dry ground, taking away from him the joy, and only giving back pain and dizziness. The sky was illuminated by hundreds of tiny stars and a round moon. Nesto stood up and found himself standing right at the edge of the fourth level. Just a breath away from the void. The wind was so strong that, if he wasn't careful enough, he could fall down to the third level, and die.

"I had almost forgotten that these islands float in the sky," said the noble, gazing at the void and the grey clouds beneath.

He wasn't exactly right. They didn't just float. Being parts of the White Tower, they tried to rise up to their initial position. To what they used to be. *Just like the dragons.* It was Lord Cornius, or perhaps Lord Mendax that had mentioned that, he wasn't sure which one. Both of them were crazy about stories and legends. Perhaps more than an actual story-teller was.

"There is something I want to tell you, now that it's just the two of us," said Nesto. "It concerns Silan-te."

Her name made Daemon's eyes turn to Nesto. "What is it?"

It probably wouldn't make any difference to Daemon as, apart from that single occasion at the lake, he always treated her badly—more or less, that's how he had treated those two girls at the Black Castle. He had taken an interest in them just to while away the time. Anyway, Nesto felt the need to tell him. "I want to make her mine. To make her my wife."

The noble looked taken aback. "Well, that makes two of us," he said. His face was all serious.

I have to admit it, this is one of those rare moments that he catches me off guard. He didn't expect to hear something like that and, maybe for the first time, Nesto got mad at him because there was no arrogance in his tone. Because…because he wasn't joking; he really meant it. "I saw all of her dreams. They were about me," he said, panicky. That lie had come out surprisingly easily. Luckily, Daemon seemed to believe it.

"She kissed me, more than once." He blurted out that lie just as easily. In the dream Nesto had seen, the noble was the one to kiss her, and not the other way around.

But he let him have that one, since Nesto also lied. "I know," he said, stressing the word. "I saw you at the lake. However, she wants to serve me forever."

"I know," he said in the same tone. "I was there. Apparently, she doesn't know what she truly desires."

"I couldn't agree more."

"So, what do we do now, commoner?" Daemon asked. "Let her decide?"

"Obviously," said Nesto, but it was quite hard not to give in to the temptation of pushing the noble over.

He was still mad at Daemon, when they started running towards dark trees and the ruins of the White Tower, to where they hoped the portal would probably be. As if that weren't enough, the flame turned up under his mark, giving him an excruciating burn. As always, out of nowhere and for no apparent reason. *A completely useless gift.* If it was indeed a gift of his divine blood. Perhaps, its usage was to warn him for an upcoming threat. Whenever he had been in danger, the mark had always burnt him. But that was highly unlikely. There was no...

The noble's hand grabbed him and dragged him under a tree trunk. He instantly knew, that meant danger ahead. *Alright. Maybe, it wasn't a completely useless gift.* He looked where Daemon was pointing, then stuck his head behind the tree. He could feel beads of sweat trickling down his forehead. He looked at the noble, the expression on his face indicating that they shared the same thought. *There's too many of them!* Cursed Ones. Dozens of them. More than they had seen in the Fortress. Why were there so many of them? They moved silently and more stealthily than night itself. Only their glassy weapons and their whitish-green masks that reflected the faint green light of their daggers gave them away.

Earlier on, he had failed to make them out because he was still preoccupied with being mad at Daemon. And what the mark did—whose purpose was supposed to warn him—was distract him even more. Once again, the noble's reflexes and instinct had saved his life. And, for some unexplainable reason—he wasn't absolutely sure, but he guessed it might have had something to do with Daemon claiming that he wanted to make Silan-te his wife—, that made him even madder at that damn noble.

Fighting them would mean jumping to their deaths; running away seemed too hard. Hiding was the best choice. And all those ruins scattered all around were favourable. Daemon had come to the same conclusion first. He pointed with his finger to some of the ruins of the White Tower that were fairly close to them. It was a great temporary hideout.

The strong wind reached their ears like a song, deadening all other noises that their footsteps could make, as they hunched hurriedly towards the bulky ruins. They were slightly taller than a plain house and, while it was full of cracks and holes, these were not big enough for them to risk being seen. They hid behind the tall weathered walls, and peeked through the holes to see if those who were sent to hunt them down had by any chance discovered their trail.

It seemed that they hadn't, although his mark was still burning. Nesto saw them running like shadows, holding their green daggers, looking around with their impersonal masks on. It was really hard picturing a face under those masks. They were so different from Silan-te. She was warm and gentle, while the others seemed too distant and emotionless. They probably numbered close to forty men…no, at least fifty. *Way too many!* Especially, considering the fact that there were only a couple on the previous level.

Their great numbers were truthfully unanticipated. Lord Zoloc had made it clear that the Order of the Lords had gathered all those men, Lords and Cursed Ones, that they had, whom they sent to the second level, as soon as they perceived the presence of an individual with the blood of the dragons. And most of them, if not all, had been burnt alive, mangled by the dragon. Those left must have died at Lord Zoloc's hands.

And, of course, from the beginning, their force had been limited, since a big part of it—Nesto guessed they must have consisted of hundreds of Cursed Ones and dozens of Lords—was busy fighting Tzenon, the demon, who had re-appeared, threatening them. Unless...*unless they decided to focus all their attention on me.* The real threat. On the face of it, it was obvious that the demon was dangerous, and it had also tarnished the Order's reputation. However, that could in no way be compared to the undeniable threat that the descendant of the dragons posed. *If I were to survive, all the dragons would come back to life.* Killing the demon, or stopping the dragons from digging out of their graves? The answer was quite clear. *They don't care about the demon or his son anymore. They only seek me, my death.*

"I guess that the portal is in the direction of where they came," said Daemon, as he peeked through the holes. "There are lots of them, though. We have to find a way to move without being seen, before the night's gone." He turned his gaze upon Nesto. "Any ideas, commoner?"

Nesto shook his head. "If only we had Lord Zoloc with us. I'm sure he would be able to think of something." The noble looked at him in a way that didn't approve of his thought. "What? His plans are crazy, ridiculous, and surely dangerous beyond any doubt, but, in the end, they worked."

"Only by pure luck," Daemon demurred. "And there's no reason why we should be discussing this right now. Lord Zoloc is not here to help us. We're left to our own devices."

The Cursed Ones came to a halt, several metres away, close to some other ruins. A loud voice made them freeze in their tracks. They made room for that person to walk. When her face was illuminated by the green sheen of their daggers, Nesto could recognise her: *Lord Ereina!*

Her appearance bore his thoughts out. The first priority of the Order of the Lords was definitely the boy with the blood of the dragons running through his veins. *And I bet Lord Commander Legris must be somewhere around here.* Maybe, he was the one guarding the portal. That wasn't good at all. Just one Lord, a Deathlord, to be precise, was more than enough to almost kill them both. And now, they had to face at least two of them, without considering the Cursed Ones, of course! Yet another obstacle that looked insurmountable. *Now, I really wish Lord Zoloc were here.*

He was too far away for Nesto to make out what she was saying to them, until Lord Ereina lifted her eyes high to the dark sky. "It has already begun," she almost shouted, and the masked men became one with the dark, spreading all around.

They were in such a hurry that they didn't even take a look at the ruins. Nesto and Daemon didn't move, though, even when the Cursed Ones were nowhere to be seen. Not until they could come up with a plan that would give them a slim hope of successfully passing the portal. Dying once was more than enough.

"I didn't expect to see Lord Ereina here," said the noble in a low voice. He was still breathing hard from that run. "I thought she was hunting the demon, along with the Lord Commander."

"Well, they were. But not anymore," said Nesto. "It seems that they consider me a bigger threat than your demon father."

"That, or they succeeded in slaying him."

I highly doubt that. Daemon couldn't have ever seen his father's real power. But Nesto had. Only that single memory was enough to see how incredibly strong he really was. He was untouchable. How come all these blades of the White Lords couldn't bite his flesh? But Nesto preferred not to tell him. Maybe, it would be better for Daemon to believe that the demon could never keep him trapped in his castle again.

His mark kept on searing him and, of course, now he couldn't tell why. It was quite certain that there were no masked men, no threat nearby. Words weren't enough to describe the rage, the hatred he felt about this useless gift of his. His nails held on to the mark tight, and it took a great deal of strength and patience to keep himself from ripping that piece of flesh off his body.

It wasn't a surprise to see the noble doing exactly the same thing. That was the noble he knew. The one he met at the Black Castle. *Always mocking me.* Even at such moments. If it weren't for the threat of the Cursed Ones warning him at the back of his head, he wouldn't be able to resist the irrepressible desire to hit him. So, he settled for a hateful glare. *But wait...* The noble's lips didn't form a smile, and there was a dark reddish light coming out of his ripped top. His hand wasn't enough to hide its glow. Nesto looked under his own top. His blue mark shone through the night...

And, suddenly, he knew. He knew why this was happening, why the Cursed Ones were in such a hurry that they didn't even look through the ruins. The two moons that were one, the marks that were burning and glowing, Lord Ereina's words. This could only mean one thing.

The alignment had already begun!

He looked at Daemon again, his look being scared, this time as it dawned on him what this exactly meant. "What?" said the noble. Except the burning sensation, he probably hadn't noticed his mark glowing, let alone the fact that the alignment was taking place.

Nesto showed his radiant mark. Now, its shape clearly showed the head of a dragon. "The dragons are rising," he only said.

CHAPTER 27

He could picture them taking shape. Their sizzling eyes waking up, blue flames billowing out of their nostrils. Using their sharp claws to dig themselves out of their thousand-year grave. The first thing, Nesto imagined, the dragons would probably do would be to spread their wings and fly back to the skies, where they belonged, with a thundering roar. And the second thing…the second thing was obvious. Their divine blood would definitely seek revenge.

Nesto knew where his thoughts, these pictures, were leading him. And he didn't want to go there, to that kind of thinking; it was dangerous. Too dangerous. He had succeeded in banishing such thoughts, when Silan-te told him about his divine blood, but he wasn't sure if he could do so, now. Because now, it was too real. And, yes, it frightened him.

He hid the mark with his top, and turned around. Behind him. No, not behind him; towards the wall to peek through a hole. He didn't know what he would like to see; probably nothing. He just wanted to fool his mind. To occupy it with something, anything but those thoughts, those images. He felt lost and, for a moment, he even forgot where he was. Daemon was trying to tell him something, but his words didn't make sense. At least, that weird sound of his voice, was somehow distracting him…

Oh, I wish this flame would stop burning me. That burning sensation was a spark, the trigger for fear to turn into pictures. He did his best to block those pictures out again, to become numb, and feel nothing, to not acknowledge them, but his efforts came to nothing. In the end, they came rushing through his mind: a sea of fire burning towns and villages. Small kids, old people, commoners, and nobles trying to escape that winged threat. All of them falling prey to the dragons' ruthless jaws. He pictured the City of the Kings going up in flames and getting destroyed, just like the Fortress of Lord Zoloc on the second level. *And I will be the one responsible for all this. Because I so selfishly survived.*

All those scary stories about the dragons would come true, and even more, harrowing stories would be written. It was likely that his own name would be mentioned in them. Not as a heroic Lord, but as the one responsible for all the atrocities. Not as a hero, but as evil itself. He would be compared to the demon Tzenon, and surely he'd come out as a far greater evil. He would, without a doubt, be known as the greatest evil to have existed.

And, believe it or not, that wasn't the worst part. Garon and Lirel would be in danger because of the dragons, too. *They might be killed because of me.* Of course, there might be a slim hope of survival for them, but the Cursed Ones, the ones that betrayed the dragons in the first place, were surely doomed to suffer their fiery revenge. And Silan-te would be no exception. *I will lose her forever.* And he couldn't handle it, he couldn't handle any of that.

Everyone will suffer because of me. It is obvious that I shouldn't exist. He turned his head towards the noble. "Daemon, kill me," he blurted out without much thought. Lord Ereina and the Cursed Ones were in a hurry to kill him, although the alignment had already begun. So, if he were to die right now, maybe, just maybe, the dragons wouldn't be able to rise from their graves and kill everyone he cared about. The chances of him coming out of this alive were already pretty slim, anyway. He would be doing everybody a favour.

"Hey, look who's back," said Daemon, after he tore his eyes away from the hole he had been peeking through. "Tired of staring at the wall already, commoner? You know that, sometimes, you have the tendency to get lost in thought, right?"

"I know, I do it all the time," Nesto replied. "Now, I need you to kill me before I change my mind, before it's too late. Just do it. Don't make me beg you."

The noble took it for a joke. "I'm honestly thinking about it, but I doubt it would, in any way, help me reach the portal. So, no. I will have to decline your offer."

"Daemon, I'm serious," Nesto insisted. "Because of me, the dragons will rise. Don't you see? I'm the greatest evil."

"Greatest evil? Clearly, you haven't met my dear father. You wouldn't say that if you had seen him."

Yet, he had seen enough memories of him to know how merciless and brutal that man was. *And I'm still a far greater evil.* "You saw what that one dragon was capable of. Cities and villages will be reduced to ashes in their wake. I can't even imagine how many will die."

The noble remained silent for a while, sizing him up. "That's not my problem," he finally said. "Nor is it yours. Let the Order of the Lords handle it. They are not that weak. They will find a way to protect most of the cities. Besides, if you wish so badly to die, then why don't you do it yourself?" Daemon got closer and took his glassy dagger. He wrapped Nesto's hands around its handle, and then aimed its sharp point at his heart. "Here you are! Just a small push, and everything will be over. All your guilt will be gone."

His hands grabbed the green dagger, while this seemed to be slipping away. The mark was still burning him, making his palms sweat. Just a small push, and Garon, Lirel, and Silan-te would be safe. He saw the noble look at him, his eyebrow raised. "You don't really think I will do it, do you?" Nesto asked.

Daemon shook his head. "No, not really. One's own survival always comes first. You are the one who said it, remember?"

He took a decisive step backwards. This wasn't a joke, a game. Killing himself ought to be the best choice, no matter what that son of the demon said. But...his father and brother knew about it and, still, they wanted him to survive. "Just keep in mind," said the noble with a smile. "If you die, Silan-te is mine. Not that you stood any chance against me, anyway. I'm just clearing it up."

That was enough to bring him back to his senses. *I think he knows me too well. Maybe, even more than I know myself.* And part of him hated him unbelievably for that, while the other part was grateful. "You'd wish, noble. She belongs to me."

"Not if you are dead. So, go on. Kill yourself. Don't worry, I'll wait patiently," Daemon said and crossed his hands above his chest.

In answer to that, Nesto put the dagger back into its case, and feigned a smile. "I changed my mind. You are right. I only care about my own survival, after all."

That smug smile turned up across his lips, as usual. "I'm always right. Can we focus on how to reach the portal without getting killed, now?"

They sat on the ground, and focused only on this, but no plan seemed to be good enough to be worth taking a risk for. From the start, they rejected the idea of messing with whoever came their way, and force their way into the portal. That would be plain stupid. Especially if the Lord Commander was guarding it. After a long dispute, Nesto managed to convince Daemon to also reject the idea of one of them being the bait, while the other would escape. The one acting as a bait would most probably die. And it was certain that, in the noble's mind, the bait would be Nesto, since he was the one that the Order of the Lords wanted so desperately to kill.

They were still thinking, when they saw a Cursed One hurriedly and clumsily heading in their direction, his green dagger glowing in the dark. They instantly separated and retreated, as silently as they could, in even darker recesses of the ruins. Obviously, the masked men had already searched a big part of the island—without finding anything—, and now they were focusing their attention on the ruins. There was only one of them, but a shout would be enough to summon all the Lords and Cursed Ones.

He never had the chance, though. Nesto sliced open his throat, coming from behind, and the masked man died in complete silence. He was ready to throw the dead body in some dark corner, when Daemon stopped him. He bent over the soulless body, removed the white mask, revealing his sparkling green eyes, and pensively checked his clothes. "I just thought of a way to reach the portal unnoticed," he said. "If we wear the mask and their black clothes, they would never be able to tell us apart. What do you think?"

Nesto had to consider it for a while. He had to admit it—it was the best thing they had come up with up until now, although it was somewhat crazy. It was worth a try; they could take the risk. "I think Lord Zoloc would be proud of you."

"Oh, shut it," he said, and began to remove the clothes of the masked man. "We'll need another mask, and a second pair of clothes. I'll dress up as a Cursed One, and go kill another one. It should be easy enough."

"Why you, and not me?"

"Why don't you trust me? Do you perhaps think that I'm going to abandon you here, or use you as a bait?" he asked. *I can't say that it didn't cross my mind.* The noble's arguments were that he had observed Silan-te for a long time, and could mimic their movements better. He was the one most likely to succeed. "And, of course, I don't even have to mention that I don't trust you completely. You might change your mind again, and ask a Cursed One to kill you before it's too late, or something like that," he added. On the other hand, Nesto's arguments were nonexistent.

Daemon put on the mask, took off his own ripped clothes to wear those of the masked man and, covering his head with the hood, took the glassy dagger. "How do I look?" he asked.

He looked like a murderous shadow. "It's more than enough to fool me," he said. "As far as I can tell, you look exactly like a Cursed One."

When the noble was gone, Nesto hid back in the dark, without even bothering to peek through a hole, for an incoming threat. His mind and emotions were in such a state that he might end up staring at the wall again. He had to strive to keep himself under control. And, somehow, he knew it wasn't just because the dragons were rising. It was far deeper than that. It might have had to do with the alignment. Lord Zoloc had mentioned that, when the alignment took place, Daemon would feel the urge to kill him because of his divine blood.

And this is what I feel because of the blood that runs through my veins. Total chaos!

At least, the noble seemed to control it, otherwise he would surely have killed him, when Nesto asked him to. *To think that only a few thoughts are enough to forfeit my life.* Blaming the alignment wasn't a good enough excuse. Daemon was right, after all, about calling him weak. And he had realised it from the beginning.

The Cursed One he had killed carried some berries, so Nesto kept himself busy chewing, while waiting for Daemon to come back. A couple of hours had passed since their last meal, but the run and all those thoughts had whetted his appetite. *Not to mention that the meat was completely burnt.*

Daemon took so long that, for a moment, Nesto doubted if he would actually come back. But, fortunately, he did. "Put them on quickly!" he said, as he took out the white mask and black garment. "I made the Cursed One share with me everything he knew before I killed him. You were right. Lord Commander

Legris is guarding the last portal, and he might not be the only one." He paused for a while, then said in a lifeless voice, "They also succeeded in slaying my demon father."

The noble stayed silent after this, behind his impersonal mask. Nesto didn't speak, either. He didn't say a word, even when he put on the black clothes of the Cursed One, and the white mask that looked like transparent glass on the inside. What were the right words to say, anyway? *How would I feel if my father was dead? How would I feel if he was a hateful demon?* He had been in a similar state the first day they met master Raizel, when he learnt about the noble's demon blood. And he didn't know what to do, back then, just like now. This kind of things, obviously, weren't his strong point. Of course, back then, a small joke would be enough to banish that irksome feeling. He could do that right now, but his instinct stopped him, for an unexplained reason. So, they set off for the portal in awkward silence.

The wind was howling, and it was heard everywhere, as they ran incessantly. At every step he took, Nesto felt his senses heightening, and his heart trying to leap out of his chest. Fear lurked deep inside of him. The noble seemed to be in a worse state. He was clumsy, and had nothing to do with Silan-te's elegant movements. He made no attempt to avoid the branches, and they avenged themselves by ripping his clothes and scratching his skin, the way they fell on him. The further they moved, the more Cursed Ones they saw. Chances were getting slimmer and slimmer.

The only redeeming feature was that their garments were enough for the few Cursed Ones not to bother taking a second look at them.

Nesto knew they were almost there, when the smell of smoke assailed his nostrils, and he saw something that looked like two big stone horns jutting above the rest of the trees. The easy part of their plan was over, and the hard part, which wouldn't forgive the slightest slip, was now unfolding before their eyes. And they couldn't just wish in like that, not when Daemon was obviously distracted. It was the noble who had accused Nesto of getting lost in thought, however he was the one lost now. "Are you alright?" he asked him in as low a voice as he could muster, since he was hiding behind a bush to observe the territory. Fortunately, no masked man was around.

The smell of smoke was coming from the swaying fires burning in some iron baskets placed on tall poles. Two such bright lines ended in the wide open jaws of a huge stone dragon with hollow eyes. From a distance, it seemed like the dragon was breathing fire. They had to go through these jaws to reach the final portal. And Lord Commander Legris would be there waiting for them, prepared to slay them with the dragonslayer.

"I'm perfectly fine," replied Daemon.

"Well, you don't seem like it. If it's because of the demo…"

"No, it's not that. It's nothing. I just remembered something that I had long forgotten, and it distracted me. A certain memory that I had promised to engrave into my mind. It's not really that important." It was obvious that it had to do with Tzenon's death. That demon was still torturing him, even after his demise.

"It certainly isn't," said Nesto. "Surely no more than our lives."

"Yes, probably not."

"Good. Because now, we need to stay focused if we want to even hope to survive this thing."

"I don't need to hear that from someone who, only a while ago, asked me to kill him, commoner."

He couldn't argue that down. At any rate, life seemed to have returned to his voice. That was somewhat reassuring.

Dawn was playing hide-and-seek, together with them. It must surely have been waiting impatiently and fearfully for the right opportunity. Two Cursed Ones that suddenly took to their heels, right in front of them, heading for the mouth of the gigantic dragon made their heart beat faster. They stood right at the entrance, with their heads bent over. Lord Commander Legris paced towards them, motioning for them to raise their heads. He knew it was him, although he had never seen his face, as he wore the silver uniform of the Commanders with the Mark of the ancient Gods drawn across his chest in purple. His long hair, as well as his thin mantle, were flying in the strong wind, while in his hand he held his sword, the famed Dragonslayer. Another two Lords dressed in crimson turned up by his side.

Nesto could barely hear them, but he thought they were saying that they had traced the two with the divine blood, and they were now chasing them. Which, of course, didn't make any sense. *We are right here, and I'm quite positive that no one has sniffed us out.*

The masked men left just as suddenly, while the other two Lords followed them, leaving the Lord Commander alone, guarding the portal.

At a glance, it seemed hard to understand what was going on. However, it became quite clear—after some thought. This was a distraction, just like the dragon, back on the second island, was supposed to be. And Lord Zoloc ought to be behind this one, too. He was trying to draw all their attention to him. And it was working!

I partly blame the alignment for this kind of thinking. But now, I really feel that we might actually get out of this alive.

CHAPTER 28

"It's him. This is Lord Zoloc's doing," he said, as he watched Lord Commander Legris go back into the dragon's stone mouth.

"Yes, there's no doubt about it," said Daemon. "I'm not entirely sure if I'm happy that he is here, or sad that he is still alive."

"Oh, you are happy. You just don't want to admit it," said Nesto. *And grateful, too.* Because now every single Cursed One and Lord, apart from the Lord Commander, that had been summoned to hunt them down were eradicated. They were blindly chasing the shadow of Lord Zoloc. And, knowing Zoloc, it was almost certain that they would never be able to catch it. The combination of his magic and his craftiness would make sure Nesto and Daemon had a lot of time on their hands to go through Lord Commander Legris' obstacle. Nestal, his father, could not have hoped to find a better ally than him.

He has succeeded in upsetting both of the forces that were sent to shed our divine blood.

After careful thinking, they concluded that facing head-on the Lord Commander wouldn't be such a good idea. They had better play it safe. To keep their disguise on and try tricking him. Surely, an opportunity would come for them to make a run for the final portal. They also added a small detail to their plan to ensure their success. A detail that was mostly inspired by the so many distractions of Lord Zoloc. They'd inform Lord Commander Legris that the ones with the godly blood were finally caught and slain. *Relief and joy will seize his body.* And those emotions ought to blind him, even if it would be just for a while, for a moment.

What was needed was for them to wait for some time, so that their words would be convincing. Maybe, he would be incredulous if they rushed into the dragon's mouth just now, after the other two Cursed Ones had left.

As he felt scared and jittery, he had no memory of that wait, nor could he recall himself leaving the protection of the bush. All of a sudden, he caught himself running between the flames, towards the dragon's jaws, with the noble next to him dressed up as a Cursed One. It was so sudden that he began to panic. He couldn't breathe properly, and he kept feeling the Deathlord's spear pierce through his chest. Everything seemed to warn him to run away: the howling wind, the black trees all around and, of course, the fire burning behind his divine mark. But he chose to ignore them.

He tried to imagine and mimic Silan-te's elegant movements, but it was far more difficult than it seemed. At least, her thought managed to calm him down a bit. They came to a halt, when they were under the not so sharp stone teeth, and bent their heads over before the Lord Commander. He stood bolt upright, on the alert, while his uniform was stained with blood. Nesto hoped it was his.

He wasn't sure if he had to blame the chaos he felt inside because of the alignment, but standing before Legris somehow made him feel as if he were standing in front of the dragon he had seen on the second level. Even his appearance looked just as menacing—that could partly be due to the mask of the Cursed Ones he wore. Who knows what kind of magic resided in it! The orange and red flames shed their light on his dark eyes, and they looked like they were burning. There were no horns on his head but, were he to make a sudden, wrong move, it was almost certain that his sword would come chasing him like terrifying jaws. *I'm glad he can't see my face, or else he would be able to read my nervousness.*

It was hard not to notice the portal behind Lord Commander Legris. A black sea, which looked as if painted exactly where the dragon's throat was supposed to begin.

He signalled to them to raise their heads. "What is it? Have they finally been dealt with?" he asked, and Nesto was somewhat surprised that he didn't breathe fire out of his mouth.

He let Daemon do the talking. "They have, Lord Commander," he replied, making sure his tone of voice was respectful. "The descendant of the dragons and the son of the demon were caught and killed. Lord Ereina pierced through their hearts with her sword."

Legris was supposed to be the one to feel relieved and blissful, but it was Nesto that experienced those emotions when the Lord Commander said: "Good. Lead me where they are. I want to witness with my own eyes their dead bodies."

As soon as they managed to keep him away from the portal, everything would be over. They turned around and paced ahead, trying to mimic the movements of a Cursed One as well as they could. Nesto was thinking that their plan was a success, when he noticed a small straight line on the ground, made by a sword probably, exactly at the mouth of the stone dragon. It bothered him enough to recall the scene with the two masked men. They hadn't entered the dragon's mouth, they hadn't passed the line, he recalled. They had stopped at the entrance, and they obediently waited for Lord Commander Legris to come out. As if they were scared, or perhaps forbidden to set foot inside…But, no matter which of the two, one thing was obvious.

They weren't supposed to pass the line!

The sudden realisation struck him like a frozen blade. And then, he heard Legris slowly unsheathing the Dragonslayer. Their plan wasn't a success, after all. He had seen through it from the beginning. Daemon turned around at the same time as Nesto. He had probably come to the same conclusion, or even sensed the danger, and it was certain that on his own chest as well had appeared the Mark of the ancient Gods, burning him with its power.

They just charged right at him. Just like that. With no more thinking, no plans, but only the desperate need to survive. Because there was only one person standing in their way, because there was a small army behind them still looking for them. And, most of all, because they were so close, just a few steps away. His father and brother were waiting where the portal led. *And I'll make sure to get there, even with a sword through my chest, if need be.*

Still, it wasn't his chest that was at risk, but his throat. Lord Commander Legris swung his sword to the side, as they jumped on him, and Nesto tried to defend by wielding his glassy dagger. At the last moment, one of the noble's black bolts struck Legris in his right eye. And, while Nesto's dagger was cut in two by the Dragonslayer, his neck was still in one piece. The tip of the sword just barely managed to graze it.

His desperate need for survival ordered his body to continue running though. He jumped-rolled forward, disregarding the danger, and somehow managed to pass through the Lord Commander and the second blade that had materialised in his hand. An acute pang of pain pierced through his leg, as he stood up to run again. A deep cut was visible on his knee. Still, he kept on hobbling. Pain was the least he was worried about right now. He ran away from Legris, away from the shadows cast by the torches, as if hunted down, towards the last portal.

He was almost a breath away from it, when he felt that something was wrong. He turned back, expecting to see two blades like claws chasing after him. But he didn't. He only saw Daemon down on his knees, unable to move, the Lord Commander pinning him down, with the Dragonslayer ready to kiss him on the neck. *That's what's wrong.*

But he wouldn't kill him. *Not yet.* The Order of the Lords was baying for the immediate execution of the descendant of the dragons. The demon's son was not their first priority. *And he doesn't know which one he is holding.* He looked him in the eye, his look warning him that he would shed the noble's blood if Nesto dared move.

One small step and he could leave. Escape the Tower, escape to safety. Daemon would probably do it. Or maybe not. *I can't be sure. I've been wrong about him before. However, I'm not Daemon...*

"One's own survival always comes first, right, son of the demon?" said the noble. And that's exactly what he was saying to him. If he had been in his position, he would have left.

The liar!

"I might have been wrong about that." Legris had surely been seriously injured, while still fighting demon Tzenon. Now, his wounds had multiplied. He could barely keep his right eye open, while Daemon had managed to stick his glassy dagger into his ribs. Nesto saw him standing with difficulty. No matter how strong he might be, he wouldn't hold out much longer. If he gained some time, if he could go closer...*I can do this. Me and Daemon together, we can do it. We can kill him.* "I am the descendant of the dragons," said Nesto, and he hobbled towards the Lord Commander. "It is me you so desperately want to kill. Let him leave. He is just the son of the demon, just the lesser evil. Because of me, all the cruel, merciless dragons will rise from their graves. I'm the greater evil for you, for the Order of the Lords. For the human ra..."

"He is lying," the noble claimed. "What are you trying to do, you foolish noble? I don't need your help. I'm a God. I'm the true descendant of the dragons."

That very moment, Lord Commander Legris pulled Daemon's head back and removed his mask. He smiled when he saw the noble's face. Because he could easily tell he wasn't the descendant of the dragons. His resemblance to Tzenon was quite obvious. *Now, he knows who the real threat is. He's going to focus on me, now.* "You are not a good liar, Lord Candidate Daemon. It's because you are still too young and innocent," he said, his tone of voice somewhat sad. And then, the Dragonslayer pierced through the noble's heart…

For a moment, Daemon's eyes shone through, red and bloodshot, then went out, and he dropped dead.

"NOOOOOO!" Nesto cried. "Why?" *I can't understand. I just can't.* His mind was desperately trying to find a reason. He was the biggest threat the Order should be worried about. Their first priority should be to kill Nesto. So, why? Why was he giving him the chance to escape? Or did he think that he wouldn't escape, not now, not after watching him kill Daemon?

If that was the case, then it had worked. Rage engulfed him, and the fiery power of the ancient Gods consumed him. Their flame seared his eyes, brushed his thoughts aside, and he materialised a flaming blade in his hand. He wasn't going anywhere now…

He charged at Lord Commander Legris, full of hatred, disregarding the pain and the blood that trickled down his leg. He attacked him with the burning blade, the broken dagger, even with his head. Whatever could be used as a weapon to inflict pain on him. To kill him, if possible. Legris seemed taken aback, confused perhaps, by the sudden attack. By all that power, all that rage and hatred. He took a step backwards, as he fended off Nesto's blows with his Dragonslayer. He took another step backwards, and another one. At the fourth step, the tip of the broken dagger stuck into the Lord Commander's belly. But the sharp blade of the Dragonslayer was already stuck into Nesto's shoulder, and didn't let him push further and deeper. Just a bit more, and he could slice open that belly of his. Nesto's teeth gritted with fury. *ARGHHH!*

His rampage came to a stop here. A powerful kick sent him flying back. He landed on one of the torches, his white mask smashed to pieces, and his head kissed the ground. The bleeding made him dizzy, and it was so difficult for him to stand up on his two feet again. He tried to, but he was pinned to the cold ground. He had managed to lean on his elbow, when he saw Legris overhead, threatening to cut his throat off with his sword. But, strangely enough, the Dragonslayer stood there frozen, looking him in the eye. He was still a bit dizzy, and his sight was somewhat foggy, so he wasn't sure he understood why the Lord Commander wasn't killing him.

Until he saw a man standing next to Legris. His one hand prevented the sharp sword from snapping off Nesto's head, while the other pressed the dagger Daemon had earlier stuck into the Lord Commander. It was Lord Zoloc. Saving him once more. His clothes were muddy and half-ripped from all that running and hiding. His face, though, was composed, as always.

"You…" That came out of Legris' mouth like a swearword. He gritted his teeth in pain, and with his free hand kept the dagger from going deeper into his flesh.

"Yes, indeed, me," said Lord Zoloc. "I really hope you don't mind, Lord Commander, but I can't allow you to kill this one, too."

The Lord's presence didn't manage to make Nesto's rage subside, even slightly. On the contrary, due to that smile hanging from his lips, it was burning him even more. Although Daemon was dead, that damn Lord wasn't the least upset. He could, at least, have the decency to hide that smile.

Everything burnt. He was probably turning into a pile of ashes because hot smoke billowed out of his nostrils. The pain, physically and mentally, was so unbearable that it made him howl like a beast, no, like a dragon. Like an infuriated dragon seeking revenge. He wanted Legris to experience that kind of pain, the suffering he felt. He wanted to burn him alive…

And burn him he did. All by itself, his hand was raised, and all that fire, all that heat left his body like a swirl and engulfed the Lord Commander with blue flames, sending his body hurtling away. Nesto couldn't hear his cries, but he hoped it was because he had instantly killed him. The flames almost burnt Lord Zoloc. *I wish they had. I hate him, too.* If he had appeared sooner, Daemon wouldn't have had to die. He knew it wasn't Zoloc's fault, but he wanted it so bad to be.

He felt his power abandoning him. Exhausted. Empty inside. All he managed was to crawl next to Daemon, next to that soulless cold body with the dead eyes. A little voice of hope whispered to him that the noble might not be dead, that his divine blood had kept him alive. Surely, he would wake up soon enough. And, this time, Nesto would be the one to make fun of him for being weak.

But, eventually, that voice died out, just like Daemon had. With the strength he had left, he held the noble's arm as tight as he could, hoping his gift would grant him with a memory, at least. One where the noble was still breathing. He wanted it so bad. It would give him the illusion that Daemon was still alive, that he was still with him. He even prayed to the three ancient Gods to give him that one last memory, almost forgetting one crucial thing.

When had the Gods ever favoured him?

Never! He only had himself to rely on. He had no power left to materialise a weapon in his hands, so he used his nails to scratch his palm, until it started bleeding. Then, he united it with the noble's blood. At first, nothing happened but, a while before he started to scream in despair, everything turned black, and the memory he sought came to whisk him off. *One last memory of his. I so hope it's a happy one…*

But, unfortunately, it never was. He saw Daemon going away from his father's castle on the sly, in the dead of night, running through the wood. Trying to escape again. Nobody seemed to be hunting him down, but the little noble never stopped looking back to make sure. And the short twigs didn't forgive him that carelessness. They scratched him, and snapped noisily to give him away. He must have been running for hours, but he didn't stop, even for a single moment, to take a breather.

He only stopped when he got out of the wood. And that was because he came across a black carriage. His demon father stood next to it, the stars over his head, while another one, a younger —but still old—, Velmar, held the bridles. Tzenon pointed to the carriage, and the boy obediently entered it.

"If I remember correctly, it's been exactly one year since you last tried to escape," said his father, as the carriage turned back. "You turn ten today. Tell me, Daemon, why do you always try to escape on your birthday?" The noble did not reply. He did not even look at him, his gaze turned outside the window. "Is it because of what I said on your eighth birthday?"

"I'm sorry, I never pay attention when you talk. What did you say, dear father?" asked Daemon, pretending to be absentminded. Tzenon simply smiled and said nothing.

Later on, in his room, Velmar brought him food and water. "This is for all that running you did," he said in a strict tone. "And this," he gave him a small greenish book, and a kiss on his forehead, "this is a gift for your tenth birthday, young master." That made the noble smile. He didn't touch his food; he lay in bed, holding the book, and started to leaf through it. The servant opened the door to leave but, before he did, he turned back to say, "I'm sorry for my indiscretion, but what was it that your father told you on your eighth birthday, and makes you try to escape on the same day every year?"

"I honestly don't remember, Velmar," said Daemon, looking at the book, avoiding the servant's eyes.

"I know when you lie to me, young master. Come on, spill it. There is no one you trust more than me."

The little noble didn't tear his eyes from the book, and thought for a while before telling him. "He said the day I would leave, he would die…because he loves me more than anything in this world."

CHAPTER 29

It started raining again. The worst kind of rain…tears.

He wanted to just stay there, next to Daemon, and cry his heart out, but Lord Zoloc had a different opinion. He reminded him that the entire force of the Order was still chasing him, and that his father and brother were waiting for him on the other side of the Portal. At the top of the Tower of the Lords.

But even this wasn't enough. He had to tear him away from the noble with force, for Nesto's hands were tightly clenched around his arm. He half-walked, half-dragged him to the portal. "Now, it's finally over," he said, as he pushed him in.

Over? Over for whom? *Surely not for me.* The pain of Daemon's death would haunt him throughout his life. So would the Order of the Lords. It would never be over. *Not until I die.* The black sea of the portal engulfed him, its darkness similar to his own, and it somehow felt right, more appropriate. A lot more appropriate than the white, frozen world that turned up before him. The dim light hurt. It demanded more helpful thoughts. Thoughts about home, about Garon, Almar, and Nestal. And it was too soon to demand something like that.

He plunged knee-high into the snow. When he looked around him, it was a uniform scene. Snow, huge mountaintops, and absolutely no sign of life. The cold must have been enough to freeze even his bones, but he was too numb to feel it, to care. Nesto had survived the ritual for the Lord Candidates without being favoured by any of the three ancient Gods. He entered the Tower, escaped the claws of a dragon, and fooled the forces of the Order. And he was finally here now, he had reached the top.

But, contrary to what Almar had promised, there was no one waiting for him…

His thoughts became darker again, despite all the white uniformity that surrounded him. And he couldn't help but think that Nestal and Almar were probably dead, killed by the Order. Or even that they had abandoned him once more. That was the sole reason he didn't want anyone to get too close to him. For, when they went away, when they deserted him, they would take a piece out of him, thus deepening the void within. And, no matter what, they were all bound to abandon him, eventually, right?

He lay on the snowy ground. He had nowhere to go, and he was tired. Really, really tired. He feared that, if he shut his eyes, he wouldn't be able to open them again. But, maybe, that was for the best. *Maybe, I should have died, along with the noble.* That last memory he had seen was reeling in his mind, as he lost his senses. Did it by any chance mean that it was Daemon's birthday today?

If so, happy birthday, then, my dear friend.

He came round only for a while, when he heard some voices. He half-opened his eyes, and saw a man, with a slash across his face, standing over him. *Lord Cornius.* "Congratulations, Lord Candidate Nesto," he said. "You succeeded in acquiring the so desirable title of a Lord. Too bad you won't be keeping it for long, though."

His eyes closed and, when they opened again, he found himself lying on an old bed. The room was small and somewhat damp, while an oil lamp was burning, trying to brighten it. It looked like the room he had, back in the Black Castle. Only its door seemed to open from the outside. There was no doubt about it. The Order had finally captured him. He was completely naked, while his wounds had been treated and bandaged. An unnecessary act. He was going to die, sooner or later.

He tried to call forth the fiery power of the ancient Gods to keep warm, but nothing happened. The Mark didn't appear on his chest, while the one across his ribs was barely visible; it was hazy and almost shorn of its bright blue colour. Even that flame was gone. He was powerless.

He looked around and found several thick woollen clothes scattered, but folded, around the room. He put them on. A blond servant with brown eyes knocked on the door, a while later, and brought him some hot soup with small pieces of meat, and burnt bread. Nesto asked him where he was, if he had somehow returned to the Black Castle. "You're still at the top of the Tower of the Lords, Lord Nesto," replied the servant.

Lord Nesto. That title sounded so weird to him, but preferable to "the descendant of the dragons" or "the greatest evil." At least officially, he was a Lord. "And what exactly is at the top of the Tower?" Nesto asked.

"The headquarters of the Order of the Lords, of course. What else would there be?"

"Oh…yes, of course," said Nesto in a melancholy tone. That was perhaps the last thing he had been expecting to hear. All this time, instead of getting away from them, he had been actually getting deeper and deeper into their hands. First, it was their entering the Tower, now their headquarters. Were they, Nestal and Almar, really trying to save him, or just condemn him once and for all? *To me, it seems that they didn't have the heart to kill me with their own hands, and chose to let the Lords do it by pushing me into the Tower.*

As the servant left, Nesto noticed that the door that held him captive was made of wood. Not only that. There was no guard outside. For a moment, it struck him as odd, until he remembered where he was. In the middle of nowhere, surrounded by snow-capped mountains. Not to mention the total absence of the Mark. Escape was deemed impossible.

He had a few mouthfuls of food, then lay down in bed, letting thoughts whisk him off far away. To a different ending. Daemon was alive, and they had gone through the last portal together. And Nesto's father and brother were waiting for him at the top of the Tower of the Lords. These thoughts were all he had left.

The next day, after breakfast, Lord Cornius, along with two Cursed Ones, stepped into his small cell. They informed him that they had orders to prepare him before leading him to the hall where his trial would be held. Where his fate would be decided. They hadn't mobilised their entire force, just to let him live, in the end. That was only a typical process as Nesto already had the title of the Lord. That was the reason why the servant was polite to him. Even the Cursed Ones didn't look too cold. *Because of the hateful title.*

"It's a shame Lord Commader Legris didn't manage to kill both the descendant of the dragons and the child of the demon," said Lord Cornius, as he showed him the way with pretentious politeness. "But, at least, he got rid of the most dangerous one. That damn noble!"

The most dangerous one? Was he so averse to the nobles as to actually prefer the death of Daemon to the one that would bring back the dragons? No, that couldn't be it. There had to be a deeper meaning to that. A proper explanation that wasn't based on pure hatred alone. But he was too mad to ask anything with the same pretentious kindness. "How's your beloved friend, Lord Mendax?" he said in response. "Still dead?" That wiped the fake smile off the Lord's face. Good, he thought. He couldn't stand that feigned kindness.

Preparation involved a visit to the baths, which were above his cell. Most likely, they didn't just want to make sure Nesto would be standing clean and tidy before the leaders of the Order of the Lords. Those baths looked similar to the ones back at the Black Castle. Numerous green and purple crystals jutted out, while the surface of the water gave off a golden colour. "It suppresses the Mark of the ancient Gods," the masked men told him. Which explained why he couldn't call forth their power earlier. This surely wasn't the first time he would be bathed in it. "Just to be on the safe side, we have to render you powerless."

He took off his clothes, and dipped into the cold water, which jogged his memories of the first day in the baths hall: the thousand commoners who died, the twenty or so candidates, the ritual of the Mark, and the lack of favour from all three ancient Gods. It was somewhat funny in its own twisted way because he had been the one least expected to survive, and yet he was the only one still alive.

After soaking in the golden water and his memories for quite some time, he was escorted by the Cursed Ones and the Lord to the higher levels. There was white marble everywhere, and almost all floors looked so much alike, as if they had been made up of snow. Statues and paintings adorned the place, but their beauty was no match for the view the windows and verandahs afforded. The headquarters of the Order were built on the side of a high mountain, and a look beneath was enough to overshadow the beauty of all the rest. Lords and servants filled most halls, verandahs, and corridors. They all looked at him with feigned kindness, talking in hushed voices.

The hall of the trial was at the top. Six old, skinny persons with grey, almost white, hair awaited him, seated on their tall chairs that looked like small thrones. Nesto didn't really care about the trial, about this formal procedure, that's why he blocked out almost whatever had to do with it. He cared more about his memories, about the past. And not when his future would end. What he managed to register was that one of the seven heads of the Order could not attend because of the wounds he had received. And that was because he realised that they were talking about Lord Commander Legris. *It's a shame that I couldn't kill him. That, at least, I couldn't take revenge for Daemon's death. It seems I'm not capable of doing even that.*

"Do you have anything to say in your defence?" he was asked at some point.

Of course, he didn't. *I don't know what they accused me of, but I'm quite sure I'm guilty of it.* "No, no. Nothing at all," he replied lifelessly, while shaking his head. All his energy had been drained. He had no strength even to hate them. He suspected the baths were the cause of that.

The trial seemed to come to an end before it even began. And the verdict was unanimous, as expected. *Death penalty!* What was left was the King's approval, then everything would be gone. He would be stripped of all the layers of protection the title provided him with. But this was going to last for a few days, as he was informed. The masked men took him back to his cell.

Days went by with him doing the same things. He ate, drank, slept, and once a day the Cursed Ones came to lead him to the baths to make sure Nesto would remain powerless. He felt nothing, not even a hint of fear. He might be expecting his death, but in fact he was already dead. He wasn't sure if he had to blame the baths for that but, apart from the fire of the ancient Gods, the very spark of life had died out inside of him.

On the morning of the fifth day, they brought him breakfast, as usual, but Nesto was off his food. He felt no hunger, and he was in no mood for life. He lay in bed. But, strangely enough, the servant didn't leave; he only looked around, and made a grimace. "Well, at least the food is not so bad," he said. "You cannot complain about that."

It took him some time to realise it. He sat up, then looked the servant in the eye to make sure. It wasn't difficult for him to make out the servant's eyes in the dim light. They were green! "Lord Zoloc," he said in a low voice, although there was no one at the door to hear him.

"You look…I was going to say fine, but you look awfully lifeless. What kind of tortures have those savages subjected you to?"

"They haven't."

"Well, that seems to be quite effective on you," the Lord said, and threw a red apple to him.

Nesto let it hit the wall and drop to the ground. "Are they dead?" he asked. "Nestal and Almar, my father and brother. Are they dead?" The Lord slightly nodded, and that was more than enough. "If you came to help me escape, then don't. I don't want to," he said. He had nowhere to go anymore. And he was sick of running and hiding all the time. It was pointless. In the end, everything he had done proved to be pointless.

"There is hardly any need for that. The King is not going to consent to your death penalty. Now that the alignment is over, and the dragons are awakening one by one, you are more valuable to him alive than dead."

That sounded to him more indifferent than reassuring. "Then, what are you doing here? You are not here to pay me a visit, are you?" He tried to sound ironic, but he failed, even in that.

The Lord shut the wooden door behind him, and leant against it. "No, not really," he said. "I just wanted to give you the flame, the motivation you will need to survive the depressing after-effects of the ordeal that you just went through. Besides, there is one last story that I want to share with you. Actually, I came mostly for the story."

"A story? You sneaked into the Order of the Lords, killing the servant and taking his form, just to tell me a story?"

"More or less. It's a really good story. It has nothing to do with all these dull stories Lord Cornius recounts, I promise. It's a story mostly about you. Would you care to listen to it?" he asked, but he didn't wait for an answer.

Zoloc told him about the White Lords, about Tzenon and their battle, about things that Nesto already knew. And then, he told him about things he didn't know. "Your father was one of the noted White Lords," he said. "He gave his life in that battle, in order to protect Daemon, thus forcing Tzenon to promise he would take care of you. When dying, he revealed that the Lords would want to kill you, too, because you shared the same mark. The mark of a God. The responsibility of raising you redounded on the demon. Yet, those hands were already more than full. That's where I come up."

Lord Zoloc had been at Tzenon's service since ever, as he pointed out. It was he who had left them with Garon with that letter, having assumed Nestal's form. And that of the storyteller. He had been the storyteller all along. He would often disguise himself as such to pay them a visit and make sure that Nesto's mark was not revealed. But, eventually, it was. In the sixteen years of his life, his divine blood would awaken, and the Cursed Ones would become aware of his presence. Then, the hunt would commence, more fierce and ruthless than ever. Because the alignment would be on the cards, threatening the entire world.

There was never anyone waiting for him at the top—Almar had actually died in the Black Castle, reduced to ashes from the fiery power of the ancient Gods. It was merely a small part of a thorough plan that was devised by Zoloc to lead Nesto to the Tower of the Lords. They did the same to the noble, so that Zoloc could keep both Daemon and Nesto safe there. Even Silante was a simple pawn in his plan. "Tzenon made sure to lure almost the entire force of the Order away, and I made sure to keep you hidden until the alignment was over," he concluded.

I can actually see my whole world dissolving in front of my eyes. He let it all slowly sink in, but it was hard. And it was even harder to accept. He found himself laughing again nervously. After finding out that he had the blood of the Gods inside of him, everything else should seem believable, and yet this was so hard to believe. Daemon might have called it horrible, ridiculous even. Just like every other plan of Lord Zoloc's. But Daemon was dead. He breathed his last in the Tower, despite this "thorough" plan. *Just thinking about it maddens me.* "Well, it didn't work," said Nesto, blaming him for it. "You failed. In the end, Daemon died."

"Yes. It was unfortunate, but Daemon had to die," said the Lord, then carried on, talking to him about the alignment, about the barrier that separated the two worlds being destroyed because of the noble, or something like that, but Nesto's mind clung to these first words.

"Daemon had to die." There were so many things hidden behind those words.

"You wanted him dead, too, didn't you?" Nesto demanded, even though an answer was unnecessary. Of course he did. He knew this would happen. Wasn't he, after all, the one that had been pulling the strings all this time? He had planned it all along. Surely, he hadn't turned up by chance, after the noble had died, to save the Lord Commander. He was waiting for his death. And Legris, Legris knew Daemon's name. Lord Zoloc must have been the one to have informed the Order about the existence of the demon's son.

Although the baths were suppressing the fiery power of the Gods, a small flame started burning on his chest, and its warmth spread everywhere, awakening him, filling the void within with rage. More and more emotions were constantly bursting out of him. It was so powerful that his head was about to burst. He got out of bed, and instantly felt the whole world reeling. He could barely stand without falling.

"You lied!" he accused him. *About everything. My father, my brother, but mostly about Daemon.* "You promised me that you would protect him."

The Lord got up to him, held his hand, and steadied him with his grip. "Didn't your brother warn you?" he asked, after shaking his head in a disappointed manner. When he smiled, his green eyes shone in the dark. Zoloc let go of Nesto's hand, and the world started going around again. The fall was imminent.

He never said the words. Yet, Nesto could hear them being whispered in his ears, as he was going down. "Trust no one!"

END OF BOOK 1

Printed in Great Britain
by Amazon.co.uk, Ltd.,
Marston Gate.